SCARLET REIGN

MALICE OF THE DARK WITCH

BY

R. D. CRIST

Second Edition

ShoRic Publishing, Colorado

Printed in the United Stated of America
ISBN 978-0-9998822-0-7 (Paperback)
ISBN 978-0-9998822-1-4 (Ebook)

Cover design by Laercio Messias,
www.facebook.com/LaercioMessias85

Edited by Paula from PaperTrue

Proofreaders & Contributors:
Shoshana, Katrina,
Karen, Sandie, Steve,
Myra, Fatima & Melissa

www.scarletreignbooks.com

Fitting in isn't hard; it's nearly impossible.

*This is for those who have the courage to challenge the masses and for who refuse to accept others' limitations:
The young leaders who forge a new fit*

...and for Sho.

TABLE OF CONTENTS

The Realm of Powers

Since the dawn of time and deep into the dark ages, man was plagued by dark powers where death, famine, and disease engulfed the lands. It was then that a band of heroines, undeterred by the all-powerful and oppressive regime, successfully united against the odds to challenge the reign of black. Thus commenced the reign of scarlet and the awakening of good.

At times, those with strong connections to evil have tried and failed to resume their reign, but prophesies tell that their era is imminent—their power will be unmatched and society, as we know it, will collapse. And it is inevitable, unless a new band of sisters finds the courage to renew the Scarlet Reign.

CHAPTER ONE

⊰⊱

NEW BEGINNING

Death was all about. It rang through Natalie's young ears, tingled her nerves, and gushed through her veins, making its way straight to her heart. Her mother, who was technically alive, was the source of this grief. Hannah, still the picture of youth and beauty, lay lifeless on a hospital bed, connected to enough machines for anyone to know that her chances were bleak. Her adolescent daughter, standing at the eve of her fourteenth birthday, remained near her mother, weeping.

The room itself—the paint, the linen, and even the air—was sterile in every way, barring only Natalie's sense of unholiness. She felt the walls draw closer and closer; the small room—barely capable of accommodating three or four people—grew smaller still. Natalie shuddered, feeling an unnatural and painful constriction. She felt this compression originate from something beyond her immediate surroundings, a feeling which was not altogether unfamiliar.

Her unease mounted as the door opened and the man she believed was the source of her discomfort entered the tiny room.

"Natalie," said the seemingly apathetic man standing at the door. "It's time." Natalie's cries grew louder to drown these words and any subsequent ones the man was to utter. He circled the room, stopping just behind Natalie as she leaned over the bed. He placed his hand on her wrist, gripping firmly the chain-linked bracelet that was a gift from him. With a slight tug, he repeated, "It's time."

"No!" Natalie screamed, pulling herself away from him, moving her mother's bed with the motion.

"Look at what you did," the man admonished, consciously restraining himself from shouting at her. "I won't let you disrespect your mother like this. Now, you will come with me and let her die in peace."

"You are not my father!" Natalie yelled. She straightened herself, her eyes widened in horrified disbelief, and backed against the wall as tears rolled down her cheeks. In five simple words she had disowned her provider, her father and negated fourteen years of bonding, if you could call his anger love. Certainly, she had no basis for such a belief. She could not understand why she had spoken so coldly, except the fact that her father had always been so very cold toward her. She knew he never liked her, and rather believed he despised her; constantly reprimanding her for being absentminded and clumsy. She once tried to argue how she was just anxious and never broke things when she was serious, but it didn't help much when she accidently knocked over his hot coffee onto his lap. She never argued again. She knew, now more than ever, she was destined to look after her home and give up her childhood now that Herold, the man who stood before her, was the only family she had. Of course, the death of her mother would mark the end of childhood for her and dwelling on it now wouldn't change anything, so she quickly accepted this fact. Her life was no longer protected by her mother; it was all in the hands of this wretched man. Her eyes lowered in surrender.

As she readied herself to leave, taking her mother's hand, Natalie was stopped by her father's next words.

"How did you know?"

Painfully clenching the infamous red ruby ring—which never left her mother's finger—inside her own fist, Natalie screamed out, "Get out, *Herold*!"

"Did your mother tell you?" he demanded.

Natalie had never been explicitly told anything, and, while she had wished at times, many times, that it were true, somehow she had always known. A picture suddenly flashed in her mind, a recurring vision she had throughout her life: her mother holding her as a baby, with a man and an older woman standing by them. The man in the picture was not the one that stood before her.

Herold aggressively approached Natalie. "Get out!" she cried out, holding her mother's hand tight. He grabbed Natalie's arms and she yelled again, but in a full, booming voice. "*Get out!*" Oddly, the man who had never paid her any respect in her entire life, numbly let her go, turned around, and left without a single word.

Natalie felt the energy drain out of her body as the emotions of the day took a toll on her. She laid her head on her mother's chest, her legs curled on the side of the bed, giving in to her exhaustion and nearly passing out, only drifting in and out of consciousness.

Natalie did not know how long she had lain there when an old, familiar smell of golden honey wafted into her consciousness. The room was peaceful; her mother was still alive with the machine-assisted heaving of her chest.

A light shining in the room and a prominent voice nudged her awake. "You've had a long day, Natalia," an unknown woman said from inside the room.

Natalie jumped up and out of the bed, in surprise. "Natalia? Who's that?" she asked as she saw an older lady who had her back to Natalie. The lady had somehow managed to slip into the room. Natalie's partial view of the lady did not eclipse the gleaming elegance the woman's noteworthy presence exuded: an aura, if you will, brighter than the light entering the room. Natalie, confused beyond any explanation, examined the formal, but dated, white-lace shirt and black skirt the lady wore and the matching black jacket hanging over her left arm.

"You are," the woman answered, staring out of the single window.

"Death is in the air, Natalia. Surely, you must have felt it a long time ago. There is nothing more we can do here but make ourselves right with it."

The elderly white-haired woman turned around and gave a welcoming smile, revealing a face that was way too youthful to match her aura of wisdom and experience. She brushed the tips of her fingers down Natalie's cheek. "Young Natalia, you have become a beautiful woman, well, almost," she smiled.

"Who are you?" asked Natalie.

"A distant relative, mentor to your mother, and former changer of your diapers, young lady."

"I meant, what is your name?"

"Oh, pardon me, sweet Natalia. My name is Ava," she said as she held out her hand, her palm facing up.

Natalie placed her free hand in Ava's, feeling more secure about letting her mother go. Ava held out her other hand, and, after some hesitation, Natalie reached out to the mysterious woman, taking a step away from her mother's attachment. The fearful leap somehow produced a healing effect. Like jumping from one ledge to another, Natalie felt she could now embrace the change and move from the safety and protection of her mother to that of Ava.

"We don't have much time," said Ava. "They'll be here for you soon."

"I don't want to go," whimpered Natalie, her hands in Ava's, the full extent of her anxiety mirrored in her eyes.

"Do you still have the memory?" asked Ava, "...of you as a baby in your mother's arms?"

Natalie's fear gave way to shock. Recognition of this woman dawned on her, and fresh tears flooded her eyes, no longer from grief. Natalie pulled Ava close and hugged her tighter than she felt was possible, bending herself to rest her head on Ava's shoulder. Ava responded warmly to the long overdue gesture of love.

Ava continued to pet Natalie's sandy blonde hair until Natalie raised her head from Ava's shoulder, bringing them face-to-face. "We must hurry," said Ava urgently. "Natalia, I know you're young, but it's time for you to start making decisions, tough decisions. I'm sorry you have to grow up this fast, but I believe you're capable. As far as I'm concerned, today you're a woman."

Natalie drew back from Ava's touch and wiped away her tears with the sleeve of her white shirt. "What kind of decisions?"

"To begin with, you have to decide if you want to stay here or come with me. If you decide to go with me, you can never come back."

Natalie turned her upper body to look at her mother. Turning back to Ava, she cleared her throat and said, "There's nothing left for me here."

Ava rubbed Natalie's face from her cheek to her ear, wiping away the remaining tears with her hand. "There's a big girl," she said. "Now, I'm sure your mother has a piece of jewelry she never lets out of her sight."

Natalie knew exactly what Ava was referring to: the ring with the dark red precious ruby set in platinum, surrounded by a series of diamond baguettes. Inspiring awe in all who saw it, and presenting an ancient appearance, the bulky oval gem sat in an oval setting that covered nearly half the length of Hannah's finger in its entirety. At times, the ruby turned so dark it appeared almost black, conjuring in Natalie's mind a stale pool of blood, a contrast to the pureness of the adjacent colorless stones.

"Yes," said Natalie. "Her ring. It's sacred for her."

"It's yours now. Take it."

"I don't think I can. It meant everything to her. You take it."

"It is forbidden for me. Only you have the right, and only you can take it."

Natalie took her time. Taking her mother's hand in her own, she kissed it, and the ring that appeared to be permanently fixed on Hannah's finger practically fell off, into Natalie's hand.

"Put it on. Quick! Get up!" urged Ava.

Natalie placed the beautiful ring, her birthright, on the ring finger of her right hand, exactly where her mother had always worn it. At that instant, the chain-linked bracelet fell from her wrist. "Now what?" she asked.

"Now, we get out of here. Put on your coat and follow me."

"But how?" asked Natalie, worried. "My father... uh, the guy out there, he has it out for me."

"Hmmm... That's interesting," reflected Ava. "Say something for me, Natalia. Quietly. I want you to say, I shall not be seen."

"What?" asked Natalie, confused.

"I want you to whisper, I shall not be seen, and I will take care of the rest."

Natalie cleared her throat and said, "I shall not be seen."

"Good. Now keep saying it softly, over and over."

"Okay," said Natalie as she continued to repeat the words.

"Now take my hand and let's go," said Ava, leading Natalie toward the exit.

Natalie turned to take in her mother's face for the last time. Remembering all the moments they had experienced together, she blew a final goodbye kiss to Hannah.

Ava did not even bother to peek out of the door, confidently exiting the room and moving into the hallway, as though there was no need for any stealth.

"That's him," whispered Natalie anxiously.

"Shh. Don't speak anything other than what I asked you to, or he will hear us."

"But he'll see us if we go this way. He's looking right at us."

"I will take care of it, just keep repeating what I told you."

Natalie continued to whisper the words despite her fear of being caught and having to leave with Herold as opposed to the almost stranger who walked beside her. It was a definitive life changer, but Natalie could not fight the overwhelming feeling of belonging she had with Ava, especially since she had the strong gut instinct that her step-father was not who he claimed to be.

Natalie's rapid thoughts distracted her from her fear about the bold escape attempt. Before she could know the exact degree of their boldness, she realized she was walking right past Herold with him staring in her general direction. Soon, they reached the dreaded oversized doors behind him. The torture of pushing past the doors, enduring the small windows laced with irreverent iron bars, reminded her of death each time she passed. The doors, which required a great deal of force to open, flung open on their own accord for the two women. Incredibly, as though the whole event were merely a vision, they passed Herold and she was free. She was free!

CHAPTER TWO

❧

INTUITION

Natalie slowly opened her eyes. She was startled by the dense, harsh cold that arose from deep within her. She felt as though she would freeze from the inside out. The chill was more than just a sensation; it was an emotion. An emotion that made her wish she were alone. She quickly learned, frost wrapped in hopelessness is a gift neither wished for nor coveted.

Natalie lifted her weary head from Ava's lap, sat up straight, and glanced at her surroundings. People were dashing up and down escalators, standing in front of monitors—monitors that posted enough schedules to make her feel dizzy—and tremendous loads of luggage were transported and transferred, more than she could believe. She could not hear any airplanes, but soon realized that she had woken up in a rather large airport. People appeared to be in a hurry—with things to do and places to go. Natalie had nothing. Not a single thing that could distract her mind from the absence she felt: a total lack of purpose. Deprived of any real connection to the living world, she could not care less about whether she was leaving with the woman beside her or walking the streets toward a meaningless destination.

"Bags," said Natalie. Feeling numb, she gazed vaguely in the direction of the industrious people all around her and repeated, "Bags."

Ava stroked her hair. "What's that, my dear?"

"No matter how many times they travel, or how far they go, they always get back to where they belong… with their owners. They have a place, a purpose, a reason. There's no question—they know where they belong. No decisions, no cares, simply a reason to exist."

"Sometimes bags get lost too," said Ava. "They could even find new owners. Perhaps, they belonged with their new owners all this time."

Natalie remained unaffected. Ava placed her hand on Natalie's shoulder and pressed lightly, pulling her closer. "Sometimes, they're even recycled. You never know when you might be called upon for a greater purpose."

Natalie pondered on the thought for a moment. "If there's more to this life, I really can't feel it. I just can't see anything to do with me having a greater purpose."

"Oh, but your intuition must tell you differently. Your mother had intuition. Good intuition."

"My mother?" whispered Natalie. Motionless, Natalie could manage to only utter an, "Ava," but nothing more.

"We all want to have things, even when they're not meant for us." Ava looked up. "Did I tell you how your mother and I became friends?" She chuckled and continued, "Your mother was quite a character when she was young. Believe it or not, her mischievous side was actually what I liked best about her. There was this guy, Roy Tassel. Oh, did I like him. My best friend and I would talk and dream about that boy. One day, he approached me. I felt like I was in heaven. Now, we weren't allowed to date back then, and your mother was quick to remind me of that, but I wasn't going to miss my chance."

Ava blushed and smiled. "Your mother would have nothing of it though. Roy and I sneaked into the park, and we sat on the bench side by side. My first kiss would be just as I had imagined—perfect. I tilted my head up and puckered my lips just enough to invite him in, and he was game. My whole body tingled in anticipation. Sixteen years I had waited for that kiss, and it would be worth every day of waiting. Just as our lips were about to touch, I got lemons instead—sour, sticky lemons. Lemonade— all over my hair, clothes, and face. Roy was upset and instantly left. We never kissed. I was horrified, embarrassed, and furious. Your mother, little Hannah, standing there with an empty pitcher, laughing at my grief, was the object of my anger, and possibly deserving of a good beating. I never caught that little girl. We made it through the lobby door where we lived, and the headmistress stopped me. I was so flustered that I almost admitted I was with a boy. I couldn't express the extent of my anger to the headmistress without getting into trouble myself, so I had to hold it in until we were alone."

Natalie lifted her head and barely managed enough emotion to display shock at learning of this different side of her mother. "My mother did that? But she was always so proper."

"Not always, sweet Natalia. Not always. But because of your mother's intuition, I learned something that day. Roy was a wild boy. He had kissed my best friend earlier the same day. He was only trying to kiss us both on a dare. He didn't care one bit about me, and somehow, your mother knew. Her intuition about him was right. That didn't mean she wasn't hard to live with, but she did keep that day a secret. That's when we started to become friends."

Natalie sighed, and then asked, "Ava, why was my mother with Herold?"

"The answer to that has to do with her intuition. Something about him was important to your upbringing. She knew what she was doing."

"You mean, my mother could sense things?" asked Natalie.

"Intuition is a little more than just that. It's a combination of all our senses and more: sight, smell, knowledge, and even probability. Once you're confident enough and learn to listen to your intuition, you'll be able to make split-second decisions before you even know it. You'll begin to surprise yourself, until you're no longer surprised by your ability. Your mother had great intuition, and I expect you do as well. We'll see that once you overcome your grief. Your mother and I became great friends at school. She was young, so I took her under my wing. But she also taught me a lot with her abilities."

"I thought you were a relative."

"Natalia, you will soon learn that we're all family. Although, technically, I am your aunt. We have a stronger bond than mere familial ties. You will see."

Ava suddenly raised her small nose above her soft, puffy cheeks and scanned her eyes from her left to her right. She then sniffed the air. "We need to keep moving," she said, standing up, and bending over to bring her face to Natalie's level. "I need you to be strong and listen to me without asking any questions. Can you do that?"

"But, why?"

"No questions, okay?"

"Okay."

Ava stretched out her hand for Natalie to grab, and as soon as she did, the two swept through the crowd like wind: swishing around people, never halting. Natalie was stunned and bewildered. She felt like her movements were slower, more controlled, than the frantic crowd, but somehow they were going faster than everyone around them—much faster.

The two of them arrived at a station where dozens of people were in line to get their tickets and deposit their baggage. Ava, undeterred, gestured her hand, palm up, across her front, as if to suggest to the person in the front of the line to go first. However, he reciprocated with the same motion and said, "Please, ma'am, take my turn."

Ava hurried to the attendant, showed her tickets, and said, "Our flight isn't for two hours, but I need one right now."

The attendant slowly typed on the keyboard, repositioned a hand to bring her cup to her mouth, peeked at the clock out of the corner of her eye, and eventually shifted the monitor, all with far less effort than Ava was willing to accept.

"*Hurry*," said Ava, in a voice that Natalie could only call crooked.

The attendant continued her search, now at an accelerated pace. "I can't get you a sooner flight to this destination, but I can get you close. You'll have to board now."

"Do it," said Ava, handing over her tickets. "*Swiftly.*"

"Here," said the attendant, stamping their new tickets and handing them to Ava. As Ava and Natalie darted away, the attendant called after them, "Have a nice flight."

Ava stopped, focusing her entire attention on the surrounding area, and then changed their direction. Natalie's anxiety was rising. To her, Ava appeared to be seriously worried. The two ladies cut through the drawn out line for security checks without so much as a word or alarm from the waiting patrons.

"Natalia," said Ava. "We have a problem."

Natalie's heart jumped and she could feel it in her throat. After the way Ava had dealt with all that had happened before as though it were a breeze, whatever was happening now must be super serious for her to call it a problem.

"Did you know that you had green eyes when you were born?"

"No," replied Natalie.

"Well, your passport says that you have green eyes, so I need you to have green eyes, or we're stuck."

"But—"

"Say it, Natalia. Say you have green eyes, say it for me."

Natalie said, "I have… green eyes?"

"Say it like you mean it, Natalia. Just like before, over and over. And I need you to hurry. He's almost here."

"Who?"

"*Say it*," said Ava in her crooked voice.

Ava and Natalie were next in line. The security attendant reached out and took the tickets and passports from them. "Is this your mother?" asked the attendant.

Natalie kept her head down as she replied, "She's my aunt." She continued to murmur under her breath, "My eyes are green. My eyes are green."

"Is everything okay?" asked the attendant.

"She's just nervous," said Ava. "She's never flown before, and we were delayed. As you can see, we might miss our flight."

"We have the best employees here," said the attendant with a smile. "You're in great hands. I just need to look at your face before I can let you through."

Natalie was frightened to her core. Who did Ava say was there? Would she have to go back with Herold? Would she go to jail for trying to run away? And above all, her eyes were brown. She felt the ring burn into her finger. A warmth spread from the spot and travelled up her arm and into her body. She felt herself relax and her confidence build. She felt the warmth enter her eyes as she looked up.

"There you go, young lady. Now, what's your name?"

"Natalie."

The attendant joked, "I take it you don't go by Natalia." He paused for a moment to look at their tickets again then continued, "You may go through, and good luck on your first flight."

Natalie and Ava quickly passed through the security check portal. As they left, Ava gave a swift pat to the wind in the direction of the ground behind her, and an argument broke out in the security line.

"We must hurry," pressed Ava. "That won't hold him for long."

Suddenly, Natalie couldn't feel the ring's warmth anymore and looked down at it. To her surprise, the ring was no longer deep red, but had turned pure white. "The ring," whispered Natalie urgently. "It's white."

Ava glanced at the ring and pulled Natalie closer. "Your mother can help you no more. We're on our own from here on. If we weren't in trouble before, we are now."

"What do you mean? What's going on? Is Herold after us?"

"No. Something worse. Quickly, this way."

Natalie felt something grab at her back, but there was nothing. She could not explain what she felt, only that something seemed to be pulling her back, and she was having trouble moving, as though she were stuck in a nightmare. Adding to the feeling of terror that gripped her was what she saw ahead of them—the door to the runway closing.

"Hurry," cried Ava, but Natalie wasn't going anywhere.

"I can't move!" screamed Natalie.

"Think positive."

Natalie felt a prickle pass from Ava's hand to hers, and she broke free from the wicked, sloth-like sensation. It felt like waking from the bad dream. The door, however, was shut. Ava continued to run toward the door, and as they almost reached it, she twisted her hand in an opening gesture. A flight attendant opened the door at that instant and politely greeted them. Within minutes, they were seated, and the plane was airborne.

Natalie, exhausted by the rush, was comforted by Ava's sense of relief. As they sat in their seats, Natalie wanted answers to some questions, but Ava said, "Rest," and Natalie did.

CHAPTER THREE

෧ඁ෧

EMOTION

The seat next to Natalie was empty. She sat staring out of the window of her second mode of transportation for the day: a moving train. Miles passed by her—miles of undeveloped terrain: grass, a few trees, and the occasional lengthy hedge. The land seemed out of this world—neither here nor there. There were small families in her car, but Natalie did not dare to make conversation. She sat with her face pasted to the window—her mind wandering about in varying realities that neither related to nor corresponded with her own. Soon, visions of her past flitted elusively through her memory: the smell of stables, the shine of steal, the sound of laughter, the marvelous feel of nature, and even the taste of blood. Once, in her much younger years, Natalie fell from her horse and tested her soft, fleshy cheek against the cold, unforgiving end of a broadsword. The taste was as pure as sunlight on her face, the salty flavor almost enjoyed in the pleasure of survival. The emotion seemed to feed a sense of power in her, a power her mother encouraged her to explore. Remarkably, she didn't scar; only her mind would mark the unforgettable sensation. When Herold later sold the horse for safety reasons she wanted to hate him more than she had ever wanted to before, but her mother had a way of keeping her sensible. "You were meant for greater things," she would say. She didn't know if her mother was responsible for her levelheadedness or whether her view of Herold's anger made her despise resentment. Often, she would see his anger as an inappropriate response, especially to her nightmares, as if she had some control over the dark, faceless presence looming over her, screeching about revenge. Each time she braced in her dream for death, but a bright light would flash and Natalie would wake without fail, tormented. Only Hannah's soothing voice could settle her, "It is merely a test of your character," as only a mother could say so pleasantly. She held her mother's ring tight in her palm, desperate to grasp onto the only physical remnant of her past and let all her emotions flood her; yet, she felt nothing.

Ava sat down next to Natalie, held out a drink, and asked, "Soda?"

Natalie neither moved nor made any sound to acknowledge Ava.

Ava held out her other hand. "Milk? You haven't eaten or spoken for some time."

Natalie shrugged. She stared straight ahead without focus on any single point as the scenery passed in front of her—like she was silently moving through time itself.

"I thought we had something going," said Ava. "At the airport. I know we haven't really talked since, but we've been busy. I could barely wake you up in time to catch this train, but now we have the time to slow down."

Natalie moaned, "I just don't really care. I don't... I can't..."

Ava waited for more, but nothing more came. She asked an employee to take the drinks away and focused all her attention on Natalie.

Finally, Natalie spoke. "I just can't describe it. Nothing seems to matter now. I'm sad, but even that's dull. I have nothing, and I don't want anything. I just want to go away, somewhere far away. And be alone. If life were a game, I wouldn't want to play anymore."

"You feel indifferent," said Ava.

Unmoved, Natalie replied, "I don't know what that means, and I don't care if that's the answer to all my troubles, I still wouldn't want to know."

"That's pretty much what it means," said Ava, sounding concerned. "You have no interest in an outcome either way—no reason or purpose to fight, or even to move at times."

"Yep, that's it." Natalie continued, "I've been angry, sad, and hurt, but nothing, nothing comes close to what I'm feeling now. It's impossible to... I... I can't live like this. I want to be angry. I want to be sad. I want to hurt myself, I just want to feel. It's like I'm dead already. At least with those emotions, any emotion, I would feel alive. I have less than nothing: I can't even feel anything."

"This can be a dangerous time," claimed Ava. "You could go looking for a cause: someone to be angry at, or to be happy with. You can be persuaded into doing things your natural thoughts or beliefs do not agree with. I can do something for you, but only if you allow me to help."

"Anything to end this nothingness."

As Natalie continued to look away, facing the window, Ava stealthily lifted her hand to the height of

Natalie's head and waved it in a circular motion. "I think you'll do a little better now."

"You don't have to worry about helping me," said Natalie. "I feel a little better already. Besides, there really isn't anything you can do to help me anyway."

Ava smirked. "You're probably right. Anyway, what you need most is time and patience. I'll be here for you when you're ready to talk."

Natalie pulled up her shoulders, straightened up, and allowed her eyes to look at individual items in the scenery. "My mother had good intuition, and here I am, unable to feel. My emotions are all out of sorts."

"Mm-hm," replied Ava.

"I have nothing," said Natalie after a long pause. "You don't have to listen the whole time. It'd help if you spoke, explained some things."

Ava smiled. "I'm glad to see that you are not only aware of your needs, but can also ask for them. Emotions are an amazing thing. Good or bad, emotions make us feel alive. But you'd be wise to neither disconnect from them, nor depend upon them. Instead, learn to work with your emotions. Emotions can inspire great strength, healing, or even weakness. Your first step is to be attentive to them. You can really learn a lot about yourself and life when you listen to them."

In a slightly more hopeful voice, Natalie replied, "If I have good intuition like my mother, then shouldn't I have control over my emotions?"

"People confuse emotion with intuition," replied Ava. "Emotion is about how you deal with what has happened. Intuition is how you sense what is happening or even what will happen. Anger will dull the blow, crying will aid in healing. I have no doubt about those. But know this, when you have dealt with and conquered everything inside you, there will be little need left for emotion. When you desire to have more or accomplish greater things, there will be a bigger need for intuition. Emotion can cloud your mind and interfere with your intuition. So, your second step is to live with emotion, but not give it precedence in your life, nor leave it behind."

"Why was my mother with that man?"

Ava knew the question was inevitable. She also knew her niece would someday require an answer for the sake of closure. The bond of family, the link of sisterhood wanted to expose the truth, but in her mind only a fool defers wisdom to emotion. She had often been the fool, but not this time. This day was long anticipated, this scenario had been a probability from the moment Hannah said her goodbye, and Ava was ready. The final embrace of two half-sisters left no promises and no reassurances, only speculation.

Hannah had learned to live by her intuition and, as she explained, Herold was the best course to protect her daughter. Emotion ran deep in the confines of magic. It facilitated power, but also hid secrets of the faith. Herold was a decent man, but Hannah knew if she could feed his anger, keep him frustrated, she could shield her legacy from the contemptuous cutthroats hiding in the shadows. Then why didn't her plan work? She said it herself, Herold was a decent man.

"I'm sure your mother had a reason."

"How could she put me through all that? I really hated her at times, only because of him."

"Life is a guessing game, sweet Natalia. We're always guessing what's best and what's right. You, your mother, even me—we all make choices, decisions whose outcomes we never know beforehand. We take chances based on our experiences, beliefs, and perceptions. We're wrong so many times, but honestly, the only time we truly lose is when we fail to make any decision."

"I want her back. More than anything else, I want her back. But... I don't feel it. I don't feel anything. It's like my tears have dried up," Natalie cried out in frustration.

"Do you feel ashamed for your lack of tears?"

"Yes. I'm a bad daughter."

"Of course you aren't. Being a child is the hardest thing to do, until you become a parent. Both sides have more love than they can show, and life often tends to muddle things."

Ava continued, "There is a normal explanation for your inability to cry. Our mind knows when to grieve and when to fight for survival. We're not free from the wolves yet. You'll grieve when you're safe to do so."

"Ava?" asked Natalie. "Are we in danger?"

Ava's demeanor altered in response to Natalie's question. Without any hint of emotion or any movement, she simply answered, "Yes."

"Is this about the man in my vision?"

"Yes."

"What does he want?" asked Natalie desperately. "Ava, what does he want?"

Natalie turned her head back toward the window. "He wants me, doesn't he? He killed my mother to get to

23

me. My mother was hiding from him. All these years...
she used Herold to hide me. I'm right, aren't I?"

"Your intuition is a thing to be coveted, sweet
Natalia. It will serve you as well as it did your mother.
Unfortunately, you're absolutely right. I'm sorry, my dear
child."

Despondent, Natalie went on, "He killed my mother
and... and he'll kill you..."

"Yes."

"You can't die!"

"Oh, I don't die so easily," replied Ava. "But he
will kill me to take you."

"I don't want you to die. I... I need you."

Natalie threw her arms around Ava, letting out a
sharp cry, and burst out in tears. "I can't lose you. I just
can't."

"Yes. Let it out, child. Let it all out."

Natalie continued to cry for some time until she fell
asleep in Ava's lap. She eventually woke up to the smell
of food and the growling of her stomach. Ava stood
before her, with food and drinks. The train was still;
suddenly, it began to move again and Ava tried to keep
herself upright.

Having recovered, as the train picked up a steady
pace, Ava presented the food to Natalie. "You haven't
eaten. Please."

Natalie accepted the food from Ava and began to
eat. She seemed to have a little joy in her again. Sitting
down beside Natalie, Ava happily noticed that a little
spark of life was back in her niece.

With her mouth half full, Natalie asked, "Why? Am
I crazy? Why do I cry now?"

Ava smiled. "Before, you had nothing. Now you have me."

"Huh?"

"Perspective changes when you have nothing to lose, and perspective is everything. Having no connection to this world, you could not care less about what was happening. Now, you have returned to the living, and so you must deal with your emotions to participate."

Natalie swallowed quickly to reply fast. "I really don't want to lose you. I don't have anything else."

"Do not fear death, sweet Natalia. Embrace it. If death was truly unfortunate, there would still be greater evils. You will soon come to know more of this, but for now, remember this much—never fear death. The way you're thinking now will only bring death closer to your person."

"How?"

"Preoccupation diminishes focus. You will limit your own capacity to prevent what you fear. Not to mention, there are the laws of attraction. Or rather, what you consume will consume you."

"I have no clue what you just said," commented Natalie.

"You'll be just fine, sweet Natalia," assured Ava.

"I will, once I find the restroom," said Natalie in a lighter tone.

This made Ava smile. She pointed behind them. Natalie took a sip of her drink and put it down. Then, she scurried past Ava toward the back with a somewhat brighter attitude and a full stomach. In the restroom, she used her time to fix her appearance a little. She thought about the things Ava had said and felt that sprucing up her looks might help. It was odd, she pondered, how water could clean not only one's body, but even one's soul.

When Natalie was done, she slowly pried open the door to listen in on a conversation that had somehow grabbed her attention even while she was inside, unable to hear everything clearly. She could only see the backside of the rather tall, slender man. Instinctively, she felt that something was wrong as he detained a young female employee with a barrage of questions.

"Again, I'm looking for my daughter. Have you seen a girl, about thirteen to fourteen years old, with blondish-brown hair and green eyes? About this high," he finished as he held his hand up to Natalie's height.

CHAPTER FOUR

❧❧

GALLANTRY

It was him! It was the man who was looking for Natalie, and he now stood an arm's length away from her. How did Ava not know that he had made it on the train? How did he find them? Natalie grew worried as he continued to interrogate the young employee. She locked herself inside the restroom, unsure that the thin aluminum would be able to shield her. She noticed that people were waiting to use the restroom. What would she do if he found Ava in the next car?

With her heart thumping in her chest, Natalie boldly cracked open the door. He was still there. "She's traveling with this woman," he said. "Have you seen her?"

Natalie inspected his ensemble carefully as he shifted, and saw him holding out a picture. It was the same picture—the one she remembered! And he was the man in the picture! A woman, waiting in line to use the restroom, began to push open the door. "Are you done?" she asked.

As Natalie saw the man begin to turn his head, she immediately forced the door shut. The woman knocked on the door, but Natalie completely zoned her out. There was no escape! She was trapped!

"I think I saw her go this way," said the employee.

"I came from that way," replied the well-dressed man. He sported a long pitch-black coat, held a straight cane that was capped with a black jewel, and had an amulet around his neck—with the same shape and design as Natalie's ring, but with a black stone instead.

"Can you describe your daughter again?"

His daughter? Natalie looked in the mirror. Her one consolation was that her eyes were light brown, not green as he believed them to be. Then she thought, "I made it through the airport, I can handle this. I have to control my emotions. No. I must work with them, work side by side." First, she must put it out of her mind that Ava could die. Ava. Ava said preoccupation diminishes focus. What else? Laws of attraction… "He will not find me?" She did not even dare to whisper it. Patience! Patience was her ally. Her position was not compromised yet; she must not act as though she had already been found out. Natalie inhaled deeply and focused entirely on listening to the conversation happening outside.

"Did you try three or four cars down?"

The slender man replied in a strange voice Natalie had heard once before, from Ava. *Did you see a young girl that direction?*

"Yes. Yes, I did."

Natalie waited until she heard the doors between the cars open and close. Then, she made her way back to Ava, positive that the man had gone in the wrong direction.

"Ava!" cried Natalie. "He's here. In the next car."

"But how?" asked Ava, springing from her seat. "This way," she said, rushing in the opposite direction.

In their haste, Natalie looked at the family sitting across from them—so conventional. She registered with a sense of shock what had come to be "normal" for her. The life she could imagine looked so appealing; yet, she felt convinced at this point that she would never have it. She and Ava bolted to the next car like criminals on the run.

Suddenly, Ava stopped between cars, holding Natalie's arm to stop her. "We can exit here."

"What!" exclaimed Natalie, certain that she had misheard her.

Ava gave Natalie a smile as she managed to pull the door open. "Trust me."

Natalie had been begging for an emotion, any emotion, and here it was, bigger than life itself: exhilaration. Not fear, not disbelief, only pure exhilaration. Her blood turned warm, her senses heightened, her strength and agility became uncompromising, her nerves, unflappable. She could see that making this escape was their only chance, and felt the thrill of the chase in her entire being. Her emotions: she utilized the exhilaration to gain courage, speed, strength, and to push away all negativity in her mind.

"Hold my hand," said Ava. "I want you to run till you hit the ground. Understand?"

"Yes, Ava."

"Go!"

"No way!" shouted Natalie as they stepped off the train. They were off and running, but she never felt the ground. They continued, still fleet of foot, on what seemed to Natalie like new-grown wings on her feet. Her body was completely unaffected by the jump; she did not even feel the wind to her face. She felt as though she were in some kind of a bubble of protection; even her hair remained unmoved, with the exception of her natural, lengthy waves. Mere seconds passed before Natalie glanced back at the train. At this point in her adventure, she was really uncertain whether anything should be surprising anymore; however, at that instant, the train must have been at least a city block behind them already.

The two went on for some time before Ava grew tired. "I must stop and rest, my dear," she said.

Despite all the marvelous events that had unfolded in front of her eyes in the last twenty-four hours, Natalie could never have pegged this older woman as being capable of running for over an hour straight. Ava then stopped and took a seat on a large stone like, well, an old woman who had just run for an hour straight.

Natalie also took a moment to recover, taking a deep breath that ended with relaxing her shoulders and lowering her body down on a separate rock. She gazed at the marvelous sunset along the horizon, across open fields— miles and miles of open fields.

"Ava," began Natalie. "I knew it was him. I knew even before I saw the picture in his hand. Before I even heard his voice."

"Yes, child. He had me blocked, but he failed to consider your skills. He will not make the same mistake again, and neither will I."

"Ava, I don't mean to sound arrogant, but... but I had something. I can't explain it, but I felt like I could do something."

"Just you wait, sweet Natalia. Just wait and see all the great things you'll be able to do once we get you home.

Now, enough of chit-chatting. Rest, child. You need it for our journey."

"Will you tell me more about your home?" asked Natalie.

"Later, I promise. We have a long journey ahead of us, and we're not safe until we cross the river. You must rest now."

Natalie slid further down to the ground. Folding her coat to make a pillow, she placed it against the rock and adjusted her body into a crevice in as comfortable a position as she could. "Ava, there's so much I want to know. And, well, you're all I have. What I'm saying is... I don't know what I'm feeling, but..."

"You're afraid of losing me," interrupted Ava, slowly making her way beside Natalie, kneeling on the ground.

Natalie, refusing to reply, lowered her head onto her coat and turned her face away from Ava in embarrassment.

"Do not fear death, Natalia. You did well back there. Very well. You must also not fear the death of others." Ava placed her hand on the back of Natalie's head and said, "*Rest* and *disregard*. We'll have plenty of time to remember. Rest." And Natalie did.

Under the full moon and starlit clear night sky, Natalie felt as though she had only been asleep for some minutes when she was hastily woken.

"Prepare yourself, Natalia" was what she heard, but Ava was too far from her to communicate anything to her without yelling it out. Ava stood some distance away, her arms swaying and her body rocking back and forth. Natalie immediately understood that they were in some kind of danger.

Natalie approached Ava, unsure of what to make of all she was witnessing. Before Natalie could ask anything, four horses came running from the four directions. The horses shoved and bit at each other until a pecking order formed from left to right in front of Ava. "Bow," she ordered, and they did.

Ava, having already made a choice in her mind, was still determined to vet each one. "This will be no ordinary task," she said out loud to the horses.

In that moment, the only thing preventing Natalie from questioning Ava's sanity was the fact that the horses were bowing. They were actually bowing to her!

"This is a commitment," continued Ava. "If you would rather run and play, then leave now." None of the horses budged. Ava began with the one on the farthest left; she glared into the horse's eyes until he lowered his head in disgrace. "You may leave," Ava told the horse, and he did. "I need someone with courage, strength, and loyalty." As she finished, the horse on the far right moved forward. "Impetuous you are, but you'll have to wait your turn." Ava vetted the second horse, but quickly moved to the third one after instructing him to rise. The last horse again stepped forward. Ava, pretending not to notice, looked into the eyes of the third horse. "Rise," she said to him. Then, she came to the fourth candidate: a restless brown horse with a black mane. She was smaller in size than her male counterparts, but rather large for a female at seventeen hands. The horse, when Ava came upon her for inspection, raised her head to Ava's eye level. "Audacious as well. Do you think you can outperform these males?" The horse neighed heartily. "I see into your soul," replied Ava. "Do you know what I see? I see gallantry. You may stay." No quicker did Ava finish her sentence than the other two horses galloped away.

"I had hoped that you'd be the one," Ava told the horse. "I have a friend for you." Ava extended her hand to Natalie, who stepped forward. Ava placed Natalie's hand on the horse's nose, and said, "Natalia, this horse's gallantry will protect you from this day forth. Therefore, I see it fit that we call her Galla. Now come, Galla. Your first task will be your most important one."

Ava whispered into Galla's ear. Then the horse nodded her head in acceptance, kneeling down for Natalie, and prompting Ava to help her mount up. Galla rose, and backed up so that Natalie and Ava could speak.

"Aren't you getting on?" asked Natalie.

"No," replied Ava. "You must go alone. Galla knows where to go, and she will protect you till her last breath."

"He's here, isn't he!"

"Listen, child, your life depends on it. This horse will take you across the river. I will meet you on the other side at dawn. If I fail to make it, you will head north. Galla knows the way. My sisters will find you. They will care for you."

"No! I won't go without you. I won't!"

"Natalia, we don't have time. You must leave. Now. Wait for me. I will be there."

Ava smacked Galla's side and the horse sped off with her distraught passenger. Natalie held on to the horse the best she could, and cried. It was a rough ride, worsened by the overpowering emotions and apprehension Natalie was feeling. After some time, she decided to pull herself up and turn her head with the shallow hope that

Ava was behind her. What she saw, however, was not very reassuring: dark clouds littered with eccentric lights across the ground and sky, a sight she had never even imagined.

Natalie put her head back down, tenaciously holding on to yet another acquired friend she was sure she would lose. There were times during the long night when Natalie was ready to give in. Again, she felt like she had nothing, and the will to fight, to stay alive, was quickly deteriorating. There was no longer a reason to run, to embrace others, when she had lost so many of her loved ones. She knew only one thing: this man did not feel right. Regardless of her mother's death at his hands, her own intuition said that she would die before being with him. Doubts crept in; answers, even from him, might tender more value than life itself.

All thoughts vanished when the dream flashed in Natalie's mind again—the catatonic dream that seized every muscle in her body, barring only her grasp on Galla's mane. Tightening her grip was all she could do to remain seated on the horse.

Natalie felt a darkness surround her and gradually permeate into her tired soul. She laid her body onto Galla's back; Galla's essence seemed to offer her a shallow field of protection, not unlike the warmth one gets from another body when one is cold. The darkness enveloped Natalie and entered her core, clutching all but her hold on the mane of the horse. Then, it traveled to her mind. "Give up," it told her; she wanted to do just that. The force pushed her down the right side of the horse, and she gave in, sliding down, feeling that was the right thing to do. As Natalie began to fall, Galla bucked her rear and efficiently saddled Natalie, perfectly in the center.

Just then, the darkness materialized into a black cloud, which progressively engulfed and preceded them. They were surrounded. "Give up and Ava will live," it spoke.

Compelling, yes. Natalie's life, future, and present were all to be filled with grief. She had nothing. Nothing but the ability to sacrifice. The dream had made life seem weary, worthless. Natalie felt the tug again. All was dark—there was neither ground nor sky, just the black cloud. Unable to move, she had accepted its complete dominance. The voice told her to jump; Natalie put her free hand onto Galla's back to push herself up and off the horse.

Galla felt Natalie shift and shook her mane. Natalie dropped back on to the horse, which steadied her balance and mind. Quickly, she said, "Ride it out, Galla. Ride it out." Galla sped forward faster and faster, moving partly outside the edge of the cloud. Natalie could sense the power of the horse that compelled the dream to fade. Galla fought harder to pull her passenger's head out of the cloud, but the force of the cloud pulled at Natalie's spine, drawing out a shriek from her and forcing her to lose her connection with the horse. The cloud began to overtake Natalie again, but before it did, reality came into focus. Natalie realized her aunt's fate at that instant. Ava was dead. She could not let this man take her too! Natalie took to the mane with both her hands, exhausted, and said, "Ride Gal, ride."

CHAPTER FIVE

ঌৄ

AURORA

The sun, not yet breaching the mountains, was making its presence felt with the preceding light blue sky, orange and pink laced white clouds, and the crisp freshness of the cold but stationary air. Morning had come, but Ava had not. This came as no surprise to Natalie; she knew she had to restart her life yet again—an effort she felt she was doomed to repeat with fewer and fewer assets each time, and more and more reason to free herself from the dull unyielding reminder that her life was pain incarnate.

Natalie—nearly lifeless—lay facing upward, gazing at the rigid clouds in an apathetic void, despite their astonishing display and the picturesque beauty she found fitting for a final end. She was cursed to be the lone observer of this miracle of nature; the clouds, however, were destined for a new beginning, as the wind forced itself upon the canvas, giving a new and unpredictable life to the scenery.

The clouds, reformed in shape, size, and color, danced across the sky in a vivid rush, as if to scream, "We are alive!"

Enter the sun: bright, uplifting, and beautifying to all that which had already registered in Natalie's mind as the most euphoric, albeit underappreciated, visual image of her life. She felt the warmth touch her face, and it bestowed upon her enough life to ready her soul for one final effort. With each new ray, Natalie gained desire, although somewhat meager at first, to strive: strive for survival.

Galla gently nudged Natalie's side with her nose. Life. Natalie would choose life. And to do so, she had to muster the energy to sit up. Almost. Galla gave her another push, and Natalie rolled to her side, listlessly forcing herself upward with both her arms. Soon, she was sitting up, soaking in the sun, perfectly aware that Ava would not be joining her. Galla put her head by Natalie's, and Natalie soon wrapped her arm around the other side of Galla's jaw, holding her in a hug.

Natalie and Galla were attached in their minds and souls. Galla's spirit guided Natalie toward the reality that life is not perfect by any means, which is hard to accept; but hope filled every gap. Natalie knew then that she and Galla had hope if they were together. From that moment forth, they would have a bond that could never be broken. As long as they had each other, there would always be a foundation to build upon; life, existence—if not happiness—all looked like possibilities as the two began to ride again.

CBEO

The last rays of sun set in the western sky, but Galla's drive and pace remained undeterred by it. Exhausted from a full day's ride, the hastening travelers clung on to hope in the northern direction as the night fell once more. Galla's valor had taken them a long way with hardly any need for rest, but fatigue finally set in. Both Natalie and Galla, nearly dead with exhaustion, were determined—it was all or nothing. Neither cared to ponder on death, but both accepted it and were willing to face off against it. Both decided to push until there was nothing left but two carcasses of failed hope. Unfortunately, Natalie's intuition told her that failure was closer than her destination. For once in her life, the ever-reasonable young lady was obstinate in sticking with her winner-take-all approach: victory or death, and death was nearer.

Natalie, on the verge of passing out, lacked the strength to carry on. Galla, who had been going on for the both of them, grew weaker in her capacity to supplement Natalie's failing will. The sky grew darker, and so did Natalie's mind. She fell unconscious a number of times, fearing each time would be the last time she closed her eyes. The line between reality and fantasy blurred in her mind, to the point that she no longer cared about anything.

Suddenly, Galla tripped, but she managed to maintain her footing enough to continue running. Natalie could feel the growing limp in her stride, and she knew that the time had come for her to give in. They would fail, but they would do so together, and on their own terms.

The night sky grew suspiciously dark when Galla began to slow down. Natalie looked around. Despite the eerie darkness, it was clear to her that they were away from any civilization. Galla slowed down to a soft gallop, her limp worsening. The time had come, and Natalie gave up her will to fight. She was satisfied with their combined heroism and felt that they went out proudly, kicking and screaming.

In time, Natalie slowly opened her eyes to what she could only describe as nothing more than a dream. She was completely uncertain about whether what she saw was a mere delusion or reality; but it was definitely something. Galla had stopped in front of three robed women. Natalie failed to understand how she could see in the absolute darkness that enveloped them. She only knew what her eyes showed her—vision in pitch-black darkness. Her eyes picked up only two colors, slightly varying shadows of black and robes of dark red, almost close to the color of her ring before it turned white. Her ring? Natalie's ring vigorously vibrated on her finger.

"You are deathly ill, child," said the first robed woman as she approached Natalie. The woman reached out her hand and placed it on Natalie. "I give you the gift of health."

The second robed woman stepped forth. "Your path forward is far more difficult." She placed her hand on Natalie and said, "I give you the gift of resilience."

Then, the third woman came forward. Her robe appeared to be a slightly different tint of red. "You will need all that you have and more to succeed and achieve your destiny. It is a unique path that you alone must navigate. There is but one gift that will aid you in a conundrum to which only you can find the answer." She placed her hand on Natalie and said, "I give you the gift of wisdom."

When the third woman lowered her hand, Natalie noticed a brooch holding her robe together at the neck. The deep scarlet color of the brooch reminded Natalie of her ring when it belonged to her mother.

The three women resumed their original positions in front of Galla, and bowed.   Galla bowed back.   The darkness subsided as the three women appeared to gravitate toward a dark, black hole-like ball and disappear. The ball took with it the last remnants of darkness, and it was morning again.   Natalie could see the sun in the sky and a stable close by before she collapsed.

CRӒ

"Wake up. Wake up, dear child," a kind voice urged her.

Natalie opened her eyes to find herself lying on a bed in a small room; the setting was quite similar to the room where she had left her mother.

"You're probably hungry," said a woman as she placed a tray of food in front of her.

Natalie groaned, put her head in her hand, and replied, "The three red robes.   Where'd they go?   The gifts?"

The woman, resembling a nurse in her white smock, dropped the drink she was holding and immediately left the room.   Shortly afterward, two girls in white button-down shirts and dark-green plaid skirts entered the room to clean the mess.   Natalie asked for water but neither girl answered her.

Then, a comforting older woman with a kind demeanor and a pleasant smile, dressed in a black robe, entered.   Nothing about this woman's appearance really stood out to Natalie.   She looked like the average suburbanite, but her aura rang with youth and compassion. The woman sat on the bed next to Natalie and uttered a single word: "Natalia."

"That's what Ava called me," replied Natalie. "But my name is Natalie."

"Of course," said the black and gray-haired woman. "It's a rare honor to be visited by one woman in red, let alone three. Can you tell me exactly what they said?"

"I remember a brooch. A brooch like my mom's... uh, my ring. But it was red." Natalie held up her hand to reveal her white ring.

"Yes, I see. Did any of these women speak to you?"

"Yes. They gave me three gifts: wisdom, health, and, uh, resilience."

The woman in the black robe tried to give her the impression that Natalie's words meant very little, but Natalie knew better. Her intuition told her that the woman was suppressing jubilance.

The door opened again. A shrewish-looking woman with pale skin and jet black hair, dressed in a black robe, entered the room, followed by a woman dressed in a red robe.

"That's it!" shouted Natalie. "Three red robes that looked exactly like hers!"

The two women stayed quiet until the woman sitting on the bed rose and addressed the woman in red, "Headmistress."

"Has she said much?" asked the headmistress.

"She only mentioned three gifts."

The woman dressed in the red robe turned her attention to Natalie. "I'm the headmistress here. You can address me as Headmistress. The woman to my left is Mara, and the woman you have been speaking with is Devia. Devia will be working to help integrate you to our school. Should you have any concerns, you will have to take them up with her for the time being. My time is very important, so I will be frank: Where is Ava?"

"I was hoping she made it here," replied Natalie.

"What does your intuition tell you?" asked the headmistress.

Natalie lowered her head. "That she's dead."

"Then we both know this to be true. What I don't know is how."

"We were followed, a dark presence. A man... A thin man with an amulet like my ring, but black."

"Saul!" exclaimed Mara.

The headmistress waved Mara's comment away. Then she asked, "How many were there?"

"One. Just one. That's all she said. I saw him too. Up close."

"You were close to him, and still made it here?"

"Yes," replied Natalie.

Mara spoke urgently, "Ava's recklessness affects us all. We should abandon her cause before whispers are renewed and a certain shadow emerges."

"No, she is our sister and she chose this path," replied the headmistress. "We must care for the child as she would. Natalia, this is very important: what did you see when you were separated?"

"Fire. Fire in the sky. Everywhere."

The two women in black gasped in shock.

The headmistress, however, remained unaffected. "We must convene" is all she said in response before waving the women out and adding, "Rest, child."

CHAPTER SIX

❧❧

RUNAWAY

Natalie lay in bed, embracing the anxiety. Attachment, relationships, bonding: what were they if they turned to nothing? All that time, effort, and commitment destroyed in a heartbeat—never complete, always fighting. Why? For the fear of loss? Her life felt like the act of repeatedly building a sandcastle, only to watch a wave demolish the half-constructed structure, each and every time, as she helplessly watched. Her relief from the piercing emotions came in form of the epiphany that fear of loss cannot exist without a connection.

Natalie rolled over to her side, facing an empty closet with no shelves and no doors. There seemed to be no point or purpose to the closet, despite the wasted efforts of some misguided person to make it. What a waste of time, thought Natalie. Just seal off the wall and let it die. She would have left it undone, because, in her mind, the closet never wanted to be made—a favor she would have known to perform at the very beginning.

The door was pushed open rather abruptly, as though the intruder were under the impression that the room was empty. Two young women entered, one after the other. Both were dressed in the white and plaid uniform that Natalie had previously seen on the other girls, but these girls seemed older. The first was blonde with penetrating, hazel eyes. With a confidence that seemed to be far beyond her years, and the schoolgirl dress, she entered with force and purpose. The second, following close behind, carried an extra uniform on a hanger and some other pieces of clothing. The blond girl stopped and turned to look in the direction of Natalie, staring. The second girl, a dark brunette, stopped close to the first girl, turned away, and hung the uniform on a hook in the closet. Ah, it did have a purpose. Then, the brunette arranged a folding table and laid the remaining items of clothing on it, barring the shoes, which she placed on the ground.

Without hesitation, the second girl made her way to the door, but paused when she noticed the blonde girl standing still. The blonde girl, her relentless eyes piercing deep into Natalie's soul, waved the other girl away. Natalie, extremely uncomfortable, turned her body to face upward; yet she could see the blonde girl from the corner of her eye.

Slowly, the blonde girl let out a few words, "So, you're Natalia."

The booming silence following those words rattled Natalie's nerves. She, however, refused to roll all the way over, as though this had somehow become a game that she refused to lose.

Before Natalie could ask her why everyone seemed to know her name, the haughty schoolgirl began to speak again. Natalie was desperate to utilize every sense at her disposal to catch every condescending syllable the girl uttered, and even slowed down her breathing to listen more carefully.

"You don't look like much to me."

What did that mean? And how could this girl, whom Natalie had never met, already harbor this much disdain for her? But Natalie refused to crack; her eyes were locked on the ceiling, her mind primed and ready to fire back.

The standoff was finally over when Devia stepped into the room. "Melissa," she said. "You are no longer needed here."

"Melissa," repeated Natalie in her mind. She would be sure to remember that name, even though she did not plan on staying there very long. Despite Devia's words, another moment passed before Melissa decided to end the game and leave the room.

Devia sat down beside Natalie. "How are you feeling, Natalie?" she asked.

Devia waited for an answer, but none came her way. Becoming a bit more reserved suddenly, as if she had intruded already too much, Devia stood up and inspected the uniform. "Yes, this should fit you really well. There are a lot of young girls your age who can relate to some of your needs."

"What could they understand?" barked Natalie.

"I think you'd be surprised, if only you gave us a chance, that is."

"What do you know?" retorted Natalie.

"I would know more if you told me."

"What's the point?"

"Natalie, I'm here to help you. You're hurt, confused... you feel abandoned. Surely, you would like to feel better. And I can help you with that."

Natalie crossed her arms. "What are you, some kind of a therapist?"

"Something like that," answered Devia.

"I don't need your therapy. I just want to be left alone."

"Oh, but we're *not* in therapy. That would require a relationship. Something that we definitely don't have. All I wish to do is show you around and perhaps learn about some of your needs and attend to them."

"And what are my needs?" asked Natalie with a little fire in her voice, which was actually meant for the Melissa girl.

"That's what I'd like to find out," replied Devia.

"You're the therapist. Shouldn't you already know what I need?"

Devia chuckled. "You're determined. I do not, however, specialize in the ways of Natalie. I deal with behaviors and patterns, but you... you're as unique as a snowflake. And only you know you. I have nothing until you show me. Will you show me?"

Natalie tried to pull herself up but collapsed back down. "I can't. It's so difficult. Why?"

"It is, but it gets better." Devia placed her hand over Natalie's forehead. "Let it out, and it will pass." Devia stepped back and held out her hand. "Shall we?"

Natalie, slightly choked up, managed to get into a sitting position, placing her legs over the side. Any movement proved tedious. "I don't want to try. Knowing me is like a death sentence. It just seems like too much work, that... That starting up..." Natalie began to cry. "I can't do anything right. It's not worth trying. I just want to sit here and rot. You can't understand. Even I don't understand."

"Help me understand, Natalie."

"It's like there's gray everywhere, and your only purpose is to avoid the gray. How do I say it? Weighed down. I feel weighed down, and sad. I can't get started. I don't want to get started. I just don't want to move. I just want to lie here and be left alone."

Devia bent over and placed Natalie's head on her shoulder. She allowed Natalie to let out some of her grief before responding. "You are overwhelmed, distant, but it's for your own protection. It's absolutely understandable, given what you've been through. We're here for you, and we'll be patient. I'm very proud of you for speaking. That's all we ask of you. Everything else will be easier than you think."

Natalie continued to cry as Devia massaged her back.

Natalie inhaled a couple of short wet breaths, but managed to gather some air in between.

Devia straightened up and patted Natalie on the back. "You're a brave woman. What you've been through takes a lot of courage. Our body is made to survive, you see. But when it does survive, all the elements that do not help survival tend to shut down. Survival is an experience of pure spiritual concentration and extreme effort; your senses, your thoughts, your physical capacity—everything is taxed to the extreme, ready, prepared to literally spring into fight or flight mode; all your energy is taken up—full throttle. This is a chore for the body and the mind, and it comes at a great expense. It's normal. *You* are normal to experience the repercussions in the aftermath of entering survival mode. This is a difficult state to return from, but you have to understand that you are not alone anymore. You don't have to do this on your own."

"I can give you something to make it easier," continued Devia.

Natalie gently moved away from Devia's hand in response. "No. That's alright. I just need some time to dry up and change. Do you mind?" she asked.

"Of course not," replied Devia. Grinning, she left the room.

Natalie lifelessly pulled herself out of the bed before tugging at the outfit she had on. She then dragged her feet to the closet, thumbed through the uniform, and looked at the shoes on the ground—shiny black, with one large silver buckle, right in the center. "Really?" she exclaimed. Everything she needed, however, was available—even the open window.

CRBO

Devia joined the headmistress and Mara, who were waiting outside the building. "She's going to run."

"I know," replied the headmistress. "Your thoughts?"

Devia closed her eyes and bowed down her head. "She's fragile. Easily susceptible to manipulation. She will take up the first cause she finds, forever. She's in danger."

"She is vulnerable," said Mara. "She will follow whoever takes her on; whoever decides to train her—be it good or evil. Ava has tasked us with this."

"Recommendations?" asked the headmistress.

Devia sighed. "We cannot force her to stay. She must remain here not only of her own will, but of her own desire. Anything less would be a disservice to her, us, and the other children."

The headmistress shook her head. "Agreed. There is nothing we can do. We cannot force her. If we do, she will grow resentful and we will lose her eventually. She must want to, choose to, stay. She must find her own way back, if she can."

Mara snorted, "It's for the best, if her mother couldn't protect her here, then how are we expected to?"

Just then, the three women saw Natalie in her new uniform, riding Galla bareback, away from them. The headmistress raised her hand in the air, her palm facing the direction Natalie had gone, and moved it up and then side to side. "May your path be clear and fortune be on your side."

Natalie rode on. Riding was all she now knew in order to live and survive. Her comfort, companionship, and trust were all removed from the world and contained easily in a single package of muscle, speed, and loyalty— the one who would die with her, even that very day if that were their destiny.

CHAPTER SEVEN

❧❦

BELONGING

Natalie dismounted Galla, reviewing all her memories of childhood. The two were stopped by a new larger river to the west, a direction about which she felt positive. It was the path away from her experience with Ava, and she felt it was the right way to continue. This was an opportunity for them to freshen up, and Natalie knew she had to walk the horse before she could drink. Going back down memory lane to her childhood, Natalie recalled moving around a lot. One of the places she remembered was a ranch. Her connection with horses ran deep. Coincidence? Could her mother have known so much about what she would need, what she would become? There were, however, so many places; she had picked up so many skills that seemed needless at the time. But were they relevant? Necessary? Would she really need to fight with swords? Although, it was true that fencing was one of her passions. Maybe her mother had just tried to teach her everything in wanting to find Natalie's natural interest. Regardless, past experiences were proving to be significant. Must she now understand her past, something she had pushed aside, to know her future?

Her disorganized thoughts, however, prevented her from finding a direction, making a decision of what to do, where to go.

Galla was drinking from the river. Natalie too decided to squat down and quench her thirst. Looking at the river, she decided that it was calm and quite safe to cross. This was the decision she had to make at the moment. Everything else would fall into place— hopefully, more easily than how her life was currently going.

Natalie took a moment to test the cold water, and then tried to lead Galla across. Galla shook her head and neighed. "Come, Gal," urged Natalie.

Galla stepped backward, shaking her head and backing away.

Natalie knew enough about horses to understand the hesitation. But Galla seemed to be more apprehensive than when they had crossed the last river. Nevertheless, desperation is a great substitute for courage, thought Natalie. Then, Natalie remembered that horses lack depth perception, as their eyes are on the sides of their heads, thus making it difficult for them to realize the actual depth of water. Of course, she was uncertain; so, Natalie decided to show Galla how shallow the water was.

Natalie trotted into the river till the water was about waist high. "Come on, Gal." She gestured toward herself. "Come on."

Galla neighed again and stomped her feet.

Natalie went on about one-third of the way and splashed some water into the air. "It's safe, Gal. Come on."

Though Natalie said it was safe, something seemed oddly amiss: an uneasy feeling about the thin man—Saul was his name. But this was different—as though he were there, but not really. He no longer had power over her as he did before, but she felt his presence: watching her, waiting.

Galla began to stomp harder on the ground, swaying her head sideways, keeping one solid eye on Natalie at all times. It was as if she was trying to say, "Come, Natalie!"

Natalie felt she could understand Galla, a feeling that far overpowered the sense of danger that she refused to accept. "What's wrong, Gal? He can't hurt us here. We're safe. Come, Gal."

Galla began to freak out and run in circles.

"Are you okay, Gal?"

Galla screeched again.

"Okay, Gal. You seem to know best. I'll listen to you," said Natalie before she began to move toward the bank of the river.

Natalie found the action of egress to be far more difficult than she had imagined. The water seemed higher, rougher. What was she thinking before? This river had become bigger than when she had stepped into it, much bigger. There were rocks in it too, and rapids. How could she have missed all this before? Had she been tricked? Saul! "Why?" she thought. Galla! Saul needed to separate her from Galla!

Quickly, Natalie attempted to exit the river. She fell and rolled, not quite touching the bottom. She came up and gasped for air. "Galla!" she screamed.

Galla's eyes followed her movements in the river, watching Natalie choke and struggle in the water.

Natalie hit a rock and tried to fight herself out of the water despite the slippery moss-like barrier between the granite and her salvation. She slipped into the water again, bobbed, and sank once more. "Galla! Help!" she repeatedly shouted as she went up and down in the river.

Galla pursued Natalie down the edge of the river, waiting for the right moment. She moved persistently to let Natalie know that she was not alone, asking her not to give up.

"Galla!" Natalie went under again and came back up propped against a rock, but this time her foot was caught in the ground. Tide after tide washed over her as she timed her breaths between them.

Galla fussed, shook, and bounced frantically.

Natalie drew some water into her mouth and lungs, coughing, gagging, and spitting it back out. She felt her fight dwindling as another bout of water gushed down her throat. She battled for trivial pockets of air. Each loss of breath made her endeavor more difficult and drastically consumed her strength.

Galla ran upstream and gauged the river. Her trepidation no longer a factor, she leaped deep into the icy rapids, struggling to balance herself. She turned her back to Natalie, allowing the water to guide her in reverse, and grant her more time to plan the rescue.

The water rolled and cracked and slapped, letting Natalie know that neither her nor Galla were in control of the situation and gaining control anytime soon appeared quite impossible. Natalie, seeing Galla quickly approach her, tried her best to stand and reach for the large and mighty beast. Galla, unfortunately, was still some distance from Natalie's grasp, but was speedily approaching.

Natalie reached for Galla's mane. Galla, however, had no control over her path, being forced downstream by the current, making her helpless to provide any assistance. Rescue was for Natalie to grab, and only Natalie could control it. Weak from all the taxation she had experienced in the water, Natalie grasped as much of Galla's mane as she could, but the water's hold on her foot was greater than her strength. Her grip was loosening. Galla fought the water to give Natalie more time, but time was slipping away. Natalie let go, and Galla tumbled in her desperate attempts to stand steady by Natalie's side.

The surge of the water increased. What seemed like splashes before, now came as waves, dancing vigorously back and forth, a celebration of nature's true dominance. The height of the river rose, and Natalie remained underwater for what seemed an eternity before she could again extend her head above the surface. She looked down the river for Galla but saw no sign of her. Her efforts seemed to be in vain. Interestingly, this moment became one of peace and tranquility for Natalie. Even if she had the strength to free herself, she lacked the capacity to reach the shore. The missing Galla was her last hope, and hope was now gone. Serenity filled her body. She couldn't win, and she didn't have to fight anymore. She came to accept this in her mind, and this calmed her.

Natalie managed to reorganize her thoughts, now that she had no fear and was rather reenergized with a new sense: a bold idea to abandon her struggle to overcome the environment. Instead, she must undermine it! This was a different feeling, albeit not quite an unfamiliar one she had often experienced in nature when she bonded with her mother. She ordered the river to calm down. "Calm," she said. And it worked!

The massive splashes dwindled to minor clatters, allowing Natalie to catch her breath. She tried to gain more command over the river, but was met with her limitations against the hostility of the water in trying to bury her forever. Still unable to free herself, Natalie looked for Galla, but she saw nothing. Natalie knew that Galla was alive—she could feel it. "Come, Gal. Come," she insisted, but again, there was nothing.

Natalie felt her control over the river slacken. She calmed herself down. "Come, Gal. You can do it." But still, nothing. "Fight, Gal! Fight!"

Suddenly, Galla shot out of the water. If ever a being had fought to drive every ounce of muscle, nerve, and energy with her will, Galla did it. She leaped out of the water, ignoring the tremendous force of nature that can even cut a canyon. Galla fought, and made her way closer and closer to her friend as Natalie clashed with the grasp of nature itself. Galla forced herself to slice through the constantly gushing water, taking advantage of the small window of opportunity. For a moment, nature gave in, allowing Galla to gain more ground. Natalie could now reach Galla, and stretched her arm out for a handful of mane; but she was no longer in control, and neither was the river. Galla, in her fit of insubordinate rage, chomped on Natalie's arm, placing it between the gap of her front and back teeth. With a firm and unassailable grip, Galla yanked Natalie free from her shoe, which remained stuck in the rocky bed, and dominated the river in her flight to the bank; and they were soon out of the water.

Galla laid Natalie down beneath a tree. Natalie lightly stroked Galla's face, "Good girl. Good girl," she repeated before she passed out. The two, worn to the bone, rested.

Natalie awakened as the sun began to set. Another day, and still no direction. "What do you think, Gal? Is there anywhere we belong?"

With her teeth, Galla picked up a single-buckled black shoe and placed it next to Natalie.

"Really, Gal? There's only one place where this shoe belongs." Saying this, Natalie flung the shoe into the river.

Galla gestured with her head, as if to say, "Come here."

"What are you saying? Do you know where we belong, Gal?"

Galla made the gesture again.

"Well, you were right about the river. So, I owe you that. Let's go."

Natalie mounted Galla, and they rode east. It was a long night, but Natalie made the most of it, her mind full of thoughts and questions. Did riding bareback hurt Galla as much as it hurt her? How nutritious was the grass that her horse ate? Anything sounded good about now. Had she been too hard on Devia? Who else would take her in so unconditionally, with so much love? None of that mattered anymore. What was done was done, and Galla knew the way.

As Natalie pondered, she pulled her body closer to Galla's back and closed her eyes. The trust that had developed between them was surprisingly superseded by another feeling—one of cohesion. In only a couple of days, Natalie could understand her horse in such a way that they seemed to ride as one. But there was more to it than just that—they were one. Natalie felt like a part of Galla, and they were never separate: one whole entity occupying two connected bodies of flesh. Natalie felt herself run and breathe with Galla. She could feel Galla's thoughts and communicate with her without speaking aloud. Even their hearts beat together.

Natalie felt the freedom of true existence—the wonder of being a horse. Running this way was greater than any euphoria she had ever felt. They ran, sprang, and flowed with each other in synch—like a body and limb, entirely complimentary. Natalie lifted her head to feel the wind in her face. This was freedom, this was contentment. Natalie lifted herself higher, her hair flying in the wind: pure delight. She and Galla were bonded forever. Natalie pulled herself close to Galla again, patted her chest, and said, "I feel you, girl."

The sun loomed over the mountains, preparing to establish its oversight of yet another day. But today was different for Natalie: there was a smell of positivity in the air. A feeling of serenity settled in her, and she believed that her life was going to change for the better.

Natalie's head was laid against Galla's neck as the horse began to slow in her stride. Natalie stretched herself and pulled away from the warmth of Galla's fuzzy body to look at their destination. Déjà vu! This morning, like the previous one, started with their arrival at the home Ava had chosen for her. This time, Natalie and Galla were greeted by dozens of women, many of whom were dressed in schoolgirl uniforms with the terrible buckled shoes.

"This is where we belong, huh, girl?"

Galla stopped, and Natalie dismounted to face the crowd of girls. A woman in a brown robe walked Galla away to the stables as the girls surrounded Natalie.

"I am an orphan," said one girl before she hugged Natalie.

A second girl announced the same: "I am an orphan." She too hugged Natalie.

Another girl followed, and another one, before all the girls embraced one another in a group hug around Natalie. All accept Melissa, the only one who stood on a porch next to two women in black robes: one, a much older, haggish woman of pale skin, and the other, a youthful pleasant-looking woman with a light bronze complexion—exact opposites in appearance. Oddly, the younger woman boasted a gray strip of undecipherable symbols down the left side of her cloak. Melissa was also in a robe, a faded green one.

In Natalie's circle of assimilation, she came to realize something: in a place where no one belongs, they all belong. She was home. It was not long until the crowd was broken up by Devia. "Come with me, Natalie. I have something for you."

Natalie followed Devia into the part of the building where she had once stayed. They went through a hallway and a different room. Devia entered first, and invited Natalie to follow her. There was a bed in the room, but it was occupied. Natalie was confused, until she saw…

"Ava!" yelled Natalie with joy. Quickly, she jumped to Ava's side and embraced her wholly. "What? What's wrong with her?" asked Natalie, noticing the pallor on Ava's face and her still, motionless features.

Devia placed her hand on Natalie's shoulder. "She's alive. That's all we could hope for, for now. So, do you wish to stay this time?"

"Yes," replied Natalie. "Definitely, yes." Natalie, teary eyed, pointed down at Devia's shoes. "But we have to talk about those buckled shoes."

CHAPTER EIGHT

WITCHES OF THREE

Making her way back from the local mall, Natalie walked beside Devia toward her new home. For the first time, she was about to properly look at the grounds. At the center of three buildings sat, in Natalie's opinion, an unromantic castle. It was indeed a castle, about five stories high, with battlements and bastions at the corners. But there was nothing really fancy like oriel windows, or a moat. There were also no towers and high rises. It was simply a building made of stone; nonetheless, it was a castle. To the right was the building in which she had stayed. Surprisingly, it was a piece of modern architecture, slightly removed from the castle, about three stories high. She already knew that the stables were behind this building. To the left of the castle sat a shorter structure that seemed to be sprawled over at least an acre, maybe two. This building was not modern in any way, but it was no castle either. There were other smaller buildings to the back, but this stadium-like structure was what stood out the most, even more so than the castle.

"Here you go, Natalie," said Devia. "This is where the girls stay."

"Luckily," thought Natalie. It was the newer structure to the right. The building boasted a rather large porch from where many girls were descending to see what Natalie had brought back.

"What do you have?" asked one girl.

Natalie lifted one foot and turned it in the air to show off her new Doc Martens. "They're called Mary Janes," replied Natalie. "Two small buckles on the side and maximum comfort. Not to mention, style you can't beat."

"Wow!" exclaimed the girls.

"Does this mean we can have them too?" asked one.

Devia sighed. "Apparently, we will be changing over."

The girls cheered and eagerly looked the shoes over as they led Natalie inward.

"I can show her the dorms," said a girl. "I'm Susan," declared the short, curly-haired student as she tried to sweep her motionless black hair away from her light-skinned face with an energetic flip. Susan placed her tiny hands on her hips, revealing a small frame that was not thin, or necessarily chunky. She had a way of showing that she was just right, especially with her extremely inviting and bright smile.

"Will you be alright, Natalie?" asked Devia.

"Yes, I'm okay."

"Good," said Devia. "If you have any questions, go to the castle and ask for me. There will be someone working at the front, in case you have an issue."

"Thank you, Devia." Natalie hesitated, "For everything."

"These are the dorms," explained Susan as she led Natalie away. "We stay on the second and the third floors. There are twenty of us. And you're our twenty-first. Oh, that's the castle," continued Susan when she noticed that Natalie's eyes were drawn to the old building. "We're really not allowed in there, except on special occasions."

"What's that big building on the other side?" enquired Natalie.

"That's the arena. We have our training and contests there."

Natalie continued to look at the odd building as Susan led her to the porch and into the dorms. Once inside, she was greeted by so many other girls that Natalie reserved the right to not memorize any names for the time being.

"Where do I stay?" asked Natalie.

"That depends on the den mother. She's the student leader." As they continued to walk, Susan went on, "But watch out for Ms. Hag. She's like the principal."

"Seriously, her name is Ms. Hag?"

"Shhh! Don't use that name. That's just what we call her, but if she hears you... I don't know what she'll do, but I'm sure you don't want to find out. Trust me."

"How will I know who she is?"

"You'll know when you see her. She looks like a hag—old and mean."

"I think I saw her standing next to Melissa when I arrived."

"If you think you saw her, you probably did. There's no mistaking her. But make sure you call her by her real name, Ms. Haggle. Do you understand?"

"Yes. I'll make sure. If it's the same lady, I don't want to get on her bad side."

Just then, they came upon an older student who had her back to them. She was dressed in the same uniform as Natalie and the other girls.

"This is our den mother. She's in charge of us," said Susan.

The den mother turned around to face Natalie, preemptively presenting a devious smile—a smile so stiff that it seemed to be pasted to her face.

"Melissa!" gasped a startled Natalie.

"Good," replied Melissa. "Just as long as you know who's in charge. You'll bunk with Emma. Your linen and clothing have already been provided in your room. Susan is your floor leader, and she will address any concerns you may have. If she is unable to do so, then I will deal with them. Under no circumstances are you to bother Devia with any of your petty concerns. That would be considered going over my head. And that, child, is intolerable in our ranks. Do I make myself clear?"

"Yes."

"Yes, Den Mother, will be your reply."

"Yes, Den Mother," replied Natalie.

"One more thing," continued Melissa. "Rebecca, Isabella, front and center."

Two older looking girls came at Melissa's call. Both stopped slightly behind Melissa, one on her each side. The brunette, Rebecca, was the one Natalie had seen before. She had straight mid-length hair, blue eyes, and light skin. Her stance had "stuck up" written all over it, but she lacked Melissa's confidence. The other one, Isabella, was very pretty. Not that the other girls weren't, but Isabella had something special about her. Her wavy long black hair nicely complimented her olive skin and dark-brown eyes. Her nose was not perfect, but it was fairly unnoticeable in comparison to her well-proportioned face and slightly angled cat-like eyes. She had an appealing charisma about her, which was completely nullified by her obstinate persona.

"These are my women of three," stated Melissa. "In my absence, they are in charge. If one gives you an order, it is to be obeyed as though it came from me. It will not be ignored, or you will have to deal with me. Do you understand?"

"Yes, Den Mother."

"Do you have any questions?" asked Melissa.

"I've just never heard of... what do you mean, women of three?"

"I'm shocked," replied Melissa. "You see, you should not have any question for me, as you have Susan to address your needs. But that is indeed not a bad question for me to answer. It has to do with the dynamics of relationships. Men are weak in terms of social skills and can work only in echelons. They need a clear leader and a defined chain of command to function. Women can work in groups and often function well in groups of equality. In our world, we tend to work in groups of three. With one leader. That would be me."

Melissa glanced down at Natalie's new shoes. "Individualism is the decay of order," she said before waving Natalie away and adding, "You may go."

Susan pulled Natalie away in the direction of her room. As Natalie was about to speak, Susan shushed her and continued to lead her up some stairs. Natalie looked back to see that Melissa and the other two girls refused to budge from their triangular position of defense.

In her new room, Natalie was greeted by a meek little girl, Emma. To her surprise, Emma seemed to only be seven or eight years old. "You look so young," remarked Natalie.

In a shy, yet excited voice, Emma said, "I'm the youngest one here."

Susan craned her neck out the door to see if anyone was lurking near the small two-bedded room. If the room had a door, she would have shut it. Then, in a lowered voice, she said, "It's a lot easier here than she made it out to be. I don't know why, but she doesn't seem to like you."

"She doesn't like anybody," said Emma.

Susan laughed. "Isn't that right! But she really can't do much to you. She was just trying to intimidate you."

Natalie scoffed. "She did a good job. And what's with that women of three?"

"More like witches of three," said Susan.

"They are like witches, aren't they?" added Natalie.

Susan controlled her expression before she gave anything away. Natalie was confused about what she was hiding. Her intuition told her that Susan was genuine and harmless, but she was sure, as she stood there, that Susan was withholding something about the "women of three."

"Women of three. What does that mean anyway?" asked Natalie.

Susan pretended her slip had gone unnoticed. She inspected the bedding left for Natalie and went back to the question. "Women of three is a pattern that you'll find here quite often. It's how we work—in threes. And there are certain characteristics to the dynamics, as Melissa put it. But it isn't exactly what she said. It's just something, you know, that you'll learn as you go."

"What kind of characteristics?" asked Natalie.

"I guess it's really not for me to say, and quite hard for me to explain. But it's basically a bonding between three women, in which they are pretty much equals. There can be a leader, but the leader may also change, especially depending on the task at hand. The three are kind of one in a sense, and inseparable in direction, I guess. It's hard to explain. All I know is that betrayal of any of the others in the group is the greatest sin possible. It would be like betraying the order. So, don't bond with a girl whose motives you aren't certain of. If you get into trouble, all of you go down together."

CHAPTER NINE

❧✦

BULLY

Monday:
"Natalie, are you ready for school?" asked Susan, dashing down the hall.

Natalie, dressed in her school uniform, was alone in her room. Since Emma was still at breakfast, Natalie thought it would be a good time to organize her newly issued clothing. She went through several black sweaters, but each one looked the same. Everything was exactly the same for every girl, except her two new pairs of shoes. Even the athletic shoes provided were all the same color. Natalie took a final glance at the mirror next to her closet and smiled in a slight approval of her outfit. In her background, she saw Susan standing in the doorway.

"Good, your bed is made. Now, are you ready to walk?"

"Walk? To where?"

"To school. It's about a mile away, so we should get going."

Natalie did a double take. "You mean we don't use the classrooms on the first floor?"

"No, silly. What do you think the uniforms are for? We go to a real school; a private school with boys and everything. These women can't teach. Could you imagine

Ms. Hag teaching math? When she was born they only had ten numbers."

"Oh, that school, by the mall. Uh, how come there are no buildings around us?"

"The orphanage owns all this, the land, the forest, everything." Susan circled her finger in the air. "We're on the edge of town because the orphanage won't allow this to be developed. Come on. We don't want to be late."

"Aren't we going to wait for your friend?"

"Oh, Toddi. She left already. Usually leaves early, comes home late. It's an academic thing. That's why they recruited her. She's the only one who's not an orphan."

About a dozen students, distributed into social groups, were on their way to school. Natalie kept an eye out for Melissa, but she was fortunately absent from Natalie's immediate surroundings. Emma, however, was quite present. "Can I walk with you?" she asked.

"No," replied Susan. "This is big girl talk."

Emma lowered her head and slowed to a pace that set her far behind the two girls to allow them some privacy.

"I've never heard her talk so much. Only since you've been here."

Shocked, Natalie asked, "You mean, she doesn't normally talk like that?"

"No. She never really fit in. Normally, the girls here aren't that young, but they took her in anyway."

"Did her parents die too?"

"No one knows. It was said a man of the cloth brought her here in the middle of the night."

"And your parents?"

"I have a mother," hesitated Susan, slowing in her step, guarding her words, and clenching her jaw. Natalie waited for more, but it was a relationship Susan often refused to discuss; a separation she cared not to relive. By her own decree, Susan had chosen the orphanage due to a disconnect and feelings of betrayal—a common result of a parent disowning a child. Not far from where they stood, she had watched her mother drive away and never look back. Susan's crime, her shame, repressed by her mother's loathing; wrestled into a shell of fear with the smack she received from the one who gave birth to her.

"Does she visit?"

"So, I heard you spoke to the headmistress."

"Yeah, she had some questions for me." Natalie knew enough of people to know when they wanted the subject to change, and enough of herself to let certain things go.

"Wow," replied Susan. "We rarely see her, and we never talk to her. I think Melissa is the only one who has. Then you know to address her as headmistress?"

"Yes," replied Natalie.

"A few other rules," continued Susan. "Ms. Hag is in charge of the sisters. Don't even think about talking to her. Only Melissa does, and she's constantly in trouble."

"Is that why she's always angry?"

"She has a history; you don't want to go there. And don't listen to what she said about Devia; she's third in charge, but quite approachable. She's like a counselor, so don't hesitate to talk to her if things get bad. Or Josephine. She's the only one here who has a gray strip on her robe. Mara is second in charge, but she can be erratic.

Some days are good, some bad, but she's always a step behind the others. Have you met her?"

"Is she the one who hangs around the headmistress?" asked Natalie.

"Never away from her side. Now, anyone in a black robe, you call her mother; anyone in a brown robe, call her ma'am; and all the students sisters, except Melissa, who's den mother. There are classes after school, so you need to do your homework during the free period. It's not bad; there'll be plenty of time. We do chores as designated by Melissa—assigned by the upper people. So, don't upset her, or you'll get a lot. Fortunately, we don't cook, clean, or do laundry."

"I'm a little nervous," confessed Natalie.

"Don't worry. See, we're here. Just go inside the front door and turn to the right. You'll find the front office. They'll make your schedule. Try to get second lunch, that's mine. If you don't though, just try to avoid Melissa. She can be tough."

Before she knew it, it was lunch time and Natalie glanced at her schedule: first lunch. "Drat," she thought. Did her life need to be so hard that she could not even avoid one person? Natalie followed the other girls to the lunch line and took out her pass for inspection. There were only a few tables inside the cafeteria, so she ventured out. As the students all knew, good weather meant an outside lunch, but everyone would have to be accommodated inside in case of poorer weather.

There was only one table that was not crowded with students, and that was where Natalie sat. A lone student, about Natalie's age, occupied one corner of the table; there was no one else. The girl was reserved, yet vibrant in an unusual way, with beautiful characteristics. The girl was neither white nor black, but rather a beautiful intoxicating mix of the two. Her long fluffy hair shined of brown and blonde and took up a huge space, even partly covering her face. It was her naturally dark bronze skin, however, that grabbed one's attention and directed one straight to her perfectly remarkable light-blue eyes.

Natalie sat away from this girl, wondering why she sat alone. The girl caught Natalie staring at her. But could one blame Natalie? Those eyes demanded attention, and Natalie, although embarrassed, felt like she should not be ashamed. Some things were just pleasant to look at, and nothing else should be made of that.

"Natalie!" called out a familiar voice, causing her to jump in surprise.

Melissa was standing right behind her with the infamous triangular formation of her entourage. "Let me see your tray."

"Excuse me?" replied Natalie.

"Your tray," repeated Melissa. "Hand me... your tray."

Natalie, still sitting, lifted up her tray of food for Melissa to take, but anxiously botched the exchange, dropping some food onto Melissa's shoes. Melissa, visibly irritated, smoothly relieved Natalie of the rest of her food, stepped backward, and turned the receptacle over as she shoved it toward the ground to completely rid the vessel of all its contents. Melissa happily returned Natalie the empty tray and left.

Natalie sighed. "Fair trade, I guess, if I don't have to see her for the rest of the day."

The blue-eyed girl sitting wordlessly at the end of the table picked up her tray, approached Natalie, left her an apple, and walked away.

Natalie walked home alone, but just as she was about to reach the dorms, Susan and Emma caught up with her.

"Whoa, didn't you want to walk home with me?" asked Susan.

"Sorry. I was just trying to avoid Melissa."

"I'm sorry too, about your lunch schedule."

Natalie groaned. "I should have known. With the way my life's going, I wouldn't be surprised if I had to share rooms with her when we get back."

"Well, you're in luck. We have class," said Susan. "I mean you don't, but we do. What I mean is, you're not a pledge. Only pledges have this class every day after school, except Thursdays. There's a self-defense class after dinner that you have to attend, but that's not until later."

"Am I the only one who sits out?" asked Natalie.

"No," chuckled Susan. "You get to hang out with Emma."

Emma enthusiastically grabbed Natalie's hand. "Do you want to play?" she asked.

"No. I think I'll go visit my aunt, Ava. See how she's doing."

Tuesday:

Natalie sat in her claimed corner for lunch, wiser, she thought. But Melissa managed to sneak up behind her and slide Natalie's tray off the table. Again, the blue-eyed girl picked up her tray and headed off, but not before she left a banana for Natalie.

After school, Susan caught up with Natalie again. "You missed self defense last night."

"I was visiting my aunt. She's in a coma."

"You're going to want to make that class, especially since you're on Melissa's hit list."

Wednesday:

Natalie saw Melissa approach her and firmly held on to both sides of her tray. Melissa stood by her for a moment before lifting the top of the tray and depositing its contents onto Natalie's lap.

The blue-eyed girl giggled but left Natalie a pear.

Again, Susan was forced to catch up with Natalie. "What do you think of the self-defense class?"

Natalie replied, "I think I need it." Then, she went straight to see Ava.

Thursday:

Natalie held on to her tray for dear life. This was now more than just lunch, it was about pride. She also made sure to slide herself more toward the center of the table, in order to use the space to her advantage. She refused to be constantly bullied by this—

"Slop!"

A big chunk of mud was dropped down on Natalie's food by none other than her daily afternoon visitor. So, what was her consolation fruit today? A peach.

Friday:

At lunch, Melissa approached Natalie from behind, excited about any new and creative way to demoralize her. As Melissa went around to Natalie's front, she was shocked at what she saw—nothing. No lunch. Natalie just sat there with nothing but a victorious smile on her face. Defeated, Melissa snarled and left.

Bully

The blue-eyed girl offered her some fruit, but Natalie pulled an apple out of her shirt.

CHAPTER TEN

❧❧

FRIENDS

Two months passed, and apart from her improved hand-to-hand skills and a little weight loss from her gluten-free lunches, Natalie's situation largely remained unchanged. It was Friday again, and with it came the Friday night challenge in self-defense class. Self defense, like most group activities, was taught in the arena. Natalie remembered her first time inside the arena. The inside, aesthetically, was a modest upgrade from the outside. She had experienced a feeling of stardom, as though she were a real athlete in the middle of an important game. The arena had that vibe—it was an oval closed dome with twenty rows of seats for hundreds, if not thousands, of people along the front and sides of the wall. The remaining section at the back contained only balcony seats, high above the ground for elite guests. The seating arrangements were separated from the dirt floor by a hip-high divider wall that encircled the inner operating area. Despite the remarkable romantic appearance of the arena, there was literally a dark side to it, which intrigued Natalie the most. Adjacent to the backside of the arena, beyond the wall and under the high-rise seats, there was an off-limits section. This area opened up to another space past the wall, which could only be described as a mini-battle arena. It looked like it belonged to an older era, not unlike the outside of the building. Most of the time, however, the modern rooms near the front foyer were used for one-on-one matches, as it was today.

The particular room chosen for today's lesson resembled a martial arts studio, with wall-to-wall mats and adjoining seats for about thirty people to watch. The girls, however, always sat on the mats for the lessons. The seats were only used if someone was injured or if there was a visitor. Devia was the sole occupant of the seats.

"Why do we practice self defense?" asked Zadie, the tall, athletic instructor. "In my experience, any dangerous encounter you might have will most certainly require hand-to-hand combat skills. It doesn't matter if you or your opponent has a weapon; combat often channels your primary physical attributes. And most of the time, it goes to the ground. That's why we practice. No matter how prepared you think you are, self defense is your last defense. Here, you stand to boost your confidence, assessment skills, and escape capacity."

"Why is she giving this speech?" Natalie asked Susan.

"I think it's because Devia's observing."

"Now," continued Zadie. "Do we have any challenges?"

Melissa stood. "I welcome all challengers." When no one replied, she turned to Natalie. "Are you scared?" she mocked, but Natalie ignored her. "Then, I take the challenge of three."

"What is that?" asked Natalie.

"Just wait and see, but don't volunteer," replied Susan.

Rebecca and Isabella stepped forth, fully aware that they were the only two out of the twenty-one students who were remotely close to Melissa in age and skill and would, therefore, be volunteered undoubtedly.

"I need a third volunteer," stated Zadie as she gathered her shoulder-length sisterlocks into a ponytail in order to prevent any obstruction of her view during the competition.

None of the younger girls so much as raised a finger as Zadie paced back and forth amongst the tremulous group.

"Toddi," she said, stopping in front of a bespectacled girl. "You're a smart girl. I'm sure you've mastered your hand-to-hand strategies."

Toddi deliberately weaved her hand through her bedraggled, light-colored hair to adjust her glasses, as though to suggest that despite being the oldest after the den three at fifteen years of age, physical activity with Melissa might be slightly daunting for her. Zadie ignored the signal, as well as the obvious fact that Toddi was rather callow in the physical sense. Just to be certain, she made sure to stumble as she rose, hoping for a rather quick reconsideration, which never surfaced. Slowly, she dragged her feet toward the older girls, dredging to mind her mediocre record in challenges, all of which she was forced to participate, and the winning half only achieved via technical wins. Even Emma, the little girl Toddi towered over, once knocked her down, but Toddi recalled a violation of the rules and called for a forfeit, which she was granted. Melissa was a different story altogether: faster, stronger, cunning, and ruthless. Timing would be her only chance.

"Fighting is ninety percent mental," reminded Zadie as the assembled team was signaled to gather in strategic positions around Melissa. "And you are our smartest student," she reassured Toddi in a softer tone before placing a wooden non-lethal knife in her slender hand.

Zadie patted Toddi on the back, stepped away, and shouted, "Go."

None of the attackers moved, but Melissa made certain to keep her eyes on all the three girls at all times by continuously moving her head and altering her stance. Then, from her most advantageous position, Rebecca advanced, prompting Isabella to follow, but before Toddi could reach Melissa, Rebecca was thrown into Isabella. Melissa was prepared: she grabbed the hand that Toddi held the knife with, and pulled it inward—along with Toddi's momentum; then, she sharply twisted the arm up and back around, slamming Toddi hard into the ground. With the knife now in her hand, Melissa exclaimed, "Did you really think you had a chance?" as the three girls fumbled on the ground, trying to scramble away.

After that display, the teacher matched the girls. Natalie was paired with Emma. Natalie was less than enthused, mostly because she already spent way more time with Emma than she desired. She meant Emma no disrespect; it was just that Emma was too young and could not understand a teenage girl's needs.

"Do you want to play later?" asked Emma.

"No thanks," replied Natalie as they went through their hand movements together.

"It's just that we have all that time together when the others are in class, and we haven't done anything at all."

"I've just been busy. We'll see on Monday, okay?"

"It's a deal! We can walk home together if you want."

Natalie brushed Emma off with a, "Uh huh."

∞

On Monday morning, as Natalie and Susan walked to school, Emma predictably trailed behind them. "What do you think of Emma?" asked Natalie.

"I don't. She's much younger, and we really have nothing in common. And she's so shy, and friendless. I noticed she got Mary Janes the day after you, though. I think she's desperate to be pledged so that she can fit in."

"Pledged? What's that?" asked Natalie.

"Oh right. A sister usually gets pledged after her first year. It's a loyalty thing, nothing else. But she's young. Girls aren't usually accepted at her age. I don't know what standards they follow, but she's been here a good two to three years."

"Do you think I'll have to wait that long to be pledged?"

"No. They'll probably pledge you during the testing next year. You'll have been here for about a year by then. That's when it usually happens. It really doesn't matter anyway. I... I'll explain after school."

Natalie was interested in continuing the conversation, but her focus was elsewhere now: the cat and mouse tactics of "lunch" were about to begin. Sometimes, Natalie ate; sometimes, she didn't. Only one thing was for certain, it was always an adventure.

Natalie was casually walking to her isolated corner when Melissa accosted her.

"Are you gaining weight?" Melissa asked. "Or are you hiding apples from me?"

Melissa reached into Natalie's shirt and pulled out an apple. "If you want to eat at my school, you're going to have to do it my way," she said as she limply let the apple roll to the ground. It traveled for about a meter before it stopped. "You can eat it now," added Melissa. Then, she and her evil sisters walked away, laughing.

Natalie sat down, accepting her fate of another day without lunch. She looked over to her silent lunch partner to see if there was any fruit on the menu for her; today was different, however. The blue-eyed girl stood up without her lunch, walked over to the apple, and picked it up. At first, Natalie thought that she was going to clean the apple, because it was still technically edible. But that is not what she did, not in the slightest bit. The girl donned a pitching pose, cocked her arm back, and hurled the apple at Melissa.

"Whack!"

Surely, the blue-eyed girl could not have imagined a better hit to the back of Melissa's head—it shattered the apple to bits and pieces that showered the three girls.

The blue-eyed girl, hunched over, left no doubt as to who had made the retaliatory move. Natalie attempted to intercept Melissa, but Rebecca and Isabella held her back in order to allow the playground lesson to commence.

"Philian, I see you're still disgruntled," said Melissa.

"Leave her alone!"—the first words Natalie heard Philian say in two months.

"I have the time and energy to bully the both of you. So, you better stay out of this."

"No," replied Philian.

Melissa forcefully pushed Philian to the ground and quickly scraped a good amount of dirt from her shoe to dirty Philian's uniform and face. "Defy me again" is all Melissa said before she walked away.

Once the zone was demilitarized, Natalie helped Philian to a seat at the table. "Why'd you do that?" asked Natalie.

"I thought it would help," Philian replied.

"I don't mean to sound unappreciative," said Natalie, "but why *do* you help me? We don't even know each other."

"Because… last year… I was you."

For the first time, Natalie became aware of more than just her own perspective. Why did she think she was the only person Melissa picked on? Embarrassed, Natalie helped her new friend brush the dirt off her hair and her shirt.

"My name's Natalie. Thank you."

"It's nothing," replied Philian.

"No, it is something to me. You were done being bullied, and yet you stood up and put yourself in harm's way instead of watching it happen to someone else. That's very courageous. Believe me, I'd do anything I can to stay out of her path."

"You're a very compassionate person," said Philian. "That's a great quality in friends."

"Friends. I like that. I think it helps that we have sympathy for each other," added Natalie.

"Empathy," corrected Philian. "Sympathy is when you can see someone else's perspective. Empathy is when you can see something *from* someone else's perspective. We both know what it feels like to be bullied, especially since it's from the same person. We not only know how it feels, but also exactly what the other has been through."

Natalie thought about that for a minute, questioning her view of relationships. Like Melissa, was she too so engulfed in her own issues that she failed to see other's needs? "You must spend a lot of time thinking, Philian."

"It's not like I have anyone to talk to." Philian chuckled. "Do you want to visit the mall after school?"

"Tomorrow," replied Natalie. "There's something I have to do today."

ርﻬ೩

After school, Emma sat crying in her room. Natalie dashed through the door, out of breath. "I'm so sorry, Emma. I was caught up after school with a teacher."

Natalie approached Emma and noticed that she was trying to wipe away her tears. Emma sniffled. "I'm used to it. Maybe tomorrow."

"I have plans tomorrow, but I have a better idea. Do you want to play now?"

Elated, Emma replied, "Can I be the good guy? I've always wanted to be a hero."

"Of course you can."

CHAPTER ELEVEN

❦

Ms. Hag

A metal trashcan tumbled its way down the hall with an earsplitting cacophony in its wake. Natalie leaped from her bed—her first instinct to defend herself. Upon her escaping from dreamland, she soon realized that the walls were not crashing in and the sky was not collapsing. She, however, wished that were the case, considering the great terror the following two menacing words set into her soul.

"Line-up!"

Natalie felt a surge of pure fear, and moved quickly to comply as adrenaline flooded her system. Immediately, she joined the other girls in the hall and swiftly assembled into a hurried line.

There she emerged, the shrew of fire and brimstone, so awfully wrinkled and dilapidated that none dared gaze at this physical manifestation of agony and torture. A foul smell constantly lingered about her presence, the boast of an unnatural, pungent odor that held the promise of death with a single breath.

Ms. Haggle.

Only one analogy was necessary to describe her appearance: "black hole." Her mere presence seemed to *suck* the life from all living things. Without wavering, her persona stayed true to the nature and science of black holes: her existence, intimidating; vicinity, terrifying; and there was no return from her "event horizon."

"Tell me!" shrieked Ms. Haggle. "Toddi," she called out as she turned toward the girl, lowering her head into the poor child's face with a slow frightening descent—as though she were a predator and Toddi the prey.

"What time is it?"

"Seven... Seven-fifteen, Ms. Hag... a-gle."

"What did you call me?" she hissed, as she drew closer. "Did you know I can devour your insides through your naval within seconds of turning them to mush?"

Toddi instantly fainted and fell to the floor.

"Rebecca!" called Ms. Haggle. "Relieve me of this miscreant's presence, immediately!"

Rebecca jumped so quickly that she could not gain a proper footing, resulting in her tripping over her own foot and crashing, head first, into the opposing wall. Dazed and terrified, she lay there, hopeful that her self-defensive attempt at playing dead would spare her life.

"That should explain my position on your seven a.m. wakeup call," said Ms. Haggle. Then, to heart-reviving relief for everyone present, she walked away.

No student made a single remark until they were a fair distance away, on their way to school. Then it began...

"Hey, girls," shouted Toddi. "You ever hear that saying, 'I used to complain that I had no shoes, until I met a man with no feet'? Well, old man Time used to complain about his age, until he met Ms. Hag."

Laughter ensued until the next girl put in her two cents, and so on.

"She's so old… her scooter runs on steam."

"She's so old… her pet turtle died of natural causes."

"She's so old… she collects disability from the pyramids."

"She's so old… her birth certificate says Pangaea."

In response to that remark, Emma asked, "What's Pangaea?"

"It was a landmass from millions of years ago when all the continents were joined into one," explained Susan. "But I got it. This is old. Ready? She's so old… when she hears about the big bang theory, she has flashbacks."

"Now, that's old," said Toddi. "And I think we have a winner."

Natalie laughed so hard on the way to school that her side still hurt during lunchtime. Lunch. Where would it go today? Given the apple incident of the previous day, Natalie decide not to join the line for lunch. She figured she would just hide, but that was before Philian found her.

"Come on, let's get lunch," said Philian.

"But Philian—"

"You can call me Phen."

"Okay. But don't you think we should play it safe?" asked Natalie.

"Trust me. Come on, let's get a full lunch."

Halfway through lunch, they were only subjected to Melissa's patented stare down, minus her signature violence.

"She's not making her daily rounds," noted Natalie. "How'd you know we could eat today? Especially after yesterday?"

"I know bullies. Their biggest fear is being called out. It's not really about winning or losing—it's all about intimidation. Do you know what would happen if I encouraged others to stand up? She doesn't want that. Bullies work with any advantage they see; so, don't show weakness. They despise weakness—in others, and in themselves."

"You're awesome, Phen. Say, if we're still going to the mall, can we take Emma along?"

"Certainly. Any friend of yours is a friend of mine."

It was a good day, and for the first time in months, Natalie went to sleep with a clear mind. Her peace, however, was not destined to last. At five a.m., Natalie woke up in full sweat, her bed soaked. "Nooo!"

"Natalie, are you okay?" asked Emma, waking with a start.

"No," she replied. "He's coming for me."

Emma grabbed her shoes. "Let's go. I'm taking you to the front desk."

Just inside the foyer of the castle was a large desk. Behind the desk sat a woman in a brown robe. Natalie was so shaken that she neither noticed nor cared about any wonder that might lie about. The woman made a call, Natalie was interviewed, and an ad hoc council was soon assembled.

When Devia visited Natalie at eight a.m., the latter was sitting on her bed. "I want you to stay home from school today."

"But what about Saul?"

Devia sat down beside Natalie. "You said in your dream that you only saw him standing there. To be safe Mara and Josephine will escort the girls. Mara is experienced, and Josephine may be young, but she'll surprise you."

Later, Natalie lay nervously in her bed when Susan rushed into her room after school. "Come quick!"

Natalie did not care to know what had transpired during the day, but in her heart, she knew that her vision would come true. She looked out the window to confirm it before Susan rushed her downstairs.

"Girls!" shouted the headmistress. "We must remain calm. Rebecca, get Mara and the others some aid; Isabella, take the students to their rooms; Devia, arrange another meeting. This issue must be resolved."

"You should have seen it!" said Toddi. "He went bip, bam, boom, and it was over. Then Melissa tried to help. She took a beating too!"

Toddi continued to explain the details, but Natalie, a great fear in her eyes, was less concerned about the fight and more about her future.

CB&D

Thirteen chairs were placed behind three tables in the council room. Two chairs remained empty. Dozens of other chairs, placed along the walls and at the center of the room, were occupied.

"Order!" called out the headmistress. "What were his exact directives?"

"The child is to be placed in his care at precisely three p.m., tomorrow, at the playground adjoining the school."

The head mistress continued, "He will not dare set a foot on our land. He knows better than that. Our options?"

Mara, just arriving with Josephine, spoke, "We can't seek help of the law. He claims that the child is his. We can seek resolution from the supreme council."

"No," said the headmistress. "Not only would such an act be seen as a weakness, but they have no authority over him."

"We can face him," said another woman. "Two, he can take, but not us all."

"Since the child has no interest in going, do we agree then?" asked the headmistress.

"No!" exclaimed a raspy old voice. "He faces us now, exposed, but if we fight him, he will run and continue with his tactics of attrition and harassment until he succeeds. You do nothing!"

"With all due respect, Ms. Haggle," the headmistress began, cautiously. "Do you recommend then that we remain inactive?"

"Precisely."

"And what of the violence that he threatened for tomorrow?"

"There will be none."

The headmistress cleared her throat. In a timorous voice, that did not wish to cast aspersions, she continued, "How can you be sure?"

"I will be present if that helps your confidence."

"Ms. Haggle, I do not wish to bother you with such trivial matters."

"Am I not responsible for overseeing the sisters? Then, I shall so be tasked."

"Very well," said the headmistress. "We are agreed. The issue is for Ms. Haggle to resolve. May pity arise."

CRBO

The next day brought about extreme trepidation from every child; yet, it appeared as though Natalie was the only one prepared to miss the afternoon's spectacle. Ms. Haggle escorted the children to school, but when they were dismissed, she was nowhere to be found. Melissa, faithful to the end, rallied the girls in the park that was near the school. He was there—the thin man with his bony malnourished face—set to act upon his threats. His head-to-toe black outfit, matching the shaded areas of his face, sharply contrasted the diamonds set in the amulet hanging from his neck.

"Child," he called out to Melissa, "come here." As she approached him, her face full of bruises from the prior day's scuffle, he said, "I gave you an order to bring me my daughter. Where is she?"

"I don't take orders from you, coward," Melissa hissed back.

"Unfortunately for you, child, I will be forced to finish yesterday's beating."

At that instant, Ms. Haggle's voice came ringing in, "You will lay no hand on that child," which prompted a smile from Melissa, who backed away with pleasure.

"Perhaps I will show you who you are dealing with, witch."

Ms. Haggle replied in a grainy voice, "Perhaps it is you who does not know with whom you deal."

Both drew close to the other, steady to a fault, while the girls took cover.

"Ms. Haggle? Ms. Haggle!" cried Saul as his intensely white face lost its last remnants of color. "Surely, you're not with these lowly girls!"

"Oh, but I am. And you *do* know with whom you deal. Yet, you dare look me in the eye."

Saul instantly reached for his amulet, but in vain: Ms. Haggle, having stealthily closed the remaining distance between the two, held it firmly in her hand as it still hung from his neck. "This pathetic device cannot aid your condition," she said as she snatched it away from his neck. She dropped it to the ground and watched Saul scurry before she stomped on it with her foot.

"I mean you no disrespect, ma'am," said Saul, pathetically bowed on the ground.

"But you *have* disrespected me by demanding one of my children."

"I have the right to—"

"You have no rights!" declared Ms. Haggle. "This order is under my absolute protection. Set foot near *my* order again, and you'll suffer seven sins from Sunday."

"Yes, Ma'am."

"If I so much as think that you are involved in any mischief within a hundred miles of *my* order, then your life and your amulet will both be mine," threatened Ms. Haggle. She then kicked the amulet toward Melissa, who picked it up. "Melissa," she continued. "Drag this malefactor out of my sight."

Every girl joined in dragging Saul through the dirt and out of the park before Melissa took over. She stood over Saul, and, as he turned over on his hands and knees, Melissa seized the opportunity to squarely kick him in the guts.

Saul gasped and coughed. Whimpering a weak "please," he stretched out his hand for the amulet.

"Yesterday," began Melissa, "I sat here, in your position. Did I beg? But here you are. Pathetic." Melissa kicked him in the face, blood gushing out from the spot she hit him.

"Do you know what this is?" Melissa demanded as she held up the amulet. "Weakness. This amulet is the symbol of your weak... worthless... life." Examining the amulet, she continued, "Hiding—the universal weakness of man. Only so long as he can cradle an imbalanced advantage." Melissa threw away the amulet and ordered, "Stone this lowlife!"

The girls took great delight in hurling rocks at Saul until he managed to grab hold of the amulet and disappeared.

CHAPTER TWELVE

❧❧

FRIGHT NIGHT

Excitement ran through the sisters' veins as Full-Moon-Friday came upon them. The faculty implicitly acknowledged this as a night of mischief, and usually allowed the girls some leeway for games and teasing. Self-defense class was all that stood between the girls and their enjoyment, and usually, Zadie let them off early on such special occasions.

Natalie had no clue why she did what she did— maybe it was the thrill of the night, maybe she had become too bold, or maybe it was just something long overdue.

"I challenge Melissa."

Melissa's eyes widened, shock stretching the now chartreuse-colored bruises and slightly puffy portions of her face from the injuries she had sustained the week prior.

Melissa smiled. "Excuse me? I thought I just heard you challenge me."

"I did," Natalie stated with feigned confidence.

Melissa laughed. "Mother," she addressed Zadie in a more serious tone. "Will you allow this?"

Zadie quickly assessed Natalie, looked back in Melissa's direction, and said, "Follow the rules." Then, she turned to Natalie and added, "Choose your weapon."

"Weapon?" questioned Natalie. "I thought we just fight."

"Then your weapon is hand-to-hand," said Zadie. "Melissa chooses the style."

"Freestyle," said Melissa. Unable to contain her joy, she got into position and scoffed. "Do you really think you have a chance?"

Natalie felt a tingling sensation in her body, and making every effort to conceal her fear, she attempted to enjoy the feeling. Something about the fight triggered her previous instinct for survival: she felt alive. She remembered the time she had felt emotionally dead; this act felt completely opposite, very fulfilling. She really, really liked it.

Natalie, positioned in a boxing stance, appeared awkward as she faced Melissa, who appeared relaxed and blatantly unconcerned. Natalie began to dance to the left, and then to the right, still maintaining a safe distance from Melissa. On the contrary, Melissa retained her pose that reflected her lack of interest, as if she were passively watching the fight, feeling bored.

Then Natalie felt something else. A connection to Melissa's essence. Her power was available for the taking. It felt like tapping into someone else's energy.

Natalie thought it was silly to assume that she could actually use Melissa's energy and turn it against her. Her senses, however, told her it was possible. Just like stealing electricity, this could prove to be an advantage; but now she could not ponder on it much, as she was in a fight.

Natalie swung, but it fell way short. She reached closer to Melissa and jabbed, but still fell short of posing any real threat—physically and psychologically. After a few more swings, she gained confidence and drew even closer. She swung again, then repeated, but reached a little closer, almost close enough to land a punch. Then, she drew even closer, and in a blink, it was all over.

Natalie tried to push herself up to stand, but stumbled back into the girls, who held her up. "It's okay, I can walk," she claimed as they let her go, and she began to fall again.

"Girls, help her to the mat and give her a few minutes," directed Zadie. "Melissa, you may be excused. In fact, the class is dismissed early."

Natalie gazed around. "Did I win?" she asked.

Emma said out loud to the other girls, "I think she's still dreaming."

"What happened?"

Susan helped Natalie sit up. "Dude, she totally jumped up in the air, wrapped her legs around your neck, and pulled you down to the ground. We told you to tap out once she had you in the choke hold, but I don't think you heard us at all."

"Are you sure I didn't land a punch? I thought I hit something."

"Just the ground," replied Susan. "Come on, there's no shame. It's time for some fun."

Zadie checked to ensure Natalie was unharmed; then, she dismissed the remaining girls to enjoy the night.

Back in the dorms, surprisingly, Natalie had a few girls congratulate her. She found, barring a few girls, most were impressed with her courage to challenge Melissa rather than making jokes about her.

A number of girls surrounded Natalie, more interested in her than in the night's adventures.

"Natalie, do you want to explore the lower levels of the arena with us?" asked one girl.

"No," said another. "We're going to Mitzi Forest, aren't we, Natalie?"

"Calm down," said Susan. "She'll decide in a minute. Give her some time, alright?"

"Yeah, she's going to need some time... after that beating," added Melissa. "Tell me, Natalie, what were you thinking before the fight? Oh, that's right, you don't remember. You looked good though... until I decided to fight."

Melissa, Rebecca, and Isabella all had a good laugh at Natalie's expense, but the other girls just mirthlessly stared at them.

"Leave her alone, Melissa. You're an anomaly. It took courage for her to face you."

Melissa's capacity to elicit fear with nothing more than a stare was enough to make even Ms. Haggle proud. "If she is indeed courageous, then she'll have no trouble at the cemetery tonight."

The girls gasped collectively, and one asked, "You... you wouldn't expect her to go to the cemetery on a full moon night?"

"Why not?" replied Melissa. "I'm an anomaly, and she stood up to me. Isn't she courageous enough to visit a little cemetery?" Changing her tone from facetious to hostile, Melissa told Natalie, "You're going to the cemetery, Natalie. To the big stone entrance, and you're going to tell me what it says above the keystone."

"Reads," corrected Toddi.

"Shut up," snapped Melissa as she swatted at Toddi. "Or perhaps there'll be another fight tonight."

"But everyone knows what it says... uh, reads," said Susan. "Here lie the dead, for all to revere. They are resting now, in peace and still."

"Not on a full moon night. Tell me what it *reads*."

"I'll go," said Natalie.

"No you won't!" exclaimed Susan. "There are things up there. Things you don't understand. You can't go!"

"She's going," insisted Melissa. "And you're going with her."

Natalie stood facing Melissa, albeit not too close. "It's okay. I'll go."

Emma took Natalie's hand. "I'll go with you," she said.

Outside, the girls waited behind the stables. One look up the hill pushed away all their thoughts to venture closer to the desolate area that evoked fear even during the day. Trees, bushes, and stone graves dotted the sullen landscape, separated from the grounds by an impenetrable iron fence. One entrance, not always accessible, defined the boundary between reality and the supernatural.

Having finished her visit with Galla, Natalie wordlessly marched past the girls in her mulish trek toward the unknown. Emma made valiant efforts to keep pace with Natalie, but the uneven ground forced her to stumble behind. Melissa pushed Susan forward. "You, too," she said.

The closer Natalie reached, the larger the compound appeared. On getting to the solid iron fence, she saw that it was much taller than her. It would be a challenge to overcome, especially with the spiked rails and tall lining of brush across the inside of the partition. The view through the brush was limited; Natalie, who had hoped for a visual to ascertain the source of the noises coming from inside, felt discouraged.

"Wild beasts!" shouted Susan.

"Shh," hushed Natalie. "Probably just wolves."

"Wolves!" shrieked Emma.

"Here," said Natalie, picking up a stick and handing it to Emma. Before she moved on, however, she grabbed a stick for herself, weighed it, and then grabbed a bigger one. Natalie felt they were safe as long as the gate was closed: there really was no other way to cross the fence. On reaching the gate, she waited several minutes, eyeing the inside for anything unnatural. There was some movement, but nothing she could see for certain. Natalie turned around and leaned against the stone post between the fence and the gate, slowly sliding to the ground to sit herself down.

"What do you girls think?" asked Natalie. "You ready?"

As she waited for a coherent answer from her fellow bravehearts, Natalie spotted a sole grave outside the cemetery. Situated down the hill, about a hundred meters away, there rested a single cross on the well-maintained grave. Who would spend so much effort to care for a grave and yet not place it inside the cemetery? The thought temporarily distracted Natalie's mind from her fear.

"Ugh, it smells like Ms. Hag in there," commented Natalie before attempting to unlatch the gate. To no avail, she used her stick to leverage the latch. "It's stuck." Grateful, Natalie gave up. "What now?" she said, stepping away from the gate.

Suddenly, the gate eerily creaked open on its own and Emma bolted down the hill, screaming. Natalie stuttered as she spoke, "If-if they didn't kn-know we were he-here, they do n-now."

Susan froze in fear as Natalie put one foot into the cemetery—the sensation contained in that one step was inexplicably surreal. Natalie, frightened out of her wits, leaned over to grab Susan for support. Susan, however, read something spooky into the touch and shot down the hill. Natalie began to tremble uncontrollably, but refusing to be beaten, she grabbed her ringed hand with the other one and entered the cemetery, prompting the gate to slam shut behind her.

ෆ෫ග

Well after Full-Moon-Friday celebrations were supposed to begin, the girls remained inside the dorms, where Melissa forced them to wait.

"Melissa, we should tell somebody," suggested Susan. "It's been way too long."

"This is our night for trouble, the Mothers know this."

"But the cemetery is forbidden for a reason. She could be hurt."

"The more reason the Mothers should not be bothered."

"I'm going," said Emma. "I'm going now."

Melissa grabbed Emma by her shirt. "You'll do no such thing."

"Let her go!" shouted Natalie.

The crowd of girls promptly gathered around Natalie in relief and surprise. Emma hugged Natalie tight while Susan sat down, exhausted from worry.

"What did it say?" demanded Melissa.

Natalie cleared her throat. "At first I was confused. It said, 'Here lie the dead, for all to revere. They are resting now, in peace and still.'"

"Then you didn't go in," accused Melissa.

"Wait. The inscription then changed before my eyes: 'Here lie the living, for all to fear. They are alive now, in turmoil to kill.'"

Melissa stepped back in disbelief. There was no doubt in Melissa's mind that Natalie had been inside the cemetery on that full moon night, braving the fear and danger that she was the only student to have done.

The girls noted the acknowledgment in Melissa's face and cheered Natalie for her courage.

"It was crazy scary," said Natalie. Then, as Natalie was deep into her descriptions, she struck a nerve: "There was something I didn't understand—the lone grave down the hill."

The air went stone silent as Melissa's anger revived. "Don't you dare talk about that grave ever again!" she shouted.

Natalie backed away from Melissa's advancing footsteps, but it was too late as Melissa lifted Natalie off the ground and pushed her down. Rebecca intervened in sheer panic. "You'll have to calm down, or I'll get Ms. Hag."

Melissa tore at Rebecca's shirt in a fit of fury; but she suddenly stopped, turned, and stomped out of the hall, into a room where she couldn't be seen by the girls, and jumped swiftly out of the second-story window.

"Thank you, Rebecca," said a distraught Natalie. Then, noticing that Melissa had vanished, she continued, "Where'd she go?"

"Mitzi Forest," replied Rebecca. "She may be there for several days to calm herself down. You're safe for now. Go to bed."

Susan accompanied Natalie and Emma to their room before she explained, "We call it Mitzi Forest because that's where Melissa goes to calm herself down. Mitzi was the nickname her mother gave her, and the forest is her only solace. So, don't belittle either of them."

"Solace? From what?" asked Natalie.

"Her mother shamed the order—a legacy she cannot shake."

Bewildered, Natalie continued, "But what does that have to do with the grave?"

"It's her mother's."

CHAPTER THIRTEEN

❧

TRESPASS

Several months passed since that eventful Full-Moon-Friday, and Natalie was beginning to fit in with the crowd at school and home. Friday nights were tough because Natalie continued to challenge Melissa without fail. In Natalie's mind, however, it was a necessary sacrifice she had to make in order to enjoy an uneventful week of school lunches. At home, Natalie, Susan, and Toddi had become good friends, so close that they were often regarded as women of three. Natalie was also able to continue her friendship with Philian and Emma, mostly hanging out at the mall after school.

"Hold on tight," said Natalie.

"I'm trying. I'm trying," replied Emma.

"Whoa, Gal! That's it. Good girl. Let's get Emma off and take you for a walk."

Galla stopped, and Natalie helped Emma off. The three walked at the small girl's pace so that Emma could relax. "What'd you think?" asked Natalie.

"That was fun! I never rode a horse before. Thank you, Galla," continued Emma as she petted the horse.

"Yeah, thank you, Galla. Now, let's get you back. We have class."

Natalie and Emma joined the other girls upstairs as they changed into their sports gear for the self-defense class. Every girl, barring the trio of Melissa, Rebecca, and Isabella, was changing out of her Doc Martens and into athletic shoes for the class. Natalie smiled, having never imagined that she would be able to create such an impact. Finally, she felt like she had something special.

Natalie regularly went to class early, practicing the moves for her Friday night challenge. Thus far, Melissa had gone easy on her, inflicting only minor scrapes and bruises. Most of the time, as Natalie had learned, tapping out prevented a lot of pain and embarrassment. "Who knows," she thought, feeling positive about the night.

"How do you plan on losing tonight?" asked Rebecca, having just arrived to class.

"Gracefully," replied Natalie, her sense of humor recovering well.

Susan laughed and gave Natalie a pat on her back. "But seriously, when are you going to give up?" she asked.

"I feel like I'm getting better," replied Natalie. To this, even her friends laughed. "No, seriously, last week I was able to stretch her shirt, you know, when I was in the choke hold. And if I hadn't passed out that fast, I could have bitten her arm. Maybe tonight." What Natalie did not say was that she had been exploring her apparently paranormal ability to tap into Melissa's strength and leveraging that energy to improve her own skills. More than the fight or winning, she concentrated on learning how to utilize the unusual energy she encountered while fighting. Natalie believed she was really stealing power from Melissa—the only way she could describe what she felt.

"I challenge Melissa," declared Natalie as she stood before the class.

"Melissa, what style have you decided on tonight?" asked Zadie.

"Arm wrestling. I plan on beating my record win of ten seconds."

Natalie's interest piqued since, until now, she had not been allowed to fight with her ring on. Jewelry was prohibited during exercises; with arm wrestling, however, she could wear the ring on her left hand to see if it made a difference in how she felt.

Back in the dorms, Natalie was massaging her arm. "Two seconds. Man, that girl is strong."

"It's okay," said Emma. "I'm practicing to take her on."

The girls were having a good time at Emma's comment when there was a loud commotion in the dorms. A pair of shoes was forcefully thrown into the hall; it struck the wall and fell to the floor. The shoes were followed by Melissa. "Where is Isabella!"

"Here, Melissa."

"Et tu, Isabella? Et tu?"

Isabella glanced down at the pair of Doc Martens on the ground, preparing to defend her actions. "They're comfortable, and what can I say, they look good on me."

"Natalie, front and center," Melissa called out.

"What? Me? How did I get into this?"

"I need you to check the stables and make sure they're secure. Do you understand?"

"Yes, Den Mother." Natalie thought that the situation could not be any more bizarre. There was no connection between the two, but she figured it was an easy task. Also, she could visit Galla while Melissa calmed herself.

When Natalie returned to her room, she noticed that Emma was missing, which was not really unusual. However, when she did not return for quite some time, Natalie began to ask around.

"Melissa sent her somewhere, and she won't say where," answered Susan.

Natalie approached Melissa. "Where'd you send Emma?"

Melissa laughed and laughed. "Your little friend is in for some big trouble."

"Where is she, Melissa!"

"Be careful how you speak to me, and maybe I'll tell you."

"Melissa, please. Den Mother. Where is she?"

"No where big. She just wanted to be as brave as her idol. So, I sent her somewhere to prove herself."

"Where?"

"I sent her to retrieve something from Ms. Hag's house, but unfortunately, the item doesn't exist. She'll be there a while before she figures it out though."

Every girl gasped. Even Melissa's women of three were shocked. "Melissa, she'll kill that poor girl," said Rebecca. "Literally."

Immediately, Natalie, followed by Susan, stormed out of the dorms and went to the castle front desk. "Ma'am, if I needed Ms. Haggle, where would she be at this time?"

"Shall I contact her?" asked the sentry dressed in a brown robe, seated behind the desk.

"No, of course not, I mean, if she's busy…" Natalie stumbled with her words, trying her best to contain the severity of the situation. "But if she's not busy, say if she's at home, then maybe I'll see about…"

"Don't you dare go to her house," replied the sentry. "Didn't you hear about the wi… woman who dared to look inside her window? You think Melissa's temperamental? Ms. Haggle's unstable. She'll… she's really hurt some people. She comes from a different time… a time when she would have the right to, uh, kill, if she felt you were trying something funny in her home. How about I call her?"

"Oh, she's in the castle?"

"Well, yes. She's in the library."

"No, thank you. I think this can wait. Oh, by the way, you haven't seen Emma, have you?"

"The little girl? No."

Before Natalie could take two steps out of the castle doors, Susan grabbed her from behind. "You're not going in there! That'd be suicide. Emma's on her own now. Ms. Hag may have mercy on her, but you… you know better."

"That's not going to stop me. I won't be long, I promise. Just go back to the dorms and wait for me, okay?"

With that, Natalie headed straight for the decrepit house that bore a most unholy look. The "dead zone," as the girls called the area, was at the center of the grounds, between the castle, the stables, and the dorms. The three buildings threw a constant shadow on the two-story house—only weeds and crooked trees could grow there.

Visibility could be very low in this area, especially once it was dark.

Natalie approached the short, rotten, wooden fence that creaked even in the absence of wind. The frail fence offered no physical protection to the property. Its wicked sight merely posed a gruff warning, marking a perimeter that bore death inside. There was no "keep out" sign: with the dead grass, lifeless trees, and dirty pathways, there was little need for one.

Natalie stood outside the fence. "Emma? Emma, are you in there?"

Natalie creaked open the rickety gate, admitting to herself that it was too late to debate the issue anymore, and that Emma needed her now more than ever. Suddenly, the gate fell off its hinges—one end of the light airy wood lay in Natalie's hand, the other propped on the ground. "I'll fix it on the way out," Natalie assured herself out loud. She marched onward—to the seemingly strategically placed stones on the "so-called" ground. Between the icky mud, sinking stones, and busted fence, Natalie was certain that Ms. Haggle never used this entrance. There must be another way, and Natalie unsuccessfully taxed her senses to look for it.

Reaching the door was no simple task, considering the webs, exceptional darkness, and strange noises that had Natalie spurting and halting repeatedly in moving towards her destination. There: a light inside and a moving shadow. Natalie arrived at the door in dire hopes to save her friend. Briefly glancing over her shoulder, she realized for the first time she was alone, abandoned by the rest of the girls. She didn't blame them: there was no point in everyone facing the brunt of Ms. Haggle's fury should she catch them. Natalie turned to face the door, jumping in shock when it creaked open on its own.

"Emma?" she whispered. "Emma, we have to go, now!"

"Eeeaaaaeek," screeched the floor as Natalie stepped into the dust-ridden museum of... old stuff—really old stuff.

"Slam!" The door banged shut behind Natalie.

"Did she go in?" asked Susan from inside the dorms as all the girls jostled for a seat next to the sole window that opened up to a perfect view of Ms. Haggle's home.

The girls went mute, however, when they saw Ms. Haggle return and inspect her broken fence.

Natalie glanced around the notorious Ms. Haggle's home. There were bookshelves covering over half of the walls of the one massive room that basically formed the house itself. Natalie shuddered at what she saw: furniture taken straight out of the Middle Ages; stuffed animals so abnormal, she would have difficulty naming them; and apparent souvenirs, so nefarious that one would have trouble giving them away.

The room was shaped as a perfect dome, with a high-rise circular ceiling. A colossal chandelier scattered light from the center of the room with candles so numerous that one would have trouble counting them, let alone light them. The dim flames shone in all directions, leaving a gloomy feel to the room. The light also touched what Natalie noted as thirteen corners in the ceiling, reaching inward from the outer walls. Having no structural value, these inelegant extensions pointed toward the center and aligned with lines on the floor! A large pentagram sat on the ground, etched in the middle of the room, where all furniture remained absent.

"Emma?" whispered Natalie in desperation.

Natalie noticed a staircase to the right—circling around the room, along the vaulted ceiling, and finally ending at the back wall to the left. The stairway to nowhere was no more unusual than the rest of the place; yet, Natalie was certain that no one in their right mind would attempt to climb those rickety stairs, not even Emma. But where, then?

Natalie veered left toward a larger-than-life fireplace. It was so spacious that she could walk right inside it if she were only hunching over slightly. That alone was not the weird part. Inside the fireplace were a bulky caldron and... green fire! Yes, green fire. And above, the mantle stretched two arm's lengths wide with thirteen black knives purposefully aligned along the wall. The sword was what caught Natalie's attention—a broadsword of brilliant shine and beauty, with a stone resembling the one on Natalie's ring set in the middle of the hilt. Natalie, sensing a connection between the two items, held her ringed hand up to the gem on the sword, feeling her hand pulsate more and more the closer they came together.

"Bang!" A noise from the other side of the house sounded like clanging of a pot or pan.

Noticing another room to the right, directly under the staircase, Natalie warily advanced toward it—past some tables decorated with skulls and dishes of dead bugs—attentive not to touch the pentagram. This other room, from what she could make out, appeared to be a kitchen. "Emma?" There was no answer, but the noise stopped abruptly. Natalie, absolutely terrified, backed away from the kitchen, keeping her eyes fixed in that direction. She passed between two tables—a smaller one with two very detailed wooden chairs and an old chess set to her right, and the other set against the back wall with beakers and tubes containing colored liquids of various shades. As Natalie continued to back away, she saw a large shadow hastily moving across the kitchen. Inadvertently, she bumped into a table, knocking over a chess piece with her hand. The shadow froze when the table made a noise from the movement. Then, it disappeared.

Natalie, momentarily secure enough to look down, saw that there was an unfinished chess game—where did the rook she'd knocked over go? Used to playing chess, Natalie decided a good, tactical place for it. When Natalie focused more closely though, she began to doubt if the piece was actually a rook. She had never seen a chess set with dragons, witches, and spellcasters, but this was surely a castle—it must definitely be a rook. But who would Ms. Haggle be playing with? The person in the kitchen? And where was Emma?

"Click!" The kitchen light went out. Panicking, Natalie ran into a bookcase as she backtracked—where she was startled out of her wits by a stuffed... crow? The animal—bigger than an eagle—was perched slightly off the bookcase, motionless. Natalie, intrigued, could not resist her urge to touch the permanently mantled recreation of something unspeakable.

"Caw!" it snapped as it spread its massive wingspan.

Natalie yelped and fumbled backward into the chess table, knocking over all the pieces. Helplessly, she attempted to recreate the former scenario—a piece here, a piece there. Then, to her horror, the front door unlocked. Natalie froze. "I need to hide," was all she could think. With the chess pieces still in her hand, she looked in the direction of the kitchen only to see a reignited light and a moving shadow. Then, she looked under the chess table— too small! The door crept open and Natalie, in response, backed into the large table, knocking over glasses and spilling fluids before she managed to grab a container and keep it from falling as well. Natalie was overwhelmed, not knowing if she should continue looking at Ms. Haggle as she walked through the front door or if she should rather put out the small fire she had started behind her. With the chess pieces in her right hand and a beaker of red liquid in her left, she did not dare take an eye off Ms. Haggle, despite the death stare flashing at her from the opening of the wicked woman's black robe.

"Ms. Hag-gle? You're never going to believe this," was all Natalie could utter before dropping the glass bottle containing the red liquid onto one of the wooden chairs. No sooner did the bottle crack open on the chair that it began to disintegrate from the chemical.

"Was that an antique?"

"Six... teenth century," replied Ms. Haggle gruffly as the onyx brooch holding her robe together at the neck appeared to beam with anger.

"He-he. It wasn't worth anything, was it?"

"More than your life."

CB&

"Melissa!" shouted Susan from inside the crowded dorm room. "You have to explain to Ms. Hag that this is all your fault."

Melissa snickered. "It's too late; they've been in there for at least twenty minutes now. What's done is done."

Rebecca grabbed Melissa. "You went too far this time! We have to stop this!"

Melissa yanked Rebecca's hands away from her shirt. "Calm down! She'll be fine. I'm just teaching her a lesson."

"Don't you remember the witch?" cried Rebecca. "Ms. Hag killed her—for nothing more than looking through her window!"

"That homeless woman had a heart attack. It wasn't Ms. Hag's fault. Besides, she didn't belong to the order. She was trying to steal from Ms. Hag, and there's some valuable stuff in there. We all know she'll kill before parting with her treasures. Natalie's just looking for Emma, she's not going to steal or destroy anything."

⊗⊗

Natalie sat in the one sixteenth century chair that stood undamaged, her hands submissively placed on the armrests. "Go ahead. Kill me. I can't take the suspense any longer."

"Don't be impatient, child. I'm merely deciding on how exactly I wish to do this."

"At this point, does it even matter?" replied Natalie.

⊗⊗

Back in the dorms, Emma pushed her way into the pile of girls. "What are you guys checking out?" she asked.

"What are you doing here?" asked Susan.

"I finished cleaning the dojo area, like Melissa instructed me to."

"You did what?" said Susan, horrified.

Melissa burst into laughter.

"She's crazy," said Susan. "Melissa sent Natalie into Ms. Hag's house to find you."

"No!" said Emma. "But the lady she killed? Not Natalie! We have to help her."

"No one goes anywhere," said Melissa, and no one did.

⚯⚲

Ms. Haggle leaned toward Natalie, over the small, ancient table. "Fine, my intolerant child. We shall finish this. I'll use my bishop. Checkmate."

"Three games," said Natalie, "and I didn't last long in any. Uh, Ms. Haggle... I'm sorry about your chair... and the table... and the glasses... and the gate."

"You'll make it up to me, child. As we discussed, you'll be here every Thursday." Ms. Haggle rose out of her chair and walked Natalie to the door, pulling it open. "I expect you to mind what we do here as personal. I have a reputation to uphold."

"Of course, Ms. Haggle." Natalie began to walk away, but she paused and turned toward Ms. Haggle. "Thank you," she said.

"About the chairs," said Ms. Haggle. "I have two more."

CHAPTER FOURTEEN

༄ঌ

TRIFECTA

It was Friday after school, and Natalie and Emma were standing outside the restroom, watching people at the local mall. The girls called it a mall and in every way it had the attributes of a mall; it, however, fell short of Natalie's shopping standards. The mall had two stories of shops inside—a rather large grocery store and a prominent retailer at each end—qualifying the area as a mall; but the reality of its limited walking space and its single strip helped exaggerate the definition. "Sometimes, a girl just needs to clear her head with a good shop-walk," thought Natalie as she glanced at the multitude of people shifting and tracking past her.

"Finally!" exclaimed Emma when Philian exited the restroom.

In Emma's defense, Philian had been inside the restroom for a while. Natalie decided not to comment, as she could tell that Philian was not feeling well; she suspected the girl had been crying. And there it was: Natalie spotted the corner of a card sticking out from Philian's purse. The cards were usually a different color every month—this time a brilliant red—but, without fail, each time Philian carried one of these cards, her mood altered for the worse. Natalie wanted to help, and had often tried to; but this was a subject that Philian was determined to deal with on her own.

"You know what we need?" said Natalie. "A good shop."

"Yeah," seconded Emma. "But I don't have any money."

"You don't need money to try things on," said Natalie.

"Awesome," said Emma. "I missed you yesterday. How long do you need to keep going to Ms. Hag's?"

"Well," began Natalie. "Four weeks down. Let's see… just forty more years left."

Emma and Philian laughed. "I missed you too," said Philian.

Natalie gave Philian a sideways hug, her usual pick-me-up when she received a card, and they both smiled. "I'm buying something today," said Philian, and the girls marched off with a purpose.

Within minutes, Philian was in one of the dressing rooms with her friends just outside when Natalie screamed out, "Who is that!" Natalie moved over to the corner of a wall to spy a better view. Emma followed close behind as Philian was delayed and temporarily unable to join in on the girls' excitement. Emma pushed Natalie, and Natalie pushed back so as to avoid being exposed.

"I want to see," whined Emma.

Natalie couldn't speak, so Emma squeezed in front of her and crouched on the ground.

A boy. Not any boy, but *the* boy—tall, thin, light skinned, black haired, dark-blue eyed. Blue eyes—like Philian's—had always intrigued Natalie. But the boy's eyes were dark blue, complementing his black hair. He had a fashion style that Natalie highly liked, but there was more—the entire package. Never had she been so attracted to a face—one that pleasing to look at. He also had a similar clothing style to hers, one that only an awesome few could pull off—all black. The face, the style, and the black hair with beautiful blue eyes: "Sold" was all that Natalie could say.

"Sold on what?" asked Philian, having just joined her friends.

"On him," replied Emma, pointing to the boy.

Natalie's engrossed response was to bite her lip, cling to the wall, and breathe more heavily.

"He is cute," replied Philian. "What are you going to do about it? Natalie? Nat?" Philian jokingly pretended to wipe drool from Natalie's mouth to get her attention. "Eww, it's wet," she replied as she wiped her hand on Natalie's back. "What are you going to do?" asked Philian again, giving Natalie a shove to bring her back to reality.

"What can I do?" replied Natalie.

"Go for it!" cheered Philian. "You have just as much right as anyone else."

"He looks older. What would he see in me?"

"Everything we see: compassion, genuineness, honesty! You're a great friend, and you look good too. That's your man over there... now walking away! Go get him!"

Natalie turned to Philian. "Do you think he'll like me?"

"Natalie, there's only one way to find out. You can't wait for your fate to take control anymore. It's time to start taking what's yours. Life favors the bold, and that's you! You're an amazing person with so many enviable qualities—you just haven't seen it yet. You've been through so much, naturally your confidence is low. But your stock is high… real high. If he can't see that, he doesn't deserve you."

Philian continued, "I've seen it so many times. A girl thinks she looks average, or fat, or cheap, but that's just because she's her own worst critic. We don't understand that men see us differently. If you have confidence, they'll grovel at your feet. So, either he'll think you're hot, or he's not worth it. Now, let's go get him." Philian began to push forward an unresisting Natalie, but the boy had already left.

"It's probably for the best," sighed Natalie. "I'm sure there's something wrong with him and I'd just be disappointed." Her shoulders slumped and head lowered, she reassured herself, "I just want to remember him like this, you know, not mess it up."

"That's your insecurity talking. Let's go," asserted Philian, tugging at Natalie's arm.

The girls searched for some time but were unable to find the boy. "We should head back," said Emma. The three girls leaned against the wall, scanning the mall left and right, grasping at their one last chance for success. Suddenly, the mall began to appear too big to Natalie.

"Let's go home," said Natalie. As they began to walk away, the three girls laughed at their mini adventure, trying to make light of their failure. At the mall exit, Natalie opened the first set of two doors, then turned her head to look behind at Emma and Philian, and commented loudly, "He was fine!"

"Thunk!" Unexpectedly, Natalie clashed into another person entering at the door. "I'm so sorry," said

Natalie as she placed her hand on the chest of the stranger to keep her balance. She turned her head to look forward and smiled as her hand gracefully stroked outward, without breaking away from the shirt. "Nice," she involuntarily whispered before she even realized the exact extent of her forwardness.

"There you are," said the boy she had been looking for.

"What?" asked a stunned Natalie, fumbling to straighten the boy's attire that bore no hint of wrinkles.

"I saw you here on Wednesday, but lost you," said the boy. "And you weren't here yesterday. I was kind of hoping to run into you, but not literally."

Natalie laughed goofily.

"What's your name?" asked the boy.

"Nat... Natalie."

"Hi, I'm Parker. I'm on my way out, but can I see you here again?"

"Mon..." Natalie looked at her friends and then back at Parker with a little more confidence. "Monday?"

"I look forward to it," said Parker with a lop-sided grin. He gently squeezed her hand and left.

After he was out of sight, Natalie shrieked. "He heard me call him fine!"

"Don't worry," said Philian. "He was looking for you. Your stock is high!"

Then, remembering what day it was, Natalie sulked, "Oh frights! It's Friday. I won't see him till Monday. And I have to face Melissa tonight. I'm going to be bummed all weekend, and I might even have bruises come Monday."

"Do you have to face her?" asked Philian.

"No, but it's for the best." Natalie sighed. "That way, I get respect."

"Yes, we've discussed this. Does it have to be physical? You did mention arm wrestling. I mean, can you do anything else? Are you good at anything?" asked Philian.

"Fencing," said Natalie. "But we don't do that."

"Yes, we can," Emma chimed in. "I've seen them do all kinds of things, even swords."

"There it is!" said Philian. "Take your destiny in your hands! If you're going to fight, do it on your terms. Every now and then, we get a trifecta, and this is yours."

"Trifecta?" asked Natalie.

"You know, three for three."

"But this would only be two."

"What do you want me to say? I've never heard of a twofecta. The night is young, Nat. Take a chance at your trifecta."

Natalie could barely contain herself on her way home. She and Emma practically ran home to prepare for the evening's challenge. Natalie, however, was greeted in the dorms by several somber women, including Devia.

"I need to speak with you," said Devia. "Come with me."

"No. Not tonight," thought Natalie. What could possibly go so wrong as to rob her of her chance at a win?

Devia led Natalie to the section that housed the room she had first come to know as her new home. She really had no desire to relive that time, not tonight. They stopped in front of the room that Ava occupied. "Compose yourself," said Devia.

Natalie took a deep breath, expecting the worst, and entered.

"Well, look who made it here," said Ava in a weak voice. "And all by herself."

Natalie sprang to Ava's side, weeping, as she held her aunt.

"Oh please, Natalia. I'm still delicate, child."

"I'm just so happy," cried Natalie.

"And we'll have plenty of time to spend together now. I do still need my rest; I only wanted you to know as soon as possible. Tomorrow?"

"Of course!" said Natalie. "I have so much to tell you."

"Whoa. I may need a couple days then. What do you think?"

"Okay," said Natalie, following Devia out of the room.

Afterwards, Natalie did not prepare for class, her focus being elsewhere—so much so that she arrived late.

"Do we have any challenges?" asked Zadie.

"Really? Nothing?" mocked Melissa, when Natalie didn't reply.

"Not tonight," said Natalie. "I'm kind of emotional."

Emma nudged Natalie. "Go grab your destiny."

"I don't know," said Natalie, unsure, but Emma's look said it all. Natalie could not disappoint her.

"Fencing," said Natalie.

"I'm sorry," said Zadie. "The challenger chooses the weapons and the accepted chooses the style, unless it is agreed otherwise."

"Broadswords!" said Melissa.

Natalie gulped, thinking she should probably have skipped class altogether. She gave Emma a morose look, who replied with a gesture that suggested that all was going well.

"Your stock is high," mouthed Emma.

Zadie suited up the girls in protective gear, and then explained the rules. "Anything goes. Three minor hits or one major hit secures a win. Any questions?"

Obviously, Melissa had none, but Natalie could write a book with her inquiries. However, she was unable to articulate her questions to postpone the event.

Zadie separated the girls, and prepared to begin the exercise. At that exact moment, Natalie felt the warmth of her ring, still circling her finger under the protective gear. Natalie glanced down, feeling her capacity to tap into Melissa's power strengthen. Suddenly, Natalie could feel Melissa's energy surge in intensity. The "Go" had been sounded, and Natalie's intuition warned her about the oncoming flight of a bulky chunk of metal in her direction. Instinctively, Natalie pulled the sword to her side in a successful, yet offsetting, defense. The fight was on.

Melissa swung again, and again. She was aggressive, but Natalie's instinct and experience were strong and spot-on. Natalie's strategy, she realized, was flawed—all defense and no offense. She was being constantly overpowered and outmaneuvered, so much there was almost no time for offense in her moves. Consequently, Natalie soon found herself cornered. Her position was vulnerable, deteriorating every second with Melissa's swings that kept coming faster and faster.

"Hit!" exclaimed Melissa, retreating away from Natalie, with her hands raised in the air in victory. But

Natalie's hip, where Melissa had struck, had merely been grazed.

"Minor hit!" declared Zadie. "It wasn't hard enough. A major hit must be capable of passing through superficial armor. Ready?" Zadie set the girls in their respective places again. "Begin!"

Emma raised her thumb up in the air, eliciting an excited cheer from all the girls gathered—this had by far been Natalie's best performance, even without offense. Natalie heard her name being shouted. A thrill of excitement ran through her, but she still had no attack planned. All she had time to do was block.

"Offense! Offense! Offense! Offense!" chanted the girls.

Natalie, finally convinced of her capabilities, found an opportunity and thrust her sword straight forward, poking Melissa in the face hard enough to shove her head backwards.

"Hit!" shouted Zadie. Natalie couldn't believe it! After months of fights, she had finally managed to strike Melissa. Then, before she could even revel in her victory, they were set again. "Go."

Melissa swung harder. Natalie could barely resist her forceful hits with her sword. As Melissa swung again, Natalie positioned her sword sideways, enlisting the aid of her other hand that was set on the flat side of the blade. With both her hands, she was able to deflect the blow. Stunned by the solid block, Melissa never saw Natalie thrust the hilt of her sword to collide with Melissa's head. Swiftly, Natalie swirled her entire body and sword around for the second of her one-two punch. Put off balance, Melissa raised her sword only enough to block Natalie, but

Natalie countered with a small hit, though not enough to engage a call.

Melissa balanced herself and sprung forward. Ducking a slicing swing, Natalie tucked in her sword. Loosening her grip on the handle, Natalie passed by Melissa's side and turned her sword upside down. Catching Melissa overextended and her backside exposed, Natalie, her hands raised high, thrust the sword downward into Melissa's lower back.

"Minor hit," announced Zadie.

Natalie was nervous: anyone could still win with one hit. She wanted to call a timeout, but could she? A timeout would show weakness, and Melissa thrived on weakness. "Go!"

Melissa advanced menacingly. Natalie's blocks seemed ineffective, but they were just enough for her survival. Melissa swung again, and again, utilizing her strength to overcome Natalie's years of training with swords. Natalie was tired and sore from blocking Melissa's enormous blows. All she needed was one minor hit, but felt as though she lacked the necessary strength to pull it off. Melissa feigned, and then missed in her real attack. Again, she brought her sword down hard. Natalie ducked, aiming for a minor strike as she dodged, but Melissa was ready with a block and counter attack. Melissa was a fast learner, and she was definitely not prepared for defeat. Natalie was exhausted, yet Melissa kept her onslaught raging, without even pausing to catch her breath.

Then, Natalie felt it: Melissa's power. With a stronger grasp than before, Natalie touched on Melissa's dexterity, strength, skill, and endurance. Melissa's attributes were for the taking—even more now than they ever were before. All the months of probing Melissa were seemingly paying off. Somehow, Natalie could sense Melissa's offensive moves as they were being planned in Melissa's mind. Natalie even sensed that she was in on the attack against herself.

It was time. Natalie embraced the risk. If she was correct, then this win was hers to take. In an instant, Natalie sought out the offensive measures Melissa had schemed against herself. Instinctively, she felt Melissa would push her sword against hers with two hands, forcing Natalie's sword up and away to her right, and then come around, full circle, with a mid-level kill swing from the left. If this was true, Natalie could capitalize by using this momentum to also turn around, starting from the right and finishing on the left, blindly taking a counter, high kill swing. To do this, she would have to invert her back at the exact point where Melissa's sword was to touch. If Natalie was wrong, she would be open to certain loss, but… it was time.

Sure enough, Melissa went ahead with her strike as envisioned. Natalie, in absolute terror, turned her back to Melissa, arching her mid section, angst-ridden that Melissa's sword would fail to make contact as she came back around. Remarkably, Melissa's sword grazed Natalie's unnaturally bowed mid region at the small of her back, and slipped through. Natalie spun around, looking straight into Melissa's flabbergasted eyes as the sword swung around to her neck. Quick witted and highly skilled, Melissa was capable of contorting her head around, but only at the cost of losing steady footing. Natalie missed, but she angled her sword and momentum downward, to catch Melissa's wrist. Melissa's sword fell to the ground with a "clink." Natalie swiftly kicked it behind her, effectively placing herself between Melissa and her snatched prospect of victory.

"Trifecta," whispered Natalie as she stood steady, arm and sword in a sturdy, straight line, aimed between Melissa's eyes.

But Melissa refused to back down.

"Concede!" shouted Natalie.

"Never!" replied Melissa.

"You are beaten! Concede!"

"She cheated!" shouted Melissa. "She stole my power! We can't use power!"

"Quiet," shushed Zadie. "There are others here."

"Arghhhhhhhh!" screamed Melissa clenching her fists at her side.

"Boooom!" went the room as some force shook the inside of the dojo, hurling Natalie against the padded wall across the room. Natalie slid to the floor, her arm guarding her face, and cringed at what she saw in front of her eyes.

Melissa's eyes rolled back into her head, revealing nothing but the white portion. Her hair let loose by itself and waved around her head—as though a storm raged inside the room. Her clothes altered in color and shape, reaching down to the floor in the form of a long black dress. She grew taller, or she began to float off the ground by some means. Her skin began to turn green—in fact, all her skin became a light shade of green.

Melissa shouted again—the force of her words creating a physical impact on Natalie, making her insides hurt. "You cheated! You stole my power!"

Melissa, standing completely upright, tilted her entire body unrealistically in Natalie's direction. Natalie cowered in fear—there was no natural explanation for Melissa's current state. Fog... it seemed like fog circulated beneath Melissa's dress, covering the floor near her feet and hiding it from view. In a motion Natalie could only describe as floating, Melissa moved toward her.

"You will cease!" shouted Zadie. "Cease!"

Melissa snapped her head around one hundred and eighty degrees to face Zadie. One hundred and eighty degrees! Melissa then slowly turned her head back to Natalie. *"I could destroy you, feeble child,"* she said in the crooked voice Natalie had heard before.

Melissa's body then turned mid-air, and she drifted away.

CHAPTER FIFTEEN

⊰∽⊱

PLEDGE

Inside the castle, Natalie and Emma sat in a room that resembled a court of law. Natalie counted thirteen chairs at the front of the room facing her and Emma—that is, if one were to count the three in the center, behind the large wooden counter. The remaining ten chairs, five on each side, were placed near simple tables. There were seats facing the center on both sides—twelve on the left and twelve on the right—placed in two rows of six, and about thirty seats behind them, separated from the rest of the room by a short half wall. Sitting with the two girls was Zadie, but originally they were attended to by an unknown brown robed-woman, who accompanied them from behind the front desk of the castle. Not one word had been spoken to Natalie or Emma about the "Melissa incident" that had taken place not more than an hour before.

Suddenly, twelve women in black robes filed into the room through the door facing the girls, while more—in black and brown robes—filed in from behind them. Everyone stood. Zadie instructed Natalie and Emma to stand, and they managed to push themselves up with little comfort from behind a small desk. The headmistress, dressed in her scarlet robe, entered the room and took her seat in the center chair behind the counter, between Devia and Mara and the other ten women.

"You may be seated," stated the headmistress. "We have debriefed Zadie. This special council is to address the two young women sitting with her. Devia."

Devia, being called upon, continued the proceedings. "I would like to begin by stating that the two of you are in no trouble and are completely safe here. This is merely an inquiry into the events that transpired approximately an hour ago. You are free to address this council without facing any repercussion. Do you have any questions before we begin?"

Zadie took a few moments to explain to the two girls what Devia's statement meant in relation to them.

"What happened to Melissa?" asked Natalie.

"We will address that later," replied Mara. "For the moment, we have some questions for you, so, please speak frankly."

"Yes, Mother," replied Natalie. Emma replied the same.

Devia began, "In your own words, please describe exactly what you saw."

"I can't describe what I saw," said Natalie. "But I know it wasn't right."

"Emma?" asked Devia.

Emma hesitated, but Zadie rubbed her back and whispered everything would be alright to encourage her.

"Melissa… she… turned into a monster. The room exploded, and Melissa turned into a monster…"

"Can you provide more details?" asked Mara.

"Details?" questioned Natalie. "That sums it all up. Melissa was flying about, her clothes changed, and… and she turned green. Then she hit me without hitting me. I don't know what happened, but Emma's right… Melissa turned into a monster."

"Anything else?" asked Mara, unruffled.

"Yes, Mother," said Natalie. "We were scared. Really, really scared, and no one seems surprised by what happened."

"It's okay," said Devia. "We will address the matter in time. You and everyone else are safe now."

"That matter is satisfied," said the headmistress. "We shall move on."

"Ahem," Mara cleared her voice. "Natalie. Have you been stealing power from Melissa?"

"Excuse me, Mother," replied Natalie. "But there's a monster out there! Melissa is missing, and no one is looking for her. Am I the only one who saw this?"

"Please stay focused," said Devia. "We concur with your account of events, and all will be explained. But, for now, we have a process to conclude. Can you help us?"

"I… I don't know what stealing power is, but I felt something unusual, something different, when we fought. I don't know how to explain it, but… but it was like I could… I don't know. I knew what she was going to do."

"How long have you been doing this?" asked Mara.

"Since the first challenge. For several months now, Mother."

"Emma," continued Mara. "Have you witnessed any circumstances that have appeared unusual to you since you arrived here?"

"Yes, Mother," replied Emma.

"Please explain."

"I've seen the Den Three do magic tricks that... I really couldn't explain."

"Continue," urged Mara.

"I've seen them jump off the roof, the high roof, without getting hurt."

"Anything else?"

"They can change things, control things—animals, colors, objects. But I've never said anything to anybody. I promise."

"We believe you," said Devia. "How do you explain these things?"

Natalie, in revelation from Emma's comments, contemplated a different perspective altogether. As she viewed the scene about her, she began to question the idea of reality itself as a constant. Combined with her experiences with Ava, the ring, her own feelings, and the night's enlightenment, she was prepared to accept the probability that some fantasies were, in fact, truths. Her jaw dropped as she embraced the notion that the women she was looking at around the room were... witches!

"Magic," answered Emma.

"And you?" Devia asked Natalie.

"No. It's not possible."

"What is impossible about our way of life?"

"It's just not possible."

"Only because you have never seen something, you would say it does not exist?"

"No, that's not what I meant."

"Then, what do you mean? How else could you have jumped off of a moving train without being harmed?"

"It's not that... it's just that... magic, magic doesn't exist."

"Because you have never seen it?"

"No, because—"

"Because that's what people told you," continued Devia. "The same people that said the Earth was flat, that the Sun circled the Earth, and that there were gods for the mountains and the moon. We have all been misled at some point, but I ask: Did your eyes deceive you tonight?"

"No, Mother."

"And you, Emma?" asked Devia. "What do you believe?"

"Can I do those tricks too?"

"We shall see," said the headmistress. "Zadie, will you please lead the children out?"

Once they were outside the room, Natalie asked Zadie, "Is it true?"

"That is not for me to say. You are one of us, and the council will care for you accordingly."

"I want to fly," declared Emma. "Can I fly?"

Zadie giggled. "I've always liked you, Emma. Not one disheartened bone in your body."

Before long, the three women were summoned back into the room, taking their original positions on their chairs.

"Do you know why we called you back in here?" asked Devia.

"No, Mother," replied Natalie.

"You are here to be pledged. To be pledged is to be entrusted with loyalty. There is only one sin against the order: betrayal. In order to be pledged, you must swear your absolute allegiance to the order and its secrets. Are the two of you prepared to do that?"

"Yes, Mother," replied Natalie.

"Yes, Mother," repeated Emma.

All thirteen women behind the desks nodded in approval. "Do we have a sponsor?" asked the headmistress.

"I believe Ava would like the honor," said Devia.

"Then send for her," replied the headmistress.

As ordered, two women left through the back of the room. Just then, two more women entered, each carrying a folded garment of a deep honey color. The women placed the articles on the small desk in front of Natalie and Emma. Natalie stroked the material with her fingers, enjoying the silky texture of the eye-catching robe.

"While we wait," began Devia, "I would like to explain a few things. To answer your questions, yes, we do have power. Power that you will come to understand, and may even yourself have. This power, however, comes at a price: your loyalty. No one is to be told; no one must know of what we do here. These secrets have been kept from you with the help of diminishing spells, and you will keep them from others. This concealment is not designed to control, but it is the only way to preserve our way of life. You must willfully agree to be pledged. And since you are not old enough to confirm your pledge, you must first undergo a spell of confidentiality."

Ava arrived in a wheelchair, and was placed beside the desk in front of Natalie.

The headmistress asked, "Ava, do you sponsor this child?"

"I do."

"And who is to sponsor the second child?" asked the headmistress.

Natalie looked at Ava with expectant eyes.

"I will sponsor both the children," replied Ava.

"Then we will proceed," continued the headmistress as she, Devia, and Mara dismounted the front counter to stand facing the two new pledges.

Zadie helped Ava up into a standing position, and all four women—including Natalie and Emma—faced the three topmost women of the order.

The headmistress spoke again. "You will see things that will bewilder your mind, do not fear; you will do things that defy logic, do not fear; you will feel things that one should not feel, do not fear; you will be one of us, the Order of the Sisterhood, and you will be welcome to all its knowledge, faith, and unity. You may sign the secret sign with me as I perform my spells." Then, the headmistress began to chant.

Ava showed the girls how to place their right hand up, palm facing forward, with their ring finger folded down. Emma had some trouble making the sign, but Ava assisted her to achieve the position. Then, Ava moved each girl's hand in an infinity-shaped gesture.

The headmistress motioned the secret sign to each girl, and then continued, "The palm shows friendship, peace, and loyalty; the bent ring finger symbolizes that no power will be used against another pledge; the infinity symbol signifies that this devotion is unbreakable and forever. Do you pledge your loyalty, secrecy, and devotion?"

"Yes, Headmistress," replied both girls simultaneously.

"You are now members of the Order of the Sisterhood. Take your robes." To this command, the girls were presented with their own golden honey colored robes.

CHAPTER SIXTEEN

❧

WITCH WITH POWER

Monday after school, Natalie's insides were brimmed with numerous mixed emotions: excitement that she could now attend after-school class with the other girls; exhilaration at learning about her new world; anticipation about spending time with Ava; anxiety at her restitution with Ms. Haggle; thrill of her boy interest; and disappointment over having to miss her meeting with Parker. Natalie knew not how to contain or stabilize so many balls bouncing in her head at once.

Susan and Toddi were as excited as Natalie as they led her to class. At first, Natalie was more focused on Parker. She had asked Philian to explain to him that she couldn't be there Monday, and didn't know when she would be able to meet him. This was an interesting test of their friendship. Natalie knew all too well how backstabbing women could be when it came to men. Philian could easily feel betrayed by Natalie's new obligation, and move in on Natalie's love interest in retaliation. Love? Oh, no! Natalie was smitten. And why not? The guy made her go weak at every joint. She craved more of him, and had even considered skipping class—which, she realized, would have been a mistake when she entered the room presenting her a new world.

The enormous classroom had a semicircular structure, and was connected to the backside of the dormitory. Reminiscent of an older theatre, in the room, two aisles descended toward a center stage, dividing the seating arrangement into three sections. There were balconies on the left, the right, and to the top, but they were curtained off, adding an even greater number to the already huge capacity of more than a hundred seats on the floor. Natalie and Emma were holding their robes, but noticed the other girls remove their robes from hooks placed along the back wall. Every robe—with the exception of those of the Den Three—was the same honey color as Natalie and Emma's. Natalie put hers on enthusiastically. She felt complete.

"Why do they have different colored robes?" Natalie asked Susan.

"They're Foresters. We're Honeys. We'll get our green robes after testing."

"Testing?"

"I'm so glad we can talk about this now," confessed Susan. "The Den Three are turning eighteen soon. They'll test for their brown robes and move out of the dorms. You've noticed that the rest of us are twelve to fifteen years old, right? Most of us will become Foresters after testing, and we're going to need a new Den Three. I was really hoping you'd come around, so it could be Toddi, you, and me."

"Really? What do I have to do to get my green robe?"

"Just prove yourself. It mostly concerns age and maturity. You don't have to worry; if I'm the front runner, you'll get one. Just relax and it'll happen. And then, I'll choose you for my group of three."

"Don't I need some kind of power, like Melissa?"

"Not every woman is a WWP."

"What's a WWP?" asked Natalie.

"Witch with power."

Highly intrigued, Natalie gushed out her next question: "How will I know if I have power?"

"Today is your first day. The seer will come and tell your fortune."

"I'm nervous," admitted Natalie.

"You should be. Toddi and I are the only students beside the Den Three who have power."

"What do you do if you don't have power?"

"Zadie and Devia don't have power."

"What?"

"No, they don't. Witchcraft isn't necessarily about power. Less than ten percent of us have it, and sometimes, even if they do, it remains undiscovered. Witchcraft is about spells. You have protective spells and curses: offense and defense. You can pull off a mighty lot with them. You just can't do what Melissa did, or the way she did it. You see, spells are preparatory and require a lot of magic, effort, and time. Power is instantaneous. But not all spells can be performed with power, and not all power can be mimicked with spells. The difference really is like solving a large math problem on paper as opposed to doing it with a calculator. There's just a huge advantage with power. And then, there're the seers. They're the weird ones."

"How so?"

"Please don't be one of those. Seers are eccentric. Since they can see the future, they think they're better than other witches. They can foresee, and many a time, alter the future. They know all about you and what you're going to do, so they look down on others. They're also creepy, mostly because they seal themselves within a solitary world in their quest for knowledge. They become addicted and spend all their time getting a sense of the future—so much so that they miss out on the present. They have no social skills, and they'll never give you a straight answer. It's a power thing. If they said things directly, you would be able to change the future, and probably wouldn't need them."

Just then, a hunched-over woman in a black robe, with white wiry hair fraying all about, stepped onto the stage. "Where are my new Honeys?" she asked.

"That's you two," said Susan as she nudged Natalie.

Natalie and Emma stood in response.

"And where is your sponsor?" scoffed the woman at the girls.

"Ava is on a quest," answered Ms. Haggle. "I shall sponsor them today."

"Mmm," said the squinty-eyed seer. "He-he. How fortunate for these girls!" With a few grunts, the little old lady moved closer to Ms. Haggle, leaning heavily on her cane. "Ms. Haggle. The pleasure is all theirs. We may proceed," she ended as she turned and manage to make her way off the stage.

Ms. Haggle snapped her fingers at the girls and followed the decrepit woman. Feeling a surge of energy, a product of one part fear and four parts curiosity, Natalie and Emma rushed to Ms. Haggle's side, making sure to not get too close.

They traveled through the doors that connected to a hallway in the castle and led into a waiting area.

"We're in the castle," said an eager Emma.

Natalie shushed her as the two gawked at the dusty, decaying, mid-sized room that smelled worse than Ms. Haggle. Coincidently, right then, Ms. Haggle inhaled a deep breath of air, and almost smiled. The girls giggled, but instantly stopped when Ms. Haggle turned to look at them.

"Is this woman a hoarder?" Natalie whispered to Emma.

Emma did not dare to smile again, but nodded in nervous agreement as she peered at the disorganized books, crates, and the trashy-looking stuff that filled the room. Despite the six chairs and abundant junk crowding the place, there was just enough room to navigate into two significantly marked doors; the markings looked like arbitrary gibberish, but certainly had purpose.

After about half an hour, a voice rang out from a door that was slightly ajar. "The little one."

Emma complied, cautiously opening the door enough to enter.

"This will not take long," assured Ms. Haggle. "Seers are self-absorbed, and their time is best spent without you. Pay heed to every little word. They work in mysterious ways."

"Yes, Ms. Haggle."

Not a minute had elapsed before Emma came out of the room, her eyes twinkling with joy. "I have power!" she whispered more loudly than she intended to.

"Good for you," said Natalie as she gave Emma a hug.

Their embrace was cut short with an abrupt "Next."

Natalie crossed her fingers and smiled as she walked toward the door. The door, however, closed in her face.

"The other door."

Natalie, with heightened anxiety, grinned to calm herself as she made her way there. Hopeful, Emma crossed fingers on both her hands.

Drapes shrouded the room, creating a perfect circular area that was furnished with two chairs around a round table. Atop the table, right in the middle, sat a crystal ball.

"Sit."

Natalie sat on the small chair nearest to her. She could hear the seer walk into the room from behind her. Mist filled the room, and the crystal ball shone with brilliant bright colors that were reflected in the moisture.

"It's power you want to know about. Simple. You don't have it."

Without hesitation, Natalie replied, "But I've felt it."

"You dare question me!"

"No, Ma'am."

The old woman placed her hands on Natalie's head. "There is a lot I see. A lot, a lot, a lot. I'm not wrong about this. Power is what you do not have."

Natalie sighed, almost pouting.

"Do not despair, child. There is more to you than one might think. Out!" she shouted, prompting Natalie to spring up and exit the room.

Once she was outside, Emma could tell that Natalie wanted to cry. The girls hugged until Ms. Haggle instructed them to sit down. "We will not disturb the class in progress. Your time will be spent here, quietly, in reflection of your prophecies."

Natalie searched for some positive interpretation, any positive aspect, but failed miserably. How would she ever compete with Melissa? Her whole life would be spent in that woman's shadow. Again, would she even be considered for the next Den Three?

"Let's proceed," said Ms. Haggle, after what Natalie felt was too long a time for reflection.

Ms. Haggle escorted the girls back to the classroom, into the balcony seats. The girls were excited to experience the remainder of the class from up high, but both were reserved from mulling over the news that neither could easily accept.

After the class filed out, Ms. Haggle told the girls that they could leave as well. Emma took Natalie's hand and held it as they walked down the stairs. When they reached the bottom, they let go and Emma said, "You're still my hero."

Natalie smiled and replied, "Go on now, tell the girls."

Emma zapped away with a pat from Natalie.

Natalie whiled time away before she went to meet the other girls, ensuring Emma could fully enjoy herself. It was not often, almost never, that Emma could brag to the older girls. Natalie didn't want to be a downer, especially with her being a hero in Emma's eyes.

Natalie slowly hung up her robe on one of the wrought iron hooks that lined the back of the classroom. It was at that moment that she noticed something odd: a faded and tattered green robe. Upon closer inspection,

Natalie noticed it was older than the rest of the robes that had been hung on the hooks. Indeed, some Honey robes were slightly faded, but this green was way different from those. Natalie touched the material to find that it was of the same type as all the others. Then, she noticed a shiny metal pin on the robe. The chrome pin had the shape of a snake wrapped around a black knife—just like the ones that were placed over Ms. Haggle's fireplace. "Leadership" was imprinted on the knife. Natalie opened the robe to find two sets of letters inside: "L.T.," preceded by an "M.T." above. "These are initials," thought Natalie. "Melissa Tate, but who is L.T.?"

Confused, Natalie felt that it was time to face the gossip and venture outside. As she left, the seer approached Ms. Haggle, who had been watching Natalie the entire time.

"I didn't tell her," said the seer.

"A girl should not know that she is to die so young."

"She could change the face of history."

"That is why her mother gave birth to her," replied Ms. Haggle.

"The reign of scarlet is nearly over, as is this order, and my service," continued the seer.

"You must do what is best for you."

"And you? Will you pay for your sins?"

"If that is possible," replied Ms. Haggle. "My destiny was written ten millennia ago, and I have never feared it."

CHAPTER SEVENTEEN

꙰

RECONCILE

Natalie was ecstatic. After a month of passing him notes through Philian, she was finally going to see Parker. It had been nearly thirty days since she had gazed into those fabulous blue eyes. It was Wednesday, and the supplemental class, which the girls referred to as "craft" class, was to be held in the library, affording her the freedom to skip, as many girls do, and go mall hopping instead.

After the final class was dismissed, Natalie went straight home from school to freshen up and drop off her books. After she was done, she impatiently waited for Emma on the front porch, all the while scrutinizing her uniform for any defects—she detested the thought of offering any excuse for Parker to reject her. "How do I look?" she asked Susan.

"No better than yesterday. I mean, no worse. Uh, you know what I mean. Good."

"Thanks for the confidence," replied Natalie with a friendly laugh.

"Do you think he's still into you?" asked Susan.

"His letters sound pretty sure. Giving him space has made him think more highly of me. But then again, he might also be disappointed when he sees me again if he thinks too highly, I guess."

"Stop overthinking it," said Susan. "You're so beautiful, and you'll have no problem finding a man who finds you attractive."

"Thank you," replied Natalie as she gave Susan a hug.

"Ava!" yelled Natalie.

As she saw Ava approaching, Natalie ran to greet her. "I've missed you so much!" Natalie grabbed Ava tight, as though she wanted to express all the despondence Ava's absence had brought her. "We never got to talk, and then you were gone. I was so worried I'd lose you again."

Ava hugged Natalie back, almost as tight as Natalie held her. "There was something I had to do—for you, and for your mother."

Natalie looked beyond Ava to see a hearse in the background. She lay her head onto Ava's shoulder, weeping.

Susan, who was standing close by, asked, "Shall we go without her?"

"Yes," replied Ava.

Natalie's mother, perfectly preserved in her coffin, lay on an altar in the cemetery at the top of the hill with Natalie by her side. As women continued to prepare for the evening's funeral, Natalie bawled her eyes out, releasing all her pent-up grief over her mother's death. The considerably large altar sat near the front of the cemetery; an opening in front of it held a hundred chairs, but could easily provide seating for a much larger group if necessary. The women performed ritualistic acts around the beautifully carved stone altar in preparation of the night's event.

"Natalie," said Ava. "Let's take a break."

"You… you called me Natalie," she replied, wiping her tears and lifting her head.

"Yes, I did. You have made your own name here, and I'm really proud of you."

Natalie embraced Ava. "The last time I went with you, away from my mother, she was still alive." Natalie began to break down and cry again.

Ava rubbed Natalie's back, silently casting a few spells to help her. "Come, I want to show you where she will be laid to rest. It is indeed a great honor to see our Hall of Heroines, and an even greater honor to be laid there."

"Okay."

Ava led Natalie to the mausoleum she had once explored on a full moon night. "Here lie the dead, for all to revere. They are resting now, in peace and still," it read. Four massive pillars upheld the overhang of marble with such grandeur that even the artist Bernini would have been proud. The marble carvings on the pillars were sophisticated and elegant beyond Natalie's comprehension of art—a museum almost unto itself. Lettering, indecipherable to Natalie's inexperienced eyes, covered all the sides of the mausoleum, detailing its significance. Ava commanded two stone doors to open, and they did. If the outside was brilliantly elegant, the inside put it to shame: a circular room with a stone podium placed in the center, staircases to the left and right, hundreds of niches—only partially filled with busts—and crevices of ingenious design allowing light to fill the entire room. Affixed to the stone podium, carved in its entirety, was the form of an open book that bore inscriptions in a language Natalie did not understand. Ava and Natalie descended the staircase to the left, and Natalie saw that both sets of stairs led to the same place. As the two women continued downward, stone torches lit up as if on some wordless cue. Natalie stopped to peek down the first sub-level of caverns as Ava continued to the second. She could see graves of stone by the hundreds: catacombs. The second level was where the two women halted. A solid stone tunnel, about twenty meters long, began from that point, and before it diverged to the left and right, Natalie noticed an overhead sign that stated, "Hall of Heroines."

"Where does the next level of stairs go?" asked Natalie.

"There is another level of ancient tombs, and if you're lucky, you can make your way to the castle from there, or the arena."

Magnificent tombs adorned the inside of the second level. Dozens of statues, stone coffins, and carved likenesses of women decorated the marble and gold room dedicated to heroines of the order. The hall was large enough to house statues and stone graves laid lengthwise in the middle, but most were embedded into the walls. As the two walked further, Natalie observed that the walls of the hall curved to complete a full circle, back to the entrance.

"Mom!" cried Natalie as she glanced upon an upright stone recreation of her mother, carved into the wall next to a sideways opening. Natalie caressed the wall as though the statue was her mother in flesh.

"This is where she belongs, Natalie. With us, here at the order."

Later, during the ceremony, Melissa, dressed in her green robe, stood by her own mother's grave. Natalie spent most of the night close to her mother until Ava carried her away, while she slept, from Hannah's final resting spot.

◯ॐ◯

The next morning presented a challenge for Rebecca to organize the girls for school.

"Susan, I assigned your section the morning wakeup and cleanup duties," said Rebecca.

"Yes, sinister," replied Susan.

"What did you call me?"

"Sister. I said sister. Are you sure you're hearing alright?"

"Just get it done," said Rebecca. "Toddi!" she called. "Has everyone had breakfast?"

"No," replied Toddi.

"What... what's going on here? Why haven't the girls been fed?"

"I don't know," replied Toddi. "Isabella asked me not to."

"Seriously? Where is she?"

"She already left for school."

"If anyone sees Isabella, tell her to come see me, I have something for her," Rebecca told the girls in exasperation.

Susan, Toddi, Natalie, and Emma left Rebecca in her state of breakdown, and made their way to school. On the way, Susan asked Toddi why she had put the blame on

Isabella for the breakfast mishap. "I'm doing her a favor," replied Toddi. "She needs to learn how to supervise."

Natalie finished some make-up assignments during lunch, but told Philian she could meet up with her at the mall after school even though it was a Thursday. Natalie was astonished that Ms. Haggle had taken sympathy upon her and given her the day off—well, postponed their meeting to Friday.

"Thanks for waiting here," said Natalie. "I had one last make-up assignment to turn in after school. Have you seen Parker yet?"

"He's under the impression that Thursdays are impossible for you, so he probably won't show. But I have good news! He'll start coming by on weekends and… I have a note from yesterday."

As Philian took the note out of her purse, Natalie impatiently grabbed at it and accidentally pulled out a blue card at the same time. Natalie flipped the two letters over to look at the mailing listing on the blue card.

"This is the same last name as yours. Do you have a brother that writes you?"

Philian turned her back to Natalie. "No."

"Phen, it's been months now. You have to talk about this. You've always been there for me. Let me be there for you."

"It's different," said Philian.

"Phen, who is this?" asked Natalie as she moved close to Philian to comfort her.

In a morose tone, Philian replied, "It's my father."

"Come on," said Natalie. "We need to get out of here."

Natalie found a secluded bench where they could speak in private.

"What about Parker?" asked Philian.

"That can wait. You need me right now. I'm opening this, okay?"

Philian did not reply; so Natalie, feeling that she had given Philian fair warning, opened and read the card. "This is good," said Natalie. "Your father loves you. This is good."

"You don't understand."

"Understand what? That you have a father who cares about you and wants to see you? A father that writes you every month?"

Philian stood and began to walk away, but Natalie stopped her. "I'm sorry. I'm... I don't understand. Please help me understand."

Both the girls sat back down; Philian put her face down into her hands and began to cry. "I lied... I lied about him. I betrayed him." Philian continued to cry.

"Betrayal," thought Natalie. Betrayal is the only sin. The guilt that Philian felt—did she deserve it? Surely, there must be forgiveness for betrayal, but not according to her order. Were they wrong? Was she wrong?

"I'll be here for you when you're ready to talk about it," said Natalie.

"My mom pressured me. I was afraid, you see, because I live with her. She made it sound right, like... like that was what *I* wanted. Before I knew what was happening, I had to keep telling the same story... again and again and again. I lied to lawyers, mediators, judges... my father. I can't go back; I can't face him. He'll never forgive me... I can't go back. I just want to forget the whole thing."

Natalie sat there, stumped. She wanted to support her friend; she knew there was no force on earth that could stop her from contacting her mother or father if they were alive. She read the card again. "He's forgiven you, Phen. Love transcends..." Suddenly, Natalie was reminded of Melissa and her mother—the connection between child and parent, regardless of sin.

"You once advised me to take charge of my destiny. Now, I'm giving it back to you. I buried my mother yesterday," continued Natalie in a stern voice. "A parent is a gift one should not take lightly. Reach out to your father. You owe it to yourself to give this a go. He put his number in here. Give me your cell phone."

"I can't."

"I said, give me the phone."

Philian handed her cell to Natalie, who dialed the number. She handed the phone back to Philian and said, "Push send."

Eventually, Philian did. As the phone rang, Philian shifted her weight from one foot to another in nervous apprehension. "Hello." Philian sniffled and let out a yelp in her attempt to breathe.

"Philian?" said the man on the receiving end of the phone.

"Hehp, hehp, Dad," cried Philian. She continued to cry so loudly that it drowned her father's voice. Natalie rubbed her back and encouraged her to speak. When she had calmed down a little, the father spoke again.

"Thank you," he said.

"F-for what?"

"For calling."

"But, Dad, the things I did…"

"All in the past. I love you."

"Dad, when I told you I didn't remember that day at the amusement park… I think about it all the time… and you."

"We've had some good times, haven't we?"

"I'm sorry, Dad. I'm so sorry."

"It's forgiven. Only one thing hurts me."

"What's that? I'll fix it. Anything."

"Not hearing from you."

"What about the things I did?"

"None of that mattered the second I heard your voice."

Philian cried. "I want to see you again, Dad."

"I would like that a lot," he replied.

"Will you come get me?" asked Philian.

"I'm not sure it works that way. Let me talk to some people. I'll take some time off, and you and I can do something special. What do you think?"

"You're still mad at me?"

"No, it's kind of kidnapping if I don't go through the courts. Believe me, I want to pick you up right now, but I'll be patient. I'll even wait for years if that's what it takes. This is about you. If you want to see me, it will take some time. The courts are very, very slow, but I'll never give up on you."

"Dad, can you get the process started?"

"Yes."

"I have to go, but… but I love you," said Philian.

"I love you too, Philian," replied her father.

Reconcile

Philian disconnected the phone, and Natalie held her till she stopped crying.

CHAPTER EIGHTEEN

༈

EXCEPTIONS

"Oh my gosh! What's he doing here?" shrieked Natalie, hiding her face and ducking behind Philian.

"Don't be shy," replied Philian.

"But it's Parker! What do I do?"

"Go say hi."

Natalie quickly checked her breath and ran her fingers through her hair before peeking out from behind her friend once again. "He's coming this way. Why?"

Philian stopped walking, making Natalie fumble in her clumsy attempt to regain her cover.

"Nat, it's time."

"Did you do this?" asked Natalie. But before Philian could break into her bright smile, Parker's tall head appeared over Philian, seeking Natalie's attention.

"Thank you, Philian," said Parker in an unfamiliar but deep, satisfying voice.

And before Natalie could realize what was happening, she found herself alone with Parker.

"Come on," said Parker, adjusting his backpack— which held a skateboard—with one hand and holding out his other hand to Natalie. "I'll have you back by a reasonable time."

"I normally don't have that much time after school, but our afternoon class was canceled today."

Parker smiled. "Do you have enough time for the brook?"

Natalie knew exactly what Parker was referring to: the romantic path that stretched along and crossed over the creek multiple times, decorated with aesthetic bridges, hills, and benches to rest upon. It was the perfect place for their first date.

"I might," she replied, sounding coy. "If the company's good."

"It will be."

Natalie felt the butterflies in her stomach. She wanted to shake and jiggle, but she managed to withhold as much excitement as she could, hoping her emotions were not too transparent. Then, her joy doubled when she thought about Parker's letters, especially the one part that had struck her the most: "I really enjoy your notes. They give me the chance to get to know you without being influenced by your beauty." All Natalie could think about was that he found her beautiful. Well, and that he was willing to learn more about her instead of just focusing on her looks. The ensuing silence grew unbearable, and she finally broke it with a bit of humor.

"Really, a skateboard?"

"Hey," said Parker, laughing. "What's wrong with a skateboard?"

"I don't know. Do you take all your dates on skateboard rides?"

"Dates," said Parker. "I like that word. Does that mean we'll have more?"

"That depends on whether your skateboard stays home or not."

Natalie inched a little closer to Parker, in order to allow an older couple to pass by them. She patted the skateboard, "I don't think there's anything wrong with a skateboard."

Parker unstrapped the skateboard and set it on the ground. "Come on. It won't bite."

Natalie took Parker's hand and stepped on the board. Parker led her down the hill, slightly easing away from her grip until she managed to maintain balance on her own. The ride was nothing like the experience with a horse, but it was nonetheless exhilarating in its own way, especially when Natalie looked to see the downward hill in front of her and Parker's fading form behind her.

"Parker!" she shouted as she gained speed.

"Hold on," replied Parker, sprinting to her.

"Hurry!" screamed Natalie, trembling and moving back and forth, before Parker caught up and placed his hands on her waist to slow her down.

After inhaling a deep breath, Natalie looked down at Parker's hands and smiled.

"Oh, sorry." Parker moved his hands to Natalie's arms and guided her over to the center of one of the bigger bridges: one of Natalie's favorite places along the brook.

"How old are you really?" asked Parker. "Philian said you were sixteen."

"Fourteen... and a half. And you?" asked Natalie, terribly worried that she was not old enough for Parker.

"I turned sixteen the first day I saw you—my best birthday gift ever."

Natalie's anxiety subsided as her heart melted, and she took Parker's hand in hers. The two stood for some time, in silence, observing the scene and immersed in the sound of flowing water.

"So, your friends call you Nat. What should *I* call you? How about Nattles?"

"What? Of course not. That's just weird."

Parker laughed. "I like a woman who knows what she likes and doesn't like. How about Nate?"

"Only on a trial basis." Natalie sighed. "I've been so worried that you might be too old for me. You're okay with the age, then?"

Parker just smiled and squeezed Natalie's hand.

Natalie initially twitched, but then she relaxed and began to enjoy the moment. After some thought on the subject of age, she said, "Sixteen, huh? I guess that's not so bad. Say, can you drive then?"

"Well, actually," Parker stumbled as, for the first time, Natalie seemed to have sensed a flaw in him.

"That's probably not going to happen... well... anytime soon." Parker lowered his head to peer down into the water. "You see... I guess you had to find out sometime. I'm a ward of the state."

"You don't have parents?" asked Natalie.

Parker moved his hand away from Natalie's, and put it on his other one, wringing them together. "I don't want to be a downer. I really want you to have a good time."

"I want to know," said Natalie. "If anyone understands, trust me, I do."

"I never knew my mother. And one day, my father went away and never returned. Because I've been on my own for so long, I've been afraid to get close to anyone. So, I thought I'd never date anyone. But then, on my birthday, I saw you."

Natalie reached out for Parker's hand and held it tight.

"I'm a little new at this," said Parker. "I know I come off as cool, but it's mostly an act. If you want to get to know me, you need to know that I'm nowhere near perfect."

"About your parents," said Natalie. "It's okay to cry. You wouldn't be human if you didn't."

"I don't want you to be late," said Parker. "I'm supposed to be back anyway."

As Natalie resumed riding the skateboard, Parker pulled her close to himself, tenderly holding on to her hand. The two never spoke, but they joyfully smiled, laughed, and stumbled slightly every now and then. They stopped at the edge of her home, where Parker lifted Natalie up and placed her onto solid ground. However, in no way did Natalie feel stable; Parker's proximity made her feel dizzy.

"There's something I have to tell you," said Natalie. "There's a promise I made to my mother. I told her that I'd never kiss a boy until I turned fifteen. But I could make an exception for you. I mean, not today though," continued Natalie frantically. "But eventually."

"No, Nate. You're the exception." Parker held out his hand, and Natalie placed her hand in his, reciprocating his gesture of affection. Parker added, "You, I can wait for."

Exceptions

After dinner, Natalie sat outside the dorms—still starry-eyed from her date with Parker—waiting for Ava to return.

"Natalie. Were you waiting for me?" asked Ava.

"How'd you know?"

Ava sat down next to Natalie. "I know a great many things that would surprise you."

"Then, well, there is something I have been wanting to know," began Natalie. "My friend, Philian... her father... well, when it comes to parents, I was wondering..."

"If Saul is your father?"

Natalie, unable to find the words to confirm Ava's suspicion, just lowered her head meekly in response. Ava raised Natalie's chin to bring her face to face with her again. "There is no shame, Natalie. You have every right to know who your father is—be it good or bad. Now, what does your intuition tell you?"

"No, he is not. But can I ask the seer?"

"Actually, she's gone. But we have a visit planned to an outside seer. Your intuition should be right, however. I really don't want to influence your decision in this matter, because someday, you may have to address him personally."

"That's what I was thinking," said Natalie. "I convinced my friend to contact her father. She had betrayed him, but he's forgiven her. I believe that man killed my mother, but I feel that one day we—"

"Natalie, most of us here... our mothers have died and few of us ever get to know our fathers. This is often by design in our world. Your friend is different. Human law and the courts are motivated by greed. We are motivated by a deeper connection: genetics."

"What? But... Ms. Zadie, and Ms. Josephine, well, we're from so many different cultures."

"Yes," replied Ava. "But trust me, we all have a common bloodline from ages ago. There are different orders too, and we all share a bond that continues to pull us together. This attraction is how we find new children; but we only bring them in if they become orphaned, or are in dire conditions. Then, we show them the world where they belong. Most don't even realize they have power until we show them how to use it."

"Will he come for me?" asked Natalie.

"Saul will wait for you now—this I know. His window has passed. He knows, when the time is right, you will go to him. We will make sure you are prepared."

"Thanks. There's just one more thing that's been bothering me. If you and my mother grew up together, then why do you look older than her?"

"No offense taken," replied Ava. "Your mother was much older than she looked."

Just then, some girls piled out of the dorms, ready for self-defense class.

"Natalie, you ready for class?" asked Susan.

"No. I have to meet Ms. Hag tonight; she gave me last night off because of the funeral."

Emma gave Natalie and Ava a hug before she scurried to catch up to the girls headed toward class. Without any clear direction, the girls played with weapons and wrestled aimlessly, Rebecca having completely given up on her authoritative role.

Toddi grabbed a sword from the wall. "We found Melissa's weakness, huh? If she were here, I'd challenge her to fight with swords."

Susan and a few other girls, grabbed some blunt practice swords and began to engage in play fights.

"I bet we could take her on," said Susan.

"Do you really think you have a chance?" challenged a voice from the shadows.

As the girls looked in the direction the voice had sounded from, they saw a figure dressed in a faded green robe, seated in the corner. Fear gripped their hearts.

Refusing to stand down, Susan gulped. "Maybe if we had swords."

Melissa stood, refusing to take off her hood. "Is that a challenge I hear?" she asked as Zadie walked into the room.

Susan looked to the other girls for their reactions before she responded. "Yes, all of us challenge you with swords."

"You might want to rethink that," said Melissa. "I'll give you a few minutes to step outside and come back with a different answer."

"We can do it!" encouraged Emma. "Let's do it!"

"Challenge accepted," said Zadie, prompted by a nod from Susan. "However, we only have equipment for ten people. Choose your nine, Susan."

"One more thing," said Melissa. "This area is too small. We'll fight outside, by the bunker."

◢◣

Natalie waited again—this time outside Ms. Haggle's broken gate. Natalie felt a surge of guilt every time she looked at the broken gate that stood propped up against the fence, knowing she had promised to fix it. Truth be told, she was afraid to destroy more of the fence, and if she did fix the gate, then she would still have to use it, making it a prime target for further damage at her hands. It was a lost cause in Natalie's mind, but one that still elicited remorse in her.

Ms. Haggle's front door opened, and Natalie knew that was her cue to enter. As Natalie went inside the door, she caught a glimpse of a shadow rushing up the staircase to nowhere, disappearing as though a door stood where the path actually ended.

"What was that?" asked Natalie.

"What was what?" replied Ms. Haggle.

"The... you know, uh... the thing that... Never mind."

"Good. Let's begin then." Ms. Haggle sat down at the chess table, resetting the pieces. "How are the girls?" she asked.

"Well, kind of out of control. Since Melissa's been gone, that is."

"Hmmm. What do you think the difference is?" asked Ms. Haggle.

"Nobody seems to listen to Rebecca."

"Lack of respect?"

"Yeah," replied Natalie. "Why is that?"

"For many reasons. It is difficult to be in charge," replied Ms. Haggle. "There are different types of leadership, and your job now is to discover which one works the best for you. Melissa's style is entirely different from yours. Hers is an authoritarian style. Her being tough offers the girls something to unify against—a direction, and motivation to achieve an objective. This style is so effective that boot camps use it as well. Yours is different, but equally effective."

"Will Melissa come back?" asked Natalie.

"She is already back."

"I saw her, at her mother's grave during my mother's funeral."

"She was paying her respect to both your mothers," replied Ms. Haggle. "We have a deeper connection with our mothers than most other people, even when they wrong us."

"What happened between them?" asked Natalie.

"Checkmate," said Ms. Haggle.

Natalie reset the chess table, figuring that Ms. Haggle had no intention of answering her question.

"How are your classes?" asked Ms. Haggle.

"I wonder if there's a point, with me having no power and all."

"Spells. Spells are more powerful than one might think."

"Really?"

"Come," said Ms. Haggle as she rummaged through a wooden chest. Pulling out a baseball from the chest, Ms. Haggle said, "This ball crashed through my window last spring, breaking that pane," pointing to a four-paned window that had only one of the four panes left unbroken. "Let me show you what a spell can do." Ms. Haggle threw the ball to Natalie and said, "Hit me with the ball."

"I can't."

"Go ahead. I take full responsibility for your throw."

"Okay," said Natalie, and she chucked the ball at Ms. Haggle from where she stood—two meters away from her mentor. Incredibly, the ball missed its mark, going past Ms. Haggle and breaking the last portion of undamaged glass behind her. Ms. Haggle gave a disgruntled look, remembering that she bore all responsibility for the throw. "How did I miss?" asked Natalie.

"I can't be hit," replied Ms. Haggle.

"But how?"

"Spells are proactive, preparatory, and not typically action based. More can be done with spells than by power. Power you will definitely want in a fight, but you may desire deflective and preventive spells just as much. And spells can be cast on areas too. Melissa has acquired protection in the forest through years of casting spells, just as we have on our land."

"You mean that I can deflect stuff too?" asked Natalie.

"Not yet," replied Ms. Haggle. "You're limited to primary spells. Mine are much more advanced."

"Primary spells are for children. When do I get to learn the more advanced spells?"

"Never underestimate the power of primary spells," explained Ms. Haggle. "They are the base we build upon, and they have the privilege of being immune to some magic. You must master your primary spells; else, you will be overwhelmed by the secondary spells."

Natalie fiddled through the wooden chest and found another baseball. "Can I try again?" asked Natalie.

This time, Ms. Haggle moved to stand with the fireplace to her back, facing Natalie. "It is of no use, child, but you may try."

Natalie, now three meters away, planned the perfect throw while Ms. Haggle continued to speak, unwary of any potential threat. "Many years I have spent layering protective spells onto myself, so much…"

Natalie threw the ball as hard as she could.

"…that even without any thought on my part, I cannot be hit."

"Kink!" The ball struck the sword hung over the fireplace and it fell toward Ms. Haggle.

"Eeeaaak," screeched Ms. Haggle as she dodged the sword. "Is nothing in my house safe from your destructive behavior?"

"Why'd you dodge the sword?" asked Natalie. "I thought you couldn't be hit."

Straightening herself and regaining her composure, Ms. Haggle picked up the sword and explained, "Mind you, there is an exception to every rule."

"That sword can hit you?" asked Natalie.

"This sword can hit anything," replied Ms. Haggle. "There are barriers—limits to magic, if you will. This sword is unaffected by magic, as is your ring. They present a zone of protection from magic, each in its own different way. Some spells can mimic their power, but none will ever match their true potential."

"The sword," said Natalie. "My ring. They have something in common?"

"There are seven weapons that bear the design on your ring," answered Ms. Haggle. "Any witch would be fortunate to even touch one."

Ms. Haggle handed the sword to Natalie, who tested its weight on her palms.

"You have now touched two of the seven," said Ms. Haggle.

"What can my ring do?" asked Natalie.

"What do you feel it does?"

"Conceal," answered Natalie. "And the sword strikes."

"Correct, conceal and strike," said Ms. Haggle.

As Natalie brought the sword near her ring, she could feel both subtly vibrate in each other's presence. "If I don't have power and there are spells that can mimic my ring's power—which is a zone void of magic—then can I bring another witch to my level with a spell, leveling the playing field in a way?"

"Now you're thinking," replied Ms. Haggle. "Sit," she said. As Natalie took her original place, she continued, "The more rules and exceptions you know, the greater are your chances of success." Ms. Haggle placed two kings, side-by-side, on adjacent squares. "What's wrong with this scenario?" she asked.

"A king cannot put itself in danger," answered Natalie. "Neither king is allowed to move into the area of the other."

"Precisely," replied Ms. Haggle. "By rule, both the kings are equal, bound by a force that repels them. Likewise, theoretically, one can bind another to one's own limitations. The spell is somewhat contradictory, as the spell can only be performed by one who is highly experienced. By the time you master the spell, you would have no need for it. Moreover, one with great experience would be immune to the spell, but, in theory, it's always possible. The goal is for you to find a way."

"So," replied Natalie. "By the two-king rule, I can force-bind another to my skill level, making the fight purely physical?"

"Difficult, but possible," replied Ms. Haggle. "According to the purely theoretical ideology, a field is generated over the two combatants, void of magic, which limits them to primary spells. This is why we preach mastering the primaries and physical combat. But again, these are highly advanced spells."

Ms. Haggle's clock announced the half hour with a wicked ring. "You may leave early," said Ms. Haggle. "Reflect on my lessons, and join your friends."

౨ೋ

Between the dorms and Mitzi's forest lay a meadow of mostly mid-length grass. This meadow was divided into three sections by two unmistakable landmarks: a lone, lifeless oak tree and a small hill. "The cove"—a smaller region that was perfect for picnics due to its sporadically growing tall and short grass—lay somewhat between the dorms and the oak tree. Beyond the cove, lay "the field," a well-maintained larger area—usually reserved for organized sports—that was defined on the far end of its perimeter by a small hill, or as the girls called it, "the bunker." Marked by a steep incline on the side of the field and a natural curved alcove facing "the grasslands"—an open area of knee-high grass leading to the forest—the girls used the bunker as a hiding place when they wanted to avoid organized activity. Tonight was exceptional as every girl, sans Natalie, watched Melissa decimate nine smaller girls, victims of their overconfidence.

Melissa stood, the sword in her hand pointed at the ground where nine bruised and battered girls lay, desperately searching for their egos.

"That should explain my position on discipline," snapped Melissa. "Susan, have your crew clean up the gear. Toddi, your crew will organize the dorms in the way they should have been all this time."

Susan and Toddi both accepted their orders. "Yes, Den Mother."

Back in the dorms, no one spoke of the brutality that had gone down at the bunker, choosing to, instead, fall into order exactly where they had been when Melissa had left, with only a single exception. Inside Melissa's locker lay a pair of Doc Marten shoes, her size, with a note that read, "Good to have you back."

CHAPTER NINETEEN

❧❧

MASTER SEERS

Saturdays, typically a free time for the girls, had quickly become Natalie's favorite day of the week, as these were the days on which she could spend time with Parker. Natalie's last four Saturdays had been dedicated, with absolute satisfaction, entirely to her boy interest. However, it was not the same on this particular Saturday. Yet, her inability to be with Parker did not diminish Natalie's excitement—today was indeed a special day for her, and for everyone else. Once a year, the girls were taken to the Master Seers—three of the best fortune tellers who resided together in a rickety old house that would certainly make Ms. Haggle proud. It was a three-hour trip, and a school bus was requisitioned for the travel. The whole group of girls sat on the bus, eagerly waiting for the leaders to board. The first on board was Melissa, who stood between the aisles in her Doc Marten shoes, looking for any disorderly conduct.

"Nice shoes," said a random voice from the back.

"Isn't the joke getting a little too old?" replied Melissa.

"Nice shoes," said another girl, managing to stay undetected.

"It's getting old," reasserted Melissa in a stern, but tolerant tone. "Okay, listen up!" she continued. "Today, we visit the Master Seers. Most of you know the drill. Do not, and I mean, do not agitate the seers. They will tell you what you need to know and nothing more. Also, we know there will be other orders there. You may interact with them, but ensure that you are on your best behavior. The last thing we need is some ill-mannered girl to reflect poorly on our order. Understood?"

"I have a question," said Toddi, raising her hand.

"Yes," replied Melissa.

"Do you like those shoes?"

"I'll give you the answer to that question tomorrow morning—early… morning," replied Melissa before assuming a seat near the front of the bus.

Ms. Haggle and Devia boarded the bus, seating themselves near the front. When the two women sat down, Melissa moved to the rear of the bus to be with Rebecca and Isabella. At last, Zadie stepped on and assumed the driver's seat.

"Are we ready?" asked Zadie.

Devia checked with Melissa for a head count, and then instructed Zadie to start the bus. The girls were on their way, and the back-seat fun had begun in full swing.

The girls were girls—loud and rowdy for almost the entire trip, which, however, somehow failed to wake Ms. Haggle, whose head lay awkwardly propped against the window. Then, a paper sack sailed through the air.

"That's my lunch!" said a girl.

The sack continued to float back and forth before a cupcake spilled out. The girl recovered the sack, but Rebecca removed the cupcake from its packet. "Do you remember not listening to me?" asked Rebecca as she pretended to eat the cupcake. "This is payback."

The girl reached for the cupcake, but Rebecca tossed it to Natalie, and the girl pounced on Natalie to get hold of her cupcake. Quickly, Natalie rid herself of the cupcake, throwing it toward the front of the bus. The cupcake struck Ms. Haggle in the face, and ultimately landed on the floor by Zadie. Ms. Haggle shrugged her shoulder and moved her head around. Then, feeling the pink frosting that stuck to her face, she tried to swat it away with her hand. Unintentionally, Ms. Haggle only smeared the frosting more rather than removing it, but still remained asleep all the while.

The bus went pin-drop silent. Every girl could hear the tread of tire course along the road, the pistons push and pull their way into the block, and even the squeak of the wheel with the most minute of turns.

"Eeew, I'm not eating it now!" announced the girl, prompting an eruption of laughter.

"Melissa's been in a good mood," Natalie observed to Susan.

"I bet she is," replied Susan. "Before you got in trouble with Ms. Hag, she had to spend every Thursday there."

"You mean she was seeing Ms. Hag every Thursday?"

"Yes," replied Susan. "It's like you took over, and now she doesn't have to anymore."

"Or get to," mumbled Natalie.

Susan missed Natalie's comment, but her observation was irrelevant as the girls finally arrived at the Master Seers' house. Hundreds of girls stood outside the house, awaiting their fortunes. Honey, green, and even several blue-colored robes lined about the house in colorful formations, sparking a sense of belonging in Natalie.

"You're going to like this," said Susan. "It's like a mystery to find out what they've prophesized for you."

"What do the blue robes mean?" asked Natalie as the bus came to a halt.

"They're the Order of Power," replied Toddi. "Don't mess with them. Not all of them have power, but rest assured: they're strong."

"Look!" said Emma. "A purple robe."

"Oh, her," said Toddi. "That's Mariska. She's the headmistress of the Order of Power. You'd do well to not even look at her. She's all powerful. Legend says that no woman holds her degree of power."

"They have more than one shade of blue," noted Emma.

"Yes," said Toddi. "The super light blue is equivalent to Honey; the next light blue means a Forester; and then onward, the darker the blue, the more power the woman has. If you don't have power in that order, you don't get a dark blue robe. I've even seen a blue so dark, it nearly looks black. The whole order is really powerful."

The girls began to dismount the bus, each passing a disheveled Ms. Haggle who had pink frosting on one side of her face and drool on the other.

"Do you think she's still alive?" asked one girl.

Another girl replied, "I don't think we'd know, seeing how she looks dead even when she's walking around."

The girls laughed. Then, one of them asked, "Hey, Natalie, is it true that she doesn't have a shadow?"

"What do you mean?" asked Natalie.

"You've been in her house. I've heard she doesn't have a shadow. Haven't you noticed that we never see one when she's in the dorms?"

"She has one," answered Melissa. "Now, let's stop with the rumors and get into formation."

Twenty girls from the Order of the Sisterhood lined up in three ranks, headed by Melissa herself. Other orders had full-fledged witches in front of their formations, but Melissa was large and in charge as Devia and Zadie socialized with the other orders and Ms. Haggle lay asleep against the bus window.

"That's us," said Melissa. "Rebecca, take the first group in. And remember girls, anyone in a dark grey robe is a Master Seer; do not speak to her unless spoken to first."

Other witches looked down upon Melissa in her faded green robe, disgusted that an order would allow a student, a Forester, to wield such power. Melissa could not care any less about their thoughts or her reputation. To her, the other orders were weak in terms of their leadership and power. Soon, the first girl was out of the Master Seers' house.

"What'd she say?" asked another girl.

"I don't know," replied the first girl. "I went this way; she went that way; she said, where'd she go; I said, where'd who go. And I was outside again."

Even Melissa let her guard down to laugh before instructing the next group to be prepared as more sisters came out of the house. When Natalie came outside, she was also asked about her fortune.

Natalie replied, "That which does not kill you, will only make you stronger. That's all she said, and she was gone. The door opened, and I left."

"What did she say?" asked a witch from a different order who stood nearby. "Her exact words, please."

"That which does not kill you, will only make you stronger. What does it mean?" Natalie asked her back, but the witch had already disappeared.

Gossip raged as elders spread Natalie's prophecy amongst the different orders.

"Melissa, what does it mean?" asked Natalie.

Unsurprisingly, in contrast with the other witches, Melissa replied, "Sorry, that's for you to discover. Next group, you're coming with me."

Melissa led the last group in as the rest of the girls heckled over each other's potential futures. Shortly afterward, Melissa came out to find the girls socializing with other orders, which was not an infraction or something to be frowned upon, as long as order was maintained. Melissa decided to consult with her fellow members of the Den Three.

"Will you tell us yours?" asked Rebecca of Melissa.

"I already know what it means," she replied. "But I'll tell you: Be prepared, it is never too late to ask for the ultimate favor."

After some time, Natalie brought an issue to Melissa's attention. "Melissa, Emma hasn't come out yet."

"She must have," said Melissa. Counting the girls, she asked them, "Has anyone seen Emma?"

No one answered positively, so Melissa decided to act on her own. "Rebecca, you're in charge while I look for Emma."

⊂⧽⊃

Five girls in light blue robes, equivalent the Foresters, surrounded Emma behind a school bus. The leader, an older blonde, held Emma against the bus. "I said, who has power in your order and what are their weaknesses?"

"I won't tell you anything!" replied Emma.

"*You will*," said the girl in a crooked voice.

"No, she won't," answered Melissa as she stepped into the scene.

Melissa faced off with the blonde girl. A set of twins backed the blonde girl, and another two of the order circled to Melissa's left.

"What are you going to do about it, you cantankerous crone?" mocked one twin.

"Yeah, you haggish shrew," jeered the other twin.

"You two have dirty mouths," said Melissa.

In a quick, hurried response, the blonde girl in front of Melissa grabbed her by the throat and drew herself closer to Melissa's face. The blonde girl's eyes turned red, and her mouth opened, exposing a set of yellowish teeth with black crud lining each tooth. Green smoky breath pushed its way out of her mouth.

"*I have a dirty mouth*," she said. "*What are you going to do about it?*"

Cool and composed, Melissa replied, "Nothing. I'm going to do nothing. Because you're more worried about that burn on your arm."

"*What burn?*" she asked.

"The one on your arm," replied Melissa as she used her right hand to grab the girl's left forearm that was supporting the grip on Melissa's throat.

The girl went down on her knees in pain. "It burns!" she screamed as a sizzle began to melt away her skin at the spot where Melissa's hand held tight.

"*Whisper*," Melissa cast a spell on the girl, and her screams dwindled to mere whispers.

The twins began to cast spells, but Melissa beat them to the act.

"*Silence*," said Melissa, and they were stopped mid-spell. "*Kneel*," she continued, and the twins dropped to their knees.

The two girls to Melissa's left advanced on her. In response, Melissa turned her hips clockwise, all the way around, landing a side kick to the stomach of the girl farthest to her left, making her crumble to the ground. Melissa came back around—never releasing the blonde girl's arm the entire time—to face the last girl, a finger in her terrified face.

"You have no power," remarked Melissa.

"No, I don't," replied the girl.

"I didn't *ask* for your opinion," said Melissa. "I was noting your pathetic weakness."

The girl turned and tried to run.

"*Halt*," ordered Melissa. Then, she said, "*Whisper*" to the two powerless girls on her left. Melissa returned her attention to the girl who had once confidently held her throat. "*It burns... so bad*," she said.

"Yes," replied the girl as she tried to scream, but ended up only with a feeble whisper. "It burns," she continued as Melissa's hand burned deep into her flesh.

"And you two," Melissa said to the twins. "If you're going to act like you have a dirty mouth, then you'll have a dirty mouth. *Eat dirt*."

The twins bent over and placed their faces above the dirt, putting chunks of earth in their mouths, chewing, and swallowing, before they repeated the process all over again.

"And you," said Melissa to the girl who was just beginning to recover from the kick to her stomach. "You have really nice hair. Too bad *it's falling out*."

The girl sat up and tried to shout as she began to pull out fistfuls of hair from her head.

"Why, you're just melting away," said Melissa to the blonde girl as more flesh continued to dissolve from her arm. "And where were you running to?" Melissa asked the halted girl. "*Be truthful*."

The girl replied in a monotone voice, "To my head mistress. For help."

"Oh," said Melissa. "You're going to see her alright. But you're going to be more concerned about the *worms*. Yes, the *worms in your head—moving, crawling, eating away at your brain*."

Suddenly, the girl grabbed at her head in madness, trying to scream for relief.

"Three girls, helplessly trying to scream, while the other two can't due to mouthfuls of dirt," said Melissa. "How pathetic, wouldn't you say?" Melissa asked the blonde girl, whose forearm was now seared to the bone. "If you ever so much as look funny at anyone from the sisterhood, I won't stop until your whole body is burnt to ashes. Do you understand?"

"Please," the blonde girl pleaded. "It hurts so bad."

Melissa placed her other hand on the blonde girl's face, burning a handprint into her cheek, ear, and a portion of her scalp. "It's going to hurt much, much more next time."

"Let's go," Melissa told Emma, who had no wish to object.

"Are they going to be okay?" asked Emma.

"In a minute," replied Melissa.

Sure enough, exactly one minute later, the five girls hysterically ran through the crowd, screaming of ailments that didn't exist. Girls of different orders laughed at them as they complained: one about a burnt arm that looked completely normal, another of false hairlessness, and another trying to pick imaginary worms from her head, while the other two spit and gagged from the dirt in their mouths.

"See Emma, it was all in their heads," said Melissa.

"Line up, girls," she continued. "Let's prepare to leave this rabble behind."

However, Melissa's plan was interrupted by a woman dressed in a dark blue robe, demanding answers.

"I don't know what they're complaining about," replied Melissa. "They look just fine to me."

"Stupid child!" the woman said. "Answer me, or I'll have you flogged!"

"If your girls have a grievance, I'd be happy to accept a challenge against all five of them," said Melissa. "All at once," she added.

The woman turned to look for acceptance from her five girls, but they all lowered their heads in defeat and shame.

"I expected as much of such a weak order," said Melissa.

The woman pulled her hand back to smack Melissa, who simply stood there, steady and unflinching. Her hand, however, failed to touch its mark, as Ms. Haggle caught the woman by her wrist.

"You wish to strike a child?" she asked.

The word "fight" travelled across the gathered women, garnering ultimate attention.

"Your child attacked my children, and she now disrespects my order."

Ms. Haggle let go of the woman's wrist, closed her eyes, and sensed the past. "I'm afraid that's not how it transpired," she said. "You may wish to vet your children further."

"That doesn't excuse her disrespect of me," replied the woman.

"An adult disrespecting a child is far more out of order than a child disrespecting an adult," said Ms. Haggle. "Your concern is noted, yet it is invalid due to your own actions that divest you of your authority."

Suddenly, Mariska herself, in her purple robe, appeared out of thin air beside the two women. "Who dares to attack my order!" she shouted. "I have half a mind to—" Mariska stopped mid sentence. "Ms. Haggle," she said, her tone changing to a calmer one. "What seems to be the problem?"

Ms. Haggle replied, "Apparently your elder has seen it fit to call my personal student, stupid. Need I remind you that I have obliterated populations over lesser insults?"

"No, Ms. Haggle. You needn't remind me," replied Mariska.

"I believe your order is done here," said Ms. Haggle.

"Yes," replied Mariska. "Agnes," she said to the blue-robed woman. "Gather the girls, we're leaving."

"But we're not finished," objected Agnes.

Mariska turned her head slightly toward Agnes, not completely removing her eyes from Ms. Haggle. "When you question me, it undermines my authority and makes the order look undisciplined. Ms. Haggle said we are finished here... and we are."

"Yes, ma'am," said Agnes as she led away the girls from her order.

"All respect, Ms. Haggle," said Mariska as she bowed. "Do we stand resolved?"

"We do, for five minutes. That is the limit of my patience."

"Yes, ma'am," replied Mariska and she backed away.

Devia, having just arrived, shook her head at Ms. Haggle and said, "May I?" Then she cautiously wiped the pink frosting from Ms. Haggle's face.

"NATALIE!" yelled Ms. Haggle.

CHAPTER TWENTY

༞

THE HALLS

Natalie sat in craft class, oblivious to the demonstrations, pondering her prophecy, which was so broad that the words could mean just about anything: "That which does not kill you, will only make you stronger." How could she be certain of the statement's purpose when the time came? She didn't know how these things worked—it was her first prophecy.

"Natalie," called the instructor. "You've been summoned to the castle lobby. Ms. Haggle says she has something for you."

"Oooh," teased the other students.

Natalie gathered her belongings and proceeded as instructed without any reaction.

As Natalie waited in the front room of the castle, she took the time to look at a recent card from Philian. Natalie was happy for her; her decision to live with her father was working out beautifully. All seemed well, and her father said she could visit anytime she wanted to see her mother.

"What were you studying in class?" asked Ms. Haggle from behind Natalie.

Startled, Natalie replied, "Spellbinders."

"And what did you learn about spellbinders?"

"They're spellcasters that specialize in complex spells that bind people, areas, and battlefields."

"A very technical answer," replied Ms. Haggle. "But what can they do?"

"Well, defensively, a spellbinder locks in the conditions of a battle, constantly negotiating the rules on the field. Offensively, they oversee the finalization of difficult spells to harm, which can take hours to cure depending on the complexity of the spell."

"Ah, so spells can be important."

"I just realized that the bishop position on your chess board is a spellbinder."

"Good observation," noted Ms. Haggle. "Now, I have something very interesting for you."

Ms. Haggle led Natalie beyond the front desk and its lone, typically stern-looking guardian. As they walked further into the front room, Natalie felt a sense of pleasure. She had seen the lobby and the stairs, but she was sure there was more to this tour.

"Have you ever seen the banquet hall?" asked Ms. Haggle.

"No," replied Natalie, delighted.

Ms. Haggle and Natalie ventured deep into the front room that boasted two stories, high-rise ceilings, and two staircases—one ascending from each side, meeting at the top to form an astonishing balcony. On the ground floor, paths diverged to the left and the right before the stairs. Natalie quivered as she was led forward, under the staircases, toward beautifully crafted and oversized doors that seemed fit for eternal closure. Ms. Haggle raised her hand and the doors noiselessly opened, pulling perfectly inward.

The Halls

Inside sat a sentry. "Good afternoon, Mother."

"Good afternoon sister," replied Ms. Haggle.

Natalie, puzzled by the term mother, dismissed the comment as she was far more engrossed with the view around her: a second lobby—not nearly as grand as the first, but still remarkable. Natalie noticed another set of doors at the other end of the room. Anticipation set in—what could be in there? To her left and right were more spacious areas that led to hallways—giant hallways. All around her, Natalie could see pictures and what appeared to be art, statues, and tapestry. Clearly, a tremendous amount of effort had been put into the design of this majestic place. Natalie was flattered by Ms. Haggle's trust and willingness to share this hidden gem of a place with her.

"The Halls," read Natalie from a sign that hung directly above the two doors in front of her.

Ms. Haggle opened the doors, saying nothing; but she didn't have to.

Every worldly thing was overshadowed by the awe and beauty contained within these halls. Two stories of carved and painted posts and ceilings greeted Natalie. Literally, the ceilings were more than a single one—separated by barriers to make space for the stories that were told through the art that decorated them. A balcony, entirely circling the inside with gold railings, accentuated the ceiling art with an inset so elegant that the second floor appeared to be engraved from the structure itself. Underneath the balcony were dining tables. The center remained open but not void of beauty—presenting the most extravagant tile that abolished any thought of emptiness as a weakness. The whole room, by design, directed all attention to the opposite stage, where tables stood. Whether one was positioned underneath the balcony or on it, their eyes would move to whoever sat at the prestigious front. Everything was breathtaking, and Ms. Haggle allowed Natalie sufficient time to take it all in. Natalie's inner child took over as she rushed to the central tile—marked with a star—and spun around like she was dancing for an entire ballroom full of people.

Ms. Haggle grinned. "I take it you're pleased."

"Pleased? No. Enchanted. But I want to dance here for real."

"In due time, Natalie. For now, there is something more you may be interested in."

"What more could there be?" thought Natalie. Nonetheless, she followed Ms. Haggle out of the massive doors, giving one final look at the wonder she was leaving behind. Ms. Haggle led Natalie down the hall to the right. The hall was wide—wide enough so that each section could be a room on its own. Numerous paintings lined the outside of the wall while the inside wall had niches on which marble busts were displayed. Each bust was of a high-status affiliate. Underneath the busts, metal plaques displaying the details of the person were placed. All plaque accomplishments were prefixed with cum laude or suma cum laude.

"What do these mean?" asked Natalie.

"Cum laude means 'with praise,' suma cum laude is 'with great praise,' and magna cum laude means 'with greatest praise.' They are Latin."

"Latin?" replied Natalie. "I don't see any magna cum laude."

"There is only one magna cum laude here," answered Ms. Haggle.

"Just one? What do you have to do to get that?"

"The impossible," replied Ms. Haggle.

"What was it granted for? I mean, what did she do to get the greatest praise?"

"As a general rule," began Ms. Haggle, "one must save the order itself, or a good portion of the order to be awarded with magna cum laude."

"The order was in danger?" asked Natalie.

"There are other ways."

"Like what?"

"All in due time," replied Ms. Haggle.

Natalie turned to the paintings. They were of different classes of the order. She moved faster through the hall, quickly scanning the paintings to find anyone she knew. As she neared the end of the group portraits, she began to recognize some of the people. Then, in the very last picture was her class, and there she was. "How did I get in this picture?" she asked.

"We have an artist who makes them."

"Wouldn't it just be easier to take a picture?" asked Natalie as she studied the portrait.

"You will learn that the sisters are hesitant to be photographed. Besides, paintings add a touch of history and value."

By now, Natalie had noticed that the hall was circular, and that they were traveling counter-clockwise around the banquet area. Near the rear apex were the individual pictures of every affiliate. Oddly, although the wall allowed ample room for new affiliates, there was an empty space between the pictures, which seemed out of place. Upon closer inspection, the paint on the wall looked faded, revealing that it had once been adorned with a painting. Natalie also noticed that some of the busts had a subtle difference from the others—a red stripe around the neck of each woman, crossing over on the front like a ribbon. The plaques stated that these particular women had once been heads of the order. The first bust was of the current headmistress. Natalie noticed that they were arranged chronologically, and it did not take her long to find one particular bust of interest.

"Mother!" Natalie pressed her hand against the stone recreation of her mother, and began to cry. She then touched her hand along the plaque that bore her mother's name, and leaned against the wall near the marble figure, weeping.

Ms. Haggle patiently allowed Natalie the time she needed.

"I'm sorry. I'm sorry, Ms. Haggle. I should be more composed."

"Crying is a bandage for the soul. How much your wound needs is entirely up to you."

Natalie lifted her head and forced the words on the plaque to form a picture in her mind: "Mother Hannah Forsythe, suma cum laude. Known for her exceptional insight, and for being the youngest mother ever to lead the order." Dates related to her life and leadership were inscribed underneath, but bypassed by Natalie, as she was more interested in the date of her death, which must have been recently added.

Natalie brushed her fingers against the bust's lips. "She was in charge of the order?" asked Natalie without taking her eyes off her mother's bust.

"Yes. She did much for us."

"She was in charge of you?"

"In a way, yes."

Natalie smiled with pride.

Ms. Haggle continued, "There is a lot of meaning attached to family here, to history. We honor and respect our own, even at times when we are in disagreement. Paramount is the purpose of this hall. We shall always remember those whom we made, and those who made us. We are all destined to be one, without any pride. That is what this hall represents, and till the end, our order and this hall must survive. It is with the greatest honor that your mother remains here as one of us for eternity. We are all made great by great acts of individuals. She is, and always will be, one of us, part of us, a definition of us."

"Is that why you took me in? Because of my mother?"

"You, we would have taken in anyway. We take in new people, but you will find that most have a deeper connection."

"And Melissa? Where is the picture of her mother?"

"It grieves me to say that you will not find one here."

"But these are all paintings. Surely, you can make one—" Natalie gasped. "The cemetery!" she shrieked. "She's been removed. The missing painting! But then you are not all one. Not when one can be shunned."

"You are right, Natalie. But just as a good person will every so often make a poor decision, we are one— regardless of an individual's indiscretions. I do not intend to side with any position on this subject, but I will say that only once in the order's history of centuries has an affiliate been discharged."

"At the Master Seers," began Natalie, "you called Melissa your personal student. She saw you before I did. The razzings, harassment—it was intentional. I guess what I'm asking is, did she send me to you on purpose?"

"And are you my personal student?" asked Ms. Haggle in reply. "Yes. Both are true. Melissa is a very powerful witch. It has been prophesized that she will exceed Mistress Mariska in power. She was in need of guidance after her mother died. Sometimes when love is so great, it turns to hate. They are not far apart in emotion."

"Mistress Mariska," gasped Natalie in disbelief at Melissa's prophecy. "Is she really the best?"

"She is remarkable, but there is no one true best, just different. We all have different strengths and weaknesses that match unequally with different people. Among three equals, you may beat one but lose to another. There are different craft paths, different powers, different match-ups. So much so that one cannot master them all. Remember, it would behoove you to keep your knowledge private."

Ms. Haggle stepped closer to Natalie and placed a hand on her back. "Any time you wish to visit your mother, I will grant you access."

Natalie, wiser and more tolerant than before, stroked her mother's marble likeness and gave it a kiss on the cheek. Then, lost in thought, she lowered her eyes to the plaque. "You knew my mother?"

"I knew her well."

"They made a mistake in recording her birth date," said Natalie. "It reads 1870, but she was born in 1970.

And here it reads, 'Mistress from 1940—1950'. That's not even possible."

"An issue that is easily resolved," said Ms. Haggle.

"Oh," said Natalie as she carried on down the hall. "I want to see the first Mother." Natalie hurried forward, walking far ahead of Ms. Haggle, disappearing out of her mentor's sight. When Ms. Haggle caught up with Natalie, she found her student frozen in the face of the first bust. Natalie remained silent until Ms. Haggle came to stand beside her. "But... how?" she asked.

Ms. Haggle stood beside the much younger marble version of herself, and replied, "We are much older than we sometimes appear."

"But you do look old... I mean... No offense."

Ms. Haggle grinned. "None taken."

"There are no dates on yours, but this other one next to you is two hundred years old." Natalie was beside herself in bewilderment. "Are the dates correct on my mother's plaque?"

"Has Ava not explained to you our concept of age?"

"She has... I just... didn't listen."

Natalie read the inscription, "Madam Haggle. Magna cum laude. Member of the First Order of Witches; Founder of the Order of the Sisterhood; Eradicator of a Dark Witch."

"You're the one with the greatest praise? Wow, you've been around."

"Natalie, I've lived a long, cumbersome life."

"And my mother was once in charge of you. Cool."

Ms. Haggle moved back and walked slightly away before mumbling, "I love the simplicity of a Honey's mind."

"What's your first name?"

"Never had one."

"What's a dark witch?"

Ms. Haggle turned completely to face the opposite wall. With her back to Natalie, she leaned her face into the life-size portrait of her young self, placed directly opposite her bust.

"Ms. Haggle? Are you okay? How do you eradicate a dark witch?"

"You can't," replied Ms. Haggle. "Only when her revenge is complete, is she taken to fulfill her obligation."

"But it says here that you did."

"There is an exception to every rule," replied a dismayed sounding Ms. Haggle.

"Like the two-king rule," observed Natalie. "And a dark witch? What is that?"

Ms. Haggle hesitated, but deflection of certain subjects was not her strongest attribute. "A catalyst for revenge. Revenge, not unlike cancer, is an emotion that eats into the soul, and corrupts it. Soon, there is nothing left to care about, or so the one that is hurt believes. At the point where the person possesses nothing but the desire for revenge, they can make a deal; a sacred deed that guarantees vengeance. Be careful of how you wrong a person. When a person feels they have nothing left, they become unpredictable, unstable, and ready to lose everything for nothing more than a slight taste of satisfaction."

"But it's not guaranteed. You stopped one."

Ms. Haggle brushed some dust off the frame encasing her portrait, keeping Natalie waiting. Her last words before Natalie was called away were, "Revenge is never the answer."

CHAPTER TWENTY-ONE

꙰

SUCCUBUS

"What are you doing?" asked Susan. "It's library day; aren't we going to the mall?"

"No," replied Natalie. "We're going to the library."

"You're joking, right? To the library on library day? Who does that?"

Natalie stopped to face Susan. "Do you know what a dark witch is?"

"No," replied Susan.

"Have you been in the banquet hall? And the surrounding halls?"

Susan replied, "Yes. I mean the banquet hall. We have a dance there every year."

"So, you haven't read Ms. Hag's inscription for when she was headmistress?"

Susan gasped. "Ms. Hag was headmistress? What? Maybe two hundred years ago."

"Yes."

"Seriously?" asked Susan. "I was joking."

"You're interested now?" asked Natalie, but Susan's face said it all. Natalie continued, "Ms. Hag told me a dark witch cannot be beat, but her plaque says that she beat one. I want to know more about what a dark witch is."

"Okay," said Susan. "Let's get Toddi and go to the library then."

Natalie, Susan, and Toddi rummaged through the entire library, finding no listings and no shred of evidence for the existence of a dark witch. Natalie began to walk past an empty desk and into another room when Susan grabbed her.

"What's in that room?" asked Natalie.

"That's the witch's library," said Susan. "We can't go in there."

Natalie played with her ring, remembering her lessons with Ms. Haggle and how the ring could conceal its bearer. That night in the cemetery; the ring must have been the reason she was successful, the reason she had no encounters. Her friends praised her for nothing more than an uneventful task when anticipation was the only thing she had to fear. She wiggled the ring on her finger. "We'll see about that."

"Don't do it," pleaded Susan, but Natalie was determined.

Susan and Toddi sat in wait for what could only be trouble. When Natalie had entered the secondary room, there was no one sitting at the desk; but now there was a brown robed sentinel.

"Bonk!" Natalie dropped a voluminous encyclopedia onto the desk in front of Susan.

"D for dark witch," said Natalie. "Let's read," she continued as she assumed a seat between Susan and Toddi.

Frantically, Natalie searched through the pages till she found her target.

"Dark Witch—Revenge Incarnate."

"Prophesy: If she cannot have it, then no one will."

"Commonality: Extremely rare."

"Weaknesses: None known."

"Ahem," sounded a familiar voice from behind the three girls.

"Yes, Den Mother?" replied Natalie, only turning her shoulder in an effort to hide the encyclopedia.

"What do we have there?" asked Melissa.

"Just a book," replied Susan. "We're trying to study."

"It wouldn't be a book from the witch's library, would it?" asked Melissa.

"Yes," replied Natalie as Susan kicked her under the table in an attempt to shush her.

"And how, pray tell, did you acquire this material?" asked Melissa.

"I sneaked in," replied Natalie.

"Good," said Melissa. "Then you'll have no trouble returning this book once you're finished with that one."

Melissa then dropped a second encyclopedia onto the table—the S section—and walked away, laughing.

"Now we're in double trouble if we get caught," sighed Susan.

"Don't worry," said Natalie as she continued her search.

"A dark witch is a soulless catalyst of power, directly channeling great sums of energy from another realm through her lifeless body, with a single purpose— revenge. Once the transformation to demonhood is complete, an otherwise normal witch of power no longer exists in her human form. Instead, all that remains in physical form after her pact is the manifestation of her hatred and scorn, making her the most dangerous entity in existence, as she remains in this world, immortal, until her revenge is complete."

"Power: Ultimate. Derived from demons of dark forces, it is considered unmatched by any known worldly power."

"Initiation: When a witch has allowed her hate to control her emotions so abnormally that her cause has breached the limits of obsession, she may be sought out by external forces to guide her into darkness—a state in which her soul is given to the highest bidder for eternal damnation, in exchange for deliverance from that which ails her."

"Frequency: A dark witch is extremely rare; appearing once per century, if that. The abnormality of darkness comes not from a lack of desire, but rather an unwillingness of external forces to deal with less than worthy, contemptuous witches. A transformation cannot be done unless the abhorrence is of such magnitude that the witch's soul is already considered inert—a state of mind marked by a complete desire for nothing more than pain and destruction, irrespective of the consequences. Otherwise, external forces lack the wherewithal to create a dark witch, and subsequently lose their bid for a fallen soul. These instances create a so-called "false dark witch" in pre-darkness—a condition where the witch maintains some amount of dark powers, which was a form of down payment for the process to proceed. The power derived, although far from the powers of darkness, remains with the witch of power forever, and is lost to the dark forces, compelling the forces to never negotiate a contract unless a favorable outcome is guaranteed. This production of a false dark witch was not uncommon, until the dark forces came to realize that their quests were extremely complex. A pre-darkness condition has not been recorded since the Middle Ages, despite the fact that one would not broadcast such a revelation of power when revenge is still a strong motivation."

"Here, here," said Toddi. "Is that Ms. Haggle's name?"

"How to Defeat a Dark Witch: It is noted with significance that a dark witch has no weakness and no discovered strategy for defeat, barring one case—that of Hag Glena."

"No," replied Natalie. "At first I thought—"

"Hag Glena—also known more recently as Haggle…"

"No way!" exclaimed Natalie.

"Continue," urged Susan.

"… was a part of the Hag Three. Their long ago story of betrayal and revenge has been passed down for centuries as a warning to avoid war amongst fellow witches (Refer to the Hag Three: Hag Glena, Hag Isha, and Hag Age—pronounced 'aj'). Unfortunately, no information regarding the means of defeating a dark witch, or how it came to be done, was ever revealed from the passage or the story. No one, with exception of Hag Glena, has ever been known to survive the fury of a dark witch. It has been suggested that only the power of one of the seven weapons of light, or seven weapons of dark, can exert an effect on a dark witch (Refer to the Seven Weapons of Light/Dark). These theories, however, shed no light on what effect each or all of them might have; yet, considering that magic cannot exist in the presence of these fourteen weapons, which compound when used in combination with each other, theoretically a dark witch can be defeated using this method."

"What are you doing?" asked Susan.

"I'm looking through the index for the Hag Three, but this book only contains the D's," replied Natalie. "Toddi, check in the other book."

"But this is the S's," replied Toddi.

"Then check for the seven weapons of light," said Natalie.

"What are you looking for now?" asked Susan.

"Anything to do with Hag," replied Natalie. "I don't see anything else in here about her. Here, Hag Glena is the only known living witch of the Hag Three."

"Do you know what this means?" asked Susan. "Ms. Hag is the baddest thing to come out of witchery since a dark witch."

"Badder," said Natalie. "She defeated one."

"Natalie!" exclaimed Toddi as she spotted something of significance in the book.

"Hold on," replied Natalie. "That's why everyone's so scared of Ms. Hag. She's actually more powerful than Mariska. Probably a lot more powerful."

Susan added, "These are common encyclopedias, not made only for this order. Everyone who's anyone knows who Ms. Hag is."

"Natalie!" interrupted Toddi again with zealous excitement. "I've been reading more on this. You *have* to see this."

"Sorry, Toddi," said Natalie. "I was thinking out loud." Natalie pulled the second book over to read. "Succubus? What does this have to do with Ms. Hag?"

"Just read!" said Toddi.

"Succubus—Consumer of Power."

"Prophesy: That which does not kill her, will only make her stronger."

"That's your prophecy!" said Toddi. "You're a succubus."

"That's not possible," said Natalie. "I have no power, remember?"

"Keep reading," said Toddi. "The power part."

"Commonality: Extremely rare. There are only a few known cases."

"Power: Technically, a succubus has no power, only that which she steals from others."

"Oh, wow!" said Natalie, drawing out a shush from the sentry.

"Keep reading," said Toddi.

"No witch can learn or perfect every discipline. Power is inherently differential, and is limited to each witch; however, a succubus, having no power of her own, can literally steal, mimic, and transfer any and all powers with little limitation. This quality, paradoxically, makes this the most powerful of all powers. Potentially, a succubus can channel, maintain, and control every known power inside one being with very little discipline. As such, the only known succubae have gone insane with, and through the accumulation of, power—a quest that often leads them to their own demise."

"Limitations: None (Note exceptions). Although the power of succubae is highly coveted, considering the limitless potential, one flaw exists for the individual that proverbially puts a target on her back. On her death, the entirety of her power can be transferred to any person, with or without power, for future use by this transferee.

This possible scope for transfer has made most, if not all, succubae subject to extreme, literal witch hunts, sacrificial activities, and eventual death."

"Exceptions: There are three conventional exceptions to a succubus' power.

1) Unique gifts: Some powers are so very unique in nature to a certain individual that their transfer is not possible (Refer to Unique Gifts). It has been estimated that less than 10% of witches possess unique gifts, and that the said gifts were strongly established to be nontransferable.

2) Estopple: Estopple is a defensive, and most often, temporary spell that can limit or restrain the succubus' ability to mimic, drain, or steal power from the caster. In some cases, estopple can become offensive, altering the capacity of the succubus' power altogether during battle; yet, it is temporary (Refer to High-Level Abnormal Spells—Estopple).

3) Succubus assassin: The name of a succubus assassin is derived from her unique ability: a succubus has no effect on this individual. Thus, a succubus assassin is often sought out to destroy or capture succubae (Refer to Abnormal Powers—Assassin; Succubus)."

"Derivation of power: A succubus steals power though interaction. The more emotional the confrontation, the greater is the capacity and likelihood of power theft."

"Defense: Combat against a Succubus often results in failure and is therefore highly discouraged. There is no known defense mechanism to prevent a succubus from stealing one's power. It has been proven that if a witch does not use power and controls her emotions in a fight against a succubus, then her powers are not susceptible to theft; however, even in instances where power is not used, some succubae have the added capacity to sense and even predict movements and thoughts before the combatant themselves are aware of these."

"Defeat: Death of a succubus must be brought about swiftly, before she can derive and utilize the witch's power against her. It is advised that one facing a succubus completely void themselves of any emotion, rid their mind of all thoughts of aggression, and withhold any attempt of attack till the exact moment of combat, in which a witch's best chance is to strike with all force at once, hoping for a brief melee. Should the encounter last, one must break off and attempt to escape before the succubus can complete the transfer of power. The more advanced a power or spell, the longer it takes the succubus to mimic, transfer, or steal. The Seven Weapons of Light and Dark affect succubae. But be warned: in one reported case, a succubus had been seen to develop the ability to mimic even the power of these weapons."

"Altar of Aroas: A succubus has a unique association with the Altar of Aroas. It is an interaction that is not fully understood; however, this is where her power can be taken by force through a ceremony (Refer to Altar of Aroas). There have been reports of succubae mimicking power and then utilizing the Altar of Aroas to transfer the power to another being, even without death eminent, but only at lower levels. These reports have not been substantiated."

"Shh, shh," hushed Susan. "Someone's coming."

"Give me the books, and meet me outside," said Natalie.

The sentry approached the girls and said, "What are the two of you doing here, making so much noise?"

"The two of us?" asked Toddi.

"Yes," said Susan, looking around for Natalie. "It's just the two of us. Uh, we're done, just about to leave. Do you need anything from us before we go?"

"No," said the woman. "Just keep it down please."

CHAPTER TWENTY-TWO

❧✦❧

TRIALS

"Featherweight!"

"Ah," sighed Natalie in frustration. "Featherweight," she declared in another attempt. "Featherweight!"

"What are you doing?" asked Susan.

Natalie sat on the floor of the porch in front of the dorms, her legs dangling over the edge while she threw rocks. "Obviously, nothing," she replied.

Susan crouched down next to Natalie and took a seat. She rummaged through a stack of rocks piled between the two, picked up a small one, and enclosed it inside her palm. The two sat quietly, staring indistinctly into the distance, far into Mitzi Forest.

"How?" said Natalie. "How am I supposed to be this great thing when I can't even perform a simple spell after all these months? It's been months... months since I've learned my prophesy." She flung a rock at a lone oak tree that stood just beyond her range. "I'm like that stupid tree. Everyone's over there in the forest and I'm stuck here—a lonesome, half-dead, misshapen freak of nature." Natalie cast another rock at the tree.

"Actually," said Susan. "The forest used to come to that oak tree. It's survived floods, fires, development, and even lightning."

Natalie threw another rock. "Lightweight!"

"Do you see that scar spiraling around it from top to bottom? Lightning. If you notice closely, you can see it's been struck twice. Being strong and unique is not so bad."

Natalie reached for another rock, but Susan stopped her. Susan opened Natalie's fist and then her own, revealing an acorn where she had placed a rock before. Susan placed the acorn in Natalie's hand. "Even that tree began this small. Every oak tree was once an acorn, and every acorn can someday be a mighty oak. It just takes time."

Natalie closed her hand around the acorn. "How does it help me today?" she asked.

"Is that what this is about?" asked Susan. "I should have known. You're worried about the trials."

"Aren't you?" asked Natalie.

"We'll get our green robes," replied Susan. "It's more about age than power."

"Yes," said Natalie. "But I feel like more is expected of me now. Before I knew about this power, there was no pressure, but now…"

"Imagine if that acorn felt the same way you do. To go from this small thing to that gigantic tree seems insurmountable to us, but it can be accomplished—one day at a time."

Natalie put the acorn into her pocket, and the two settled into quietude again, staring into Mitzi Forest.

After some time, Emma approached them. "I'm still a Honey. But I'm not the only one."

"I'm sorry," said Natalie.

"Why," replied Emma, "I'm still young, and someday I'll have power. Anyway, it's your turn. Just you three, then the Den Three. The dance is tomorrow. That's what I'm excited about."

"Come on," urged Susan. "We have nothing to lose."

"That's what I'm afraid of," replied Natalie as the two left.

Natalie, Susan, and Toddi sat on the chairs placed outside the arena. Eventually, Zadie came out to call Toddi in. Natalie and Susan, engrossed in contemplation, did not display even a single emotion for the next twenty minutes until Toddi reappeared with Zadie. Toddi gave the girls a thumbs-up and left.

"Susan," called Zadie, and Susan followed her in.

Less than twenty minutes later, Susan exited the arena with a big smile and a thumbs-up sign.

"Natalie."

Natalie stepped onto the dirt floor of the arena. Never before had she seen the floor so perfectly leveled, with exception of the center, where thirteen occupied chairs were lined in front of a battle-torn area. One other single chair was placed facing the thirteen seated head witches.

"Here," said Zadie, motioning Natalie to the center chair. "Do not sit," added Zadie, before she left for the stands.

The headmistress waved her hand, moving the chair back and re-leveling the dirt at the center of the stadium. "Show us your fighting skills," she said.

Natalie spent a few minutes demonstrating everything she had learned in self-defense class. Then, Zadie came forward with a rack of weapons.

"Demonstrate your skills with these weapons," ordered the headmistress.

Natalie felt comfortable in focusing her skills away from power and toward her physical ability, especially swordsmanship.

"That's enough," said Mara. "Let's get to the reason we're really here. Sit," she added as the chair came back to Natalie.

Natalie sat, nervous, yet less so than before. She realized that the display of her physical skills had helped her avoid thinking about the process.

"Do you have power?"

"Yes," replied Natalie to the witch seated on the farthest right.

"Show us then," she replied.

"I mean…"

"Do you have power or not?" asked another witch.

"I… I think so."

"Now you're uncertain. So, did you lie to us?" asked yet another witch from a different direction.

Repeated, apparently unanswerable questions hit Natalie from different directions, one after the other, in rapid fire—as though by design. Natalie, on the verge of breaking down, did not know how much more she could take. This seemed more like abuse than testing.

"Stop," interjected Devia. "Child. Do you have power or not?"

"No," replied Natalie.

"Did you not feel power during your exercise with Melissa, or during your adventures with Galla?" asked Devia.

"I thought I did."

"You can relax," said Devia. "This inquisition is over. There were no correct answers. We were merely testing your confidence. Had you been trying for your brown robe, you would have failed. This was merely a demonstration to help you remember what is expected of you. You did well in not breaking down; however, we will expect you to excel during your brown robe trials."

"So, I've qualified to Forester?" asked Natalie.

"Hmppt. I've never seen such a turnaround in confidence," noted Ms. Haggle. "The good news is that you will leave here having qualified to Forester. But the bad news is that you will *not* leave here until you display some power."

Natalie pulled the acorn out of her pocket. "Featherweight," she said as she threw it up into the air. She watched it fall normally to the ground and picked it up. "Featherweight." The acorn fell again, and again, until Natalie fumbled it and stumbled while trying to keep it from falling. The witches lowered their heads.

Ms. Haggle's body dissipated into the air in a mesh of backlit pitch-black residue, and magically scattered around to form a distorted background. She reappeared behind Natalie. "You are thinking too small, Honey. I have your life in my hands, and I could not care less whether you survived."

Suddenly, a sharp constriction seized every muscle in Natalie's body, making it difficult for her to even expand her chest in order to inhale. "Please," she pleaded for the pain to stop.

"I do not follow the rules of mercy. You are responsible for your own survival today. Now," continued Ms. Haggle as she reached out from behind to set her face next to Natalie's. *"Steal my power."*

"I ca-can't," stammered Natalie.

"Oh, but you must, if you wish to survive."

The fear registered in Natalie's heart. She had been close to death before, but now it felt imminent. She prayed for anyone to end this madness—repeatedly chanting "stop" in her mind—but no one came to her rescue. Natalie knew Ms. Haggle was ruthless, regardless of how close a person was to her. Facing a dark witch meant that she had once betrayed a person terribly. Natalie felt that now, more than ever, she had to take responsibility for her own safety. Dependence was not the path for a succubus—it was just not for her.

"Dig into your emotions," urged Ms. Haggle. "Feel the fight for life—the fight that kept you from the river bed, from Saul, from losing to Melissa."

Natalie gasped for what felt like her last breath of air before she embraced her power to steal from Ms. Haggle.

"There!" said Ms. Haggle. "Feel it. Own it. This is what it feels like to steal."

"Remember" was the last word Natalie heard before passing out.

CR&BO

Natalie woke up in her bed. Rebecca and Isabella stood in her room waiting for her to regain consciousness.

Susan was placing a green robe in Natalie's closet. She smiled at Natalie and left.

"You don't get to wear it until after it's presented to you in the ceremony that will be held the day after the witch's ball. Two days. Do you understand?" asked Rebecca.

"No problem," said Natalie. "But aren't you supposed to be testing?" she asked.

"I think she's been out for longer than she thinks," Isabella noted to Rebecca. She told Natalie, "You see, we're done. Melissa's testing now."

"She'll be in there for a while," said Rebecca. "She's attempting to be the first person to go straight from a Forester to a witch of power. If she succeeds, she'll have a black robe in her closet by the end of the day."

Natalie held her throbbing head in her hands. "Why would Ms. Hag do that to me?" she asked.

"You've chosen this path," said Rebecca. "What made you think it would be easy?"

"Is this another trick question?" asked Natalie.

"No," replied Rebecca. "The road to power requires hard work and discipline, just like any other field. And if it didn't, there'd hardly be any respect for the power you attain—again, just like any other field in life. The more power you want, the more work it takes to attain it. Ms. Hag and everyone else here have done nothing but help you work toward realizing your potential."

"Really?" asked Natalie.

"Didn't you get the succubus book that Melissa left for you?"

"That was on purpose?" gasped Natalie.

"I don't think you get it," said Isabella. "We're all here for each other. We need to stick together. Betrayal is the only sin."

"But, Melissa... I don't understand. She's been really hard on me."

"Urgency develops power; emotion drives it," said Isabella. "She did what was necessary, the only way she knows."

"The only way she knows?"

Rebecca and Isabella looked at each other as Natalie began to stand up. "Sit down," said Rebecca as she pushed Natalie back onto her bunk. Isabella checked the hall, and then the two girls seated themselves opposite Natalie. "What we tell you never leaves this room. Do you understand?"

"Yes," said Natalie with a newfound intrigue and attentiveness.

"Betrayal is the only sin," said Rebecca.

"Melissa's mother betrayed her, and the order," added Isabella.

"What we're trying to say..." started Rebecca, "...is that Melissa's path has been..."

"Just be thankful for what you have," continued Isabella.

"What did she do?" asked Natalie.

Rebecca sighed, and Isabella shook her head, giving in.

"Okay," said Rebecca. "Never underestimate one's connection with their mother. It is our one weakness that we have to accept. And we accept Melissa's strife, despite that it is against the directives of the order."

"Melissa's mother was temporarily dismissed from the order because she was seeking power for selfish motives. Her only desire was power and control, and she did not care for loyalty or kinship. Your mother, Hannah, was the headmistress who thought it wise to banish her for a short period of time. Hannah thought separation would be best so that Melissa's mother would come back to the order with a new perspective, and be welcomed with open arms. She was wrong. Melissa's mother came back, not with a new attitude, but with a child."

"Melissa!" cried Natalie.

"Right," said Rebecca. "And she mercilessly left Melissa here. However, when she learned of Melissa's prophecy, she came back. By then, Hannah was no longer the headmistress, but that didn't stop her from campaigning against placing Melissa in the custody of her mother. Ultimately, the decision was left to the five-year-old Melissa who had been begging for her mother since she could speak. Melissa was given back to her mother, and for two years, she suffered every kind of abuse you can imagine. Melissa's mother tried to squeeze out every bit of magic in her for her own gain. By the time the order caught up with them... Well, Melissa was half dead, weeping over a rotten corpse. Melissa was returned to the order, never the same, and her mother was permanently banished from the order, despite Melissa's pleas."

Isabella continued, "When you think about your life, never forget that there are others who have suffered worse. When you judge another, think first about how their path in life may have been different. How that might have been you."

"What was her mother's name?" asked Natalie.

"We don't say," replied Rebecca. "Betrayal is the only sin."

CHAPTER TWENTY-THREE

❧❧

BALL

Red. Dark red. So dark a red that when the skirt folded over, particularly when there was almost no light, it resembled a night black. The tulle, which pushed the floor-length, silky material outward, helped minimize folds just enough to establish that the dress was a regal red, and not the forbidden black. The vintage-inspired look, designed to cascade over her hips, gracefully flowed down from the complementary strapless bodice, decorated with bright, sparkling, iridescent, dark red crystals. There were so many crystals that every direction—regardless of how acute—was bound to be caught in its eye-catching flare. The sweetheart dress, named accurately after its heart-shaped upper part, laced tastefully at the back through twelve elaborate loops— devoted to covering as much skin as possible, but only between the lower part of the shoulder blades. Everything above the lace was designed to give way to the onlooker's pleasure.

"I love it!" beamed Natalie, freshly back from her hair appointment at the mall.

Natalie pulled the wheeled rack that housed the prom dress toward her. The displaced rack revealed

Emma, dressed in a more conservative, yet very attractive, emerald green dress.

"What do you think?" asked an apprehensive Emma. Natalie circled the rack to get a proper look at Emma in her dress. "It's wonderful! It fits you very well, and I really like the green on you. It makes your eyes stand out."

"That's why I wanted green—to match my eyes," said a more confident Emma.

Natalie giggled. "Shall I try mine on?"

"Yes, yes," encouraged a tittering Emma. "Let's see how we look together."

Natalie slipped the dress out of the hanger and held it over her body. Her insides tingled so much that she was literally popping up and down.

"Oh my gosh!" screamed Emma, pointing in the direction of the dress.

"What! What's wrong?" asked Natalie.

"There," said Emma.

Natalie turned the dress around, but failed to see anything out of place. "Where? What?"

"No, your ring," said Emma. "It's… It's yellow."

Natalie lifted her hand to look at the ring—it was indeed no longer white, but a solid vibrant yellow.

"I have to go," said Natalie as she dropped the dress on the rack and rushed off.

CRWD

"Ava! Ava!" yelled Natalie as she banged on Ava's door.

"Yes, child," replied Ava, opening the door.

"My ring… It's yellow!"

"Come in, my dear. I am sure you have many questions."

Uneasy, Natalie plopped down on the nearest chair to the door of Ava's one-room apartment. Ava leisurely placed a cup on the table next to Natalie, and poured out a blue liquid for her to drink.

"What do you think it means?" asked Ava.

"In this world, it could mean anything," replied Natalie.

"True, but that ring is associated with power."

"I have power?" asked Natalie.

"Drink up," said Ava. "Tomorrow's your fifteenth birthday. You'll be all grown up according to some cultures."

"But… But I don't have power," said Natalie.

"Oh, but your ring is proof." Ava helped Natalie take a sip of the drink, and continued, "Although it may take you some time to use what you have taken, you certainly have it. Not only can you take power from people, but you may also be taking it from the ring."

"You mean I can steal power from the ring too?"

"Technically, you can only mimic the powers of the ring." Ava helped Natalie up and led her to the door. "There are many powers you cannot steal, or even mimic. You will find that there are limitations to every power…" Ava's eyes opened wider. "And many hidden secrets that are yet to be discovered."

"But, but—"

"Never you mind all that now," said Ava. "You wouldn't want to be late for your date." She then guided Natalie out of the room and eased the door to a near shut.

"But, where does power come from?"

"If we knew where gods and magic derived, they would be renamed science and method. Speak your spells, command your power; point if you must, as movement is to power as words are to spells, but don't question it."

"Hurry," said Emma, clutching at Natalie's arm. "The boys are starting to show up."

Inside the front doors of the castle, in front of the two stairways that connected at the top, several well-dressed adult sentries wandered about. A number of beautifully dressed girls, ballroom ready, stood in desperate wait for their dates at the point where the two staircases came together on the second floor. Several boys had already arrived, and were engaged in refreshing themselves below, as they were nervously being vetted by the women.

Natalie finally arrived at the scene through the upper door, and asked, "Am I too late?"

"You look fabulous!" gasped Susan. "Like a dark princess."

"Thank you," replied Natalie. "Is he here?"

"Even if he was," said Toddi, "we wouldn't be able to go in until the festivities start. I should know, given I'm the grandmaster of the events tonight."

"How did you get that job?" asked Natalie.

"Well, if you haven't noticed, my technical knowledge of history and regulations is rather astonishing. I'm being given the bookworm award, yet again."

"How do you grandmaster when you have a date?" asked Emma.

"Oh, I don't have one. I'm the DJ as well."

At that moment, a bell sounded.

"It's time for the festivities to begin," said Devia. "Will the grandmaster of the events assume her place?"

Toddi gently gave her friends' hands a squeeze, and started down the stairs, past a dozen onlooking boys. She took a turn at the bottom before she replied, "Yes, Madam."

After Toddi passed under the stairs, Devia began to announce the girls' names one by one, so they could meet their guests below.

Natalie looked around anxiously for Parker, but could not see him anywhere. "Hey, there are girls down there too," she blurted out.

"Duh," replied Susan. "Not all of us have boyfriends. Besides, in the old days, boys weren't invited to these balls."

"Really?" asked Natalie before she gasped. "Philian! What is she doing here?"

"She's my date," said Emma. "Her dad let her come back for the ball to surprise you. She wanted to thank you for your help. Well, and to visit her mom."

Suddenly, Susan was called, followed by Emma— and many other girls after that. Natalie and Isabella were the only two left when Melissa stylishly appeared on the balcony in an all-black dress.

"I thought you weren't allowed to wear black," said Natalie.

"The infamous Melissa Tate can do whatever she wants. She's AP," replied Isabella.

"What do you mean by AP?" asked Natalie.

"AP. All powerful? You mean you don't know?" asked Isabella. "That's the next level... The *last* level of power. Only one per order is all powerful. Well, that *we* know of."

A handsome boy came to stand beside Devia and Melissa's name was called. "He's in college," said Melissa as she gracefully descended the stairs.

Natalie still didn't see Parker. However, a commotion started downstairs as a gentleman entered the castle. Boys, girls, and even Melissa's college man gathered around to get a peek.

"My date is a professional athlete," said Isabella as she climbed down the stairs in response to her name being called.

Natalie stood alone, her hands locked tightly around the central railing to steady herself. She hopelessly scanned the crowd, wondering if she was being punished for having been a good girl. Months of dating Parker, and she hadn't even allowed him a kiss. If he wanted, this could be the perfect revenge.

Suddenly, the doors opened, and the crowd—including the college boy and professional athlete—parted down the middle to give way to the newest entrant. It was Parker! Somehow, Parker managed to command tremendous respect amongst the crowd. Natalie smiled from ear to ear. If her date wasn't a prince, he played the part quite well. Parker's long legs confidently carried him across the stone floor toward his prize.

"Natalie Forsythe."

Natalie stood still for a moment. She would make him, and everyone else, wait as they gazed at her beauty, which, she hoped, matched her perception of her approaching date.

Parker, however, refused to be hindered by any delay, and met her halfway up the stairs.

"You're not allowed up here," whispered Natalie.

"I'm sorry, but I simply couldn't resist your beauty."

It took Natalie everything she had to keep herself from crying midway through the first dance. After several slow dances—Toddi's strategy to fill the floor—the tempo increased, which is when Natalie led Parker off the floor, toward the tables.

"What's the matter?" asked Parker. "Don't you want to dance?"

"Dancing's not the only thing I wish to do tonight," replied Natalie as she took Parker's hand in hers and pulled him away to a secluded corner.

Meanwhile, Mara, looking annoyed, whispered in Devia's ear, "In our day, there were no boys."

"I know," said Devia. "But that was a different time."

"Regardless, we need to keep this dance clean," replied Mara, pointing to some inappropriate dancing. "Those children are grinding!" she shrieked.

"I have it under control," said Devia. "Josephine is watching them right now."

Josephine positioned herself close to the Den Three—uncomfortably close—with her arms crossed over her chest and her eyes fixed in an unwavering stare. As the dates danced closer together, Zadie also made herself present, observing the scene wordlessly. When the girls had ignored the hints for long enough, Josephine raised her hand up in the air and twirled her finger around—a signal for Toddi to change the music. Consequently, the boys were escorted off the dance floor, and every girl assumed a predetermined spot on the floor—all except Natalie.

"I have to go," said Natalie as she stood and pulled away. "Come watch," she added as she darted off.

As the music changed to a classical style, the girls began a ballroom dance full of grace and elegance. As if they had coordinated and practiced for a lifetime, they flawlessly spun, glided, and exchanged partners amongst themselves in a celebration of joy and sisterhood. Awestruck, the boys gaped, unblinking, at the old-fashioned dance. All girls had their own place—even Toddi—and not one missed a single step. This commemoration of a time long past was nothing short of an extravagant affair.

Suddenly, the girls spun outward and each girl took her date's hands, leading them into an alternate, but smooth-flowing version of the dance.

"What are they doing now?" asked Mara. "This is unacceptable!"

"Wicked moons," said Devia, sarcastically. "Lighten up."

"Lighten up?" asked Mara.

"Yes. We're witches, not monsters."

The night was brilliant, and everyone was content when the dance came to a close—all except Natalie. Yes, it had been a magical time, but she didn't want to leave Parker's side. As boys, girls, and a few men exited the castle, the escorts corralled them all to keep the event clean.

"This way," whispered Natalie as she led Parker away.

"But they'll see us," replied Parker.

Natalie bit her lower lip, twisted her yellow-stoned ring, and said, "Trust me."

Together, they slipped past the escorts and entered the arena. They didn't stop until they stood in the exact center, with Parker holding both of Natalie's hands in his.

"How—"

Natalie placed her hand on Parker's mouth. "Save your lips," she said.

Parker smiled.

"I wanted to thank you for honoring my mother's wishes and waiting to kiss me after I turn fifteen. I know it was hard for you to wait, and I feel respected."

Natalie's non-verbal cues invited Parker closer. "But you don't turn fifteen until tomorrow."

"It's almost midnight," she replied.

Parker placed one hand on Natalie's cheek. Natalie responded by wrapping her hands around the back of his neck. Parker then placed his other hand at the small of her back, and pulled Natalie closer. The bells outside struck midnight, and Parker, his thumb still brushing Natalie's cheek and his fingers entangled in her hair, pulled Natalie even closer to his body. Softly their lips touched at first, and then they moved in perfect synch. The kiss was just enough to fill them with a tingling pleasure. Natalie started to lean in for more, but the act was pointless as her body relaxed and she fell back into Parker's hold, her head held firm by his other hand.

Parker pulled away, making sure Natalie could support herself before he let her go. He took hold of her hands again. "Did you like that?" he asked.

"Ye... yeah."

"I want more," said Parker. "But I don't want to over do it."

"Three," said Natalie. "No more, no less."

CHAPTER TWENTY-FOUR

❧❧

UNHOLY NIGHT

"**K**iss Parker."

"What?" asked Susan.

"You asked me what I want to do tonight," said Natalie. "I said, kiss Parker."

"That was last night. Tonight's the unholy night. This is when we bond while the witches have their ball."

"I know, but you said I could have anything for my birthday, and that's what I want," replied Natalie as she blissfully rolled around on her bunk.

"You already got your presents, even from Parker," said Toddi. "Let's do something that we'll always remember."

"That sounds a little dangerous," scolded Susan.

"Sorry," said Toddi. "It's just that the spirit of the unholy night is getting to me."

Before the girls could decide what to do, Melissa, dressed in her green robe, entered the room. She wordlessly lingered about as though she was inspecting minute details of the room. Eventually, she made her way over to the three girls that were gathered around Natalie's bed.

"Come with me" was all Melissa said.

The three girls threw on their honey-colored robes as they followed Melissa. Melissa led the girls to the castle entrance and, after some hesitation, ushered them inside the front lobby. Melissa sat, and the girls followed. Two witches dressed in black robes and one witch in a brown robe were talking; Melissa did not dare to interrupt them.

"Personally," began one witch, "I enjoy these dances without men. In fact, I take great pleasure in tormenting them." The witch sat on the desk, closing the distance between her and the naïve-looking witch in the brown robe, sitting behind the desk. "But my hatred is nothing compared to Arlene's."

Arlene, the third and the oldest witch, ran her hand along her cheek. "You see this scar? It came from a man. I ate his tongue, while it was still in his mouth. I have a reputation for hurting men. Almost got me banished from the order."

The naïve-looking witch gasped. "Are we allowed to hurt people?"

"Not really," said Arlene. "But there are ways. Subtle ways through which no one is the wiser. I once put a spell on a man to make him go slightly off on every measurement. He was a contractor who couldn't make a living anymore. If a man so much as looks at me wrong, I put a spell on him. They're small but effective."

"Ahem," the witch sitting on the desk cleared her throat, turning toward the four girls.

Arlene also turned and approached the girls, stopping in front of Melissa. "Stand," she ordered.

"Yes, Ma'am," replied Melissa and the three Honeys.

"We are the sentries tonight," said Arlene. "As it is, we are not happy about missing the witch's ball. So, do not anger us with any mischief. I will be on patrol, and if I find you off the grounds, even in the forest, you will have to pay. Do I make myself clear?"

"Yes, Ma'am," replied the girls in unison.

"You may leave, but remember this... I do not tolerate disobedience, and I will lock you all down if one single problem arises. Now, be gone."

Natalie, Susan, and Toddi scurried away, but Melissa put on an exaggerated display of leaving with a strut. As they walked, the girls spoke badly of Arlene.

"I didn't think witches were supposed to be... well, *witches*," said Natalie.

"She should be careful," said Toddi. "Have you ever heard of a retribution spell? If she dies due to one, then all the pain she's ever dished out comes back to her tenfold."

"Whoa, wait!" said Susan. Then she turned to Melissa. "Excuse me, but why'd you take us there?"

"Beginning tomorrow, you girls will be the Den Three. You need to understand how things work. After tonight, you three will report to the front desk for instructions. But tonight, I'll let you direct the girls."

"Cool," said Natalie. "Let's go."

CB&CO

Back at the dorms, all the Honeys were trying to decide what to do in the lower recreation room where they often gathered. The Den Three sat in chairs placed along the wall, in order to allow the girls the freedom to make decisions for themselves.

"Let's go to Mitzi Forest," suggested one girl.

"We really shouldn't," said Susan.

"Oh, it's Arlene, isn't it?" the girl replied. "She doesn't mean much around here. Let's just go."

A few girls stood up and began to move, until…

"You might want to rethink that," said Melissa.

"Yeah, we should rethink that," said the girl who was trying to lead the others.

"What then?" asked Natalie. "We should do something we'll remember."

"Have you been to the caverns?" asked Toddi. "It's a storehouse of ancient history."

The group sneakily looked in Melissa's direction, who gave the tiniest of nods.

"Alright! Let's do it."

"I know the best place," said Toddi. "Follow me."

Toddi led twenty girls to the classroom, to a door in the floor behind the stage, which led underground. "This entrance leads to the caverns—miles and miles of tunnels that connect to everything on the grounds, even the forest. We can reach the arena, the cemetery, and even Ms. Hag's house, or so I've heard. There are so many tunnels that I haven't figured out where all of them lead, but I'm sure they go to a lot more places."

"What if we get lost?" asked Emma as she climbed down a spiral staircase.

"Stick to the bigger tunnels," advised Melissa. "It's the narrow, less traveled paths that you should worry about."

"You'll be fine," said Toddi. "There's an area that is dotted with statues, graves, and murals on the main path.

I call it the four corners. We can have fun exploring that, and it'll be easy to find our way back. I'll show you."

The last girl entering the stairway shut the trap door, cutting off all outside light. Emma clung on to Natalie, even after Toddi cast a spell to light the torches on the side walls. The torches lit up with a bright green flame. The stairway was nothing more than a small, carved tunnel of rock and stone, barely wide enough to fit three girls side-by-side.

The adjoining trail was equally narrow, but the area opened up when they reached the four corners—a space that eliminated all of the explorer's claustrophobic thoughts. This area, once majestic, would undoubtedly look like ruins to the modern eye; yet, a single glance to the left or right, or even straight ahead, would amaze any person who first set foot on this underground marvel.

The girls could instantly see why Toddi called it the four corners—on each corner of the massive four-way intersection, a colossal marble figure of a cloaked woman appeared to be holding up the cavern roof with her back. Each of the four women, their arms stretched to the center, held their portion of a large, circular shield that bore a stone similar to the one on Natalie's ring.

The girls took in the remains of what must have once been a beautiful and well-appreciated site: two side-by-side paths, perpendicular to the path they were on, filled with awe-inspiring architecture. Along the far wall, built into life-sized niches, stood statues—very old statues—of women the girls did not recognize. Directly at their feet lay the first of the two paths: a brick walkway covered by an archway of approximately three-meter width. The archway ran through the entirety of the tunnel curving into the distance until the girls could no longer see where it went. This curve, they were told, led to the cemetery. Parallel to the brick corridor was the path that ran along the niches, almost twice as wide as the archway with a floor made of earth instead of brick. Upon closer inspection, the girls discovered a flat stone base under the dirt. These caverns were clearly spectacles to be enjoyed, but at present, with arbitrary pieces missing throughout the structure, discarded bricks lying about—some in large piles—and unkempt decay, it could easily be classified as a hazard.

The girls scattered and frolicked within the historical remains and the creepy past of the precarious area. For some time, the Honeys enjoyed their adventure in what seemed to be a memorial site and a prophetic holy ground combined into one.

"How far do you want to go?" asked Toddi. "I can show you really far."

"Ahem," interrupted Melissa.

"Maybe we should just stick to the open area," suggested Susan. "Besides we've been here for over an hour. I'm taking a break."

Susan sat down near the Den Three, who had tired too soon, as though they had spent many nights, and not this one alone, exploring the caverns. Not all the girls were visible from where they sat, but Melissa had an unspoken way of curtailing any desire for unauthorized exploration. Something, however, caught Susan's eye. Natalie was standing down to the right of the way through which they had first entered the main cavern—in front of a niche that had been suspiciously bricked in. Susan turned her attention to the left and to the right, only to realize that this niche was different from the rest, as if someone was trying to hide something. Susan gathered herself as she approached Natalie.

"I don't understand it," muttered Natalie before Susan was close enough to make her presence known. "Something about this seems to be calling out to me."

Natalie placed her hand on the corroding brick and mortar of the oversized niche that began on a knee-high ledge and stretched on to the ceiling. She climbed on to the ledge and noted that the bricks casing the niche were old, weak, and breaking apart. At the top, several bricks were even missing.

"Hoist me up," said Natalie, and Susan did.

By this time, all the Honeys had gathered around to help unravel the mystery.

"Take a few more bricks out," suggested one girl. She then looked behind her, in Melissa's direction, and amended her order, "Maybe we should rethink this."

Melissa and the other members of the Den Three joined the Honeys. "No," said Melissa. "I think it will be okay. It's time to move the bricks away."

At Melissa's words, the Honeys took to bricks like a demolition crew.

"I can't see anything," said one.

"Get off my foot," yelled another.

Anxious and extremely tiny, Emma crept low and pulled one brick away. "Sunlight," she cast to help everyone see inside. A bright light entered through the tiny hole and spread sharply out of the many crevices that the other girls were creating. Quickly, the girls backed away.

"That's too bright," said Susan. "What are you trying to do, blind us?"

But Emma remained unaffected by the rebuke, feeling proud that she had managed to cast a spell.

"Move away," said Melissa. "I got this."

Melissa began to whisper a string of words in rapid succession, holding her hand in the direction of the brick wall. One by one, the bricks crumbled, fell, and piled themselves into a somewhat neat pile along the side of the wall. What the girls saw rendered them speechless.

"It's you!" exclaimed Toddi.

"It can't be!" replied Natalie, gasping.

"But it is," said Melissa. "Just an older version of you."

Melissa was right, and the girls, their hands all over the statue, soon came to accept that the statue was a memorial to an older version of Natalie. But how? The marble carving must have been decades old—if not older.

There Natalie stood, cast in marble, with Ms. Haggle's sword resting on her shoulder, held by her right hand. Her mother's ring adorned her right ring finger. A bracelet on her left wrist bore the same stone as her ring. Around her neck was an amulet, also set with the same stone. The statue wore a chained belt—another of the same stone gracing it. A similarly stoned brooch connected her robe at the neck, and she wore earrings that were set with a similar but smaller stone.

Natalie caressed the older version of herself. "How?" she asked.

"Someone saw you in her future," answered Melissa. "All our destinies are written beforehand. Only a few are seen."

"And the jewelry?" asked Susan.

"Natalie knows what they are," replied Melissa.

"What are they?" asked Susan.

Natalie looked at Melissa for reassurance before she answered. "The Seven Weapons of Light."

The girls ooohed, awwwed, and no-wayed in response.

"Look at the mural in the background," said Toddi. "It's Ms. Hag."

Painted on the rock wall at the back was a picture of Ms. Haggle cringing in pain on the ground as a bubble was cast around her, seemingly shifting her energy to a painting of Natalie, who heartily took it in.

"Do you steal Ms. Hag's energy?" asked Toddi.

"Or do you kill her?" asked Susan.

"Even in a mural," said Melissa, "you can't stop hurting that woman."

CHAPTER TWENTY-FIVE

❧❧

COMPANIONS

"Natalie, are you okay?" asked Susan.

Natalie leaned against the interior wall of the niche, near her own painted likeness. Her legs buckled and she slid down to the ground—her knees drawn near her face and arms wrapped around her shins.

"It... It's just too much," replied a despondent Natalie.

Susan sat with Natalie in silence while girls hovered around the memorial. Eventually, a few girls left, followed by a few more, until Natalie and Susan were left alone. They sat, quiet, until they heard a scream from the direction of the cemetery.

"What's going on?" asked Natalie as she caught up with the group that Melissa was trying to control.

In the distance, Natalie saw a witch in black, bent over something. Due to some large stones blocking her view, she could not see what was on the ground; but her attention was drawn to the witch who appeared to be neither here nor there—the best she could interpret what she saw.

"This way," said Melissa, leading the girls away. "We must get Ms. Hag."

"What is it?" asked Susan as they sneaked back toward the path through which they entered the caverns.

"You don't want to know."

Natalie peeked back as they crept away—the witch struck down, and in response, a pair of legs rose into the air, then fell limp. As the girls quickly put more distance between the witch and themselves, they heard a long ear-piercing screech.

"That's a retribution spell," said Toddi.

"What happened to Arlene?" asked a girl.

"We have to get back now!" yelled Melissa. "That's a dark witch's companion. The others must be warned. Rebecca, Isabella, can you morph?"

"I'm trying," said Isabella as her eyes suddenly turned yellow and two fangs sprouted out of her mouth.

Rebecca zapped three meters forward in what appeared to be a bolt of lightning. "I'll get Ms. Hag," she said.

"Good, go," said Melissa.

As soon as the words were out of Melissa's mouth, Rebecca flurried off down the path in a series of short bolts—out of sight.

"Isabella, you're responsible to get the girls to the top, should we have to separate."

"Yes, Melissa," she replied.

"Listen up," Melissa said to the entire group. "If we encounter the witch, everyone follow Isabella. Natalie and I will hold her off. Your job is to reach above the ground and warn the others."

"But I don't have any power," Natalie whispered to Melissa.

"You won't fight her," said Melissa. "I need you to hide and steal her power. Do not engage with her. With your ring, you can hide and steal. That's what I need you for."

"What's a dark witch's companion?" asked a girl.

Toddi answered, "A dark witch is ultra-powerful. A companion is someone who can link with a witch to utilize her power. She has all the power of a dark witch."

"Here," said Melissa as they came back to the four corners. "Straight ahead is the arena, and to the left is the way we came in through. We'll reach the arena, and come back around to the castle."

The girls continued forward, moving more loudly, sacrificing stealth for speed. Their efforts, however, were futile, as they were confronted by the companion herself. Melissa halted, casting spells under her breath while softly backing away.

"We're not afraid of you," said Melissa.

"What do you mean by we, Forester?" hissed the companion.

Melissa looked to her left and then her right to see that she was alone. "Ms. Haggle once defeated a dark witch, and I'm all powerful. I suggest you leave now while you still can."

"Oh. We're prepared for Ms. Haggle, and you as well," replied the companion.

In the meantime, the companion gained ground on Melissa, bringing herself close enough for both of them to strike at each other. The companion pulled down her hood to reveal solid black eyes, set in a grey complexion.

Melissa shrieked.

"So, you recognize me," said the companion. "You've seen your prophecy, and you know that I'm the one who kills you. But, you were surprised?" In a slow, eerie voice, the companion continued. "Did you not know I'd be here so soon?"

"I'm not afraid to die," replied Melissa. "But when my sisters find you... Then, it is you who will be afraid."

"Impossible," replied the companion in a condescending tone. "You see, your order is trapped in the castle, and will remain there until our spell is complete. Then, they die. So, they cannot *possibly* help you."

"Enough lies!" shouted Melissa. "Let's do this."

"Are you so eager to die?" asked the companion.

"I'm not dead yet," replied Melissa, constantly backing away from the companion, who pushed forward faster and faster.

"You're stalling," noted the companion. "Why?"

"You know my future, you tell me."

The companion closed her eyes and set her head back—like she had entered a trance—as her feet left the ground and she began to float. "There is another. Another power around here. Who is she? Yes. She has potential. I can use her. Who is she? Where is the child?"

"She's right here!" answered Melissa thrusting her left arm forward, then her right—sending out a bright light and a bout of dust respectively. Melissa leaped forward, feet first, kicking the companion in the face—one, two, three, and four times—as she continued to fly forward in a run-like series of kicks, connecting each time as the companion fell backward.

The companion, taken completely by surprise at the bold move, recovered enough to pull a short staff out of her robe, touching Melissa's foot with it and turning her foot to ice. Then, before Melissa could fall, the companion delivered a powerful backswing with her other hand, flinging the forester down to the ground. Quickly, Melissa cast a spell at her foot, rubbing the icy growth away, and stood up again.

"Round one, Forester," said Melissa.

"Do you really think you can harm me?" asked the companion. She laughed. "You know, we actually have something in common," she continued. "We're both companions. That's it!" she cried. "Where's the succubus? My power! Where is she?"

"Round two, Forester," said Melissa.

The companion responded by pointing her staff toward Melissa and sending a ray of ice at her. Melissa pulled up her arm to form an invisible shield, which deflected the ray, forcing it to hit a wall and rattle the caverns, bringing rocks down.

"You are powerful," said the companion. "But that doesn't change the fact that, tonight, you die. At my hands!"

With that, the companion shot forward, engaging in a close-range melee with Melissa, who was able to block a barrage of strikes and land a few herself. Then, Melissa snatched the companion's staff, twisting it away before belting her in the chin with an upward strike, then a cross thrust. The companion flopped down onto her backside.

"I underestimated you, Forester," said the companion. "I had hoped I would not need to use the dark witch's power, but you asked for it."

The companion held out her hand, summoning her staff to return to her from Melissa's grip. Then, she twirled it around, causing bricks from all about to lift up. One by one, the bricks flung themselves at Melissa. Melissa easily sliced the first brick in half with her hand, then the second, but the effort became increasingly difficult as dozens of bricks came at her all at once. With her feet, Melissa kicked two, even three, away in the air at a time, while still snatching and smashing at the bricks with her two hands, and at one point, even a head butt. The bricks, however, were too many, and one finally made its mark, striking Melissa in the shoulder. Melissa shrugged off the pain, but found her fight growing harder and harder as the companion now pulled bricks from the walls. Several more reached their target, hitting Melissa hard. Melissa refused to give in, taking each hit in her stride, waiting for the bricks to fall short; but they didn't. Melissa was shortly engulfed in bricks up to her hips, making it extremely difficult for her to defend herself. She muttered a few spells, pushing the bricks away, but now there were too many. Melissa soon took a hit to the head and fell under a storm of more bricks—buried alive, if alive at all.

"No!" screamed Natalie, rushing over to the pile, shouting, "Lightweight!"

To Natalie's surprise, the bricks began to rise up, as though they were weightless; so she quickly began to bat them away.

"There's the succubus!" exclaimed the companion, suddenly hovering over Natalie's shoulder.

Natalie tried to run, but the companion made her trip with a spell and she fell to the floor. Natalie seemed unable to push herself up—it was impossible to get higher than her knees.

"You shouldn't have used your power. Your power, no matter how limited, interrupts the power of the ring," said the companion. "I can use you though," she added. Placing her hand on Natalie's shoulder, the companion whispered into Natalie's ear, "With your gift, I can be more powerful than the dark witch."

"I'll never help you," whispered back a pained Natalie in her failed effort to shout.

"Have you ever held the hand of the Devil?" asked the companion. Moving closer to Natalie's head, she inhaled blissfully. "It's not as bad as you think."

The companion spun Natalie as she remained on her knees, around until they came face to face, then held out her hand to the Honey. "Take my hand, child. Take my hand, and I will show you power. Your friend will live if you take my hand. *Do it, child*!"

Natalie stretched her hand out toward the companion. She hesitated, but found herself giving in to the overwhelming command. Natalie placed her hand in the companion's, and soon, she could feel a connection— power slowly beginning to combine in the touching palms of their hands from both the sides.

"Hurry child," said the companion. "Hurry before we lose the connection. I need enough power. More power before I can pull it in. More. More."

Suddenly, the companion was flung back, falling to the floor, flailing. Natalie felt all the power from both the sides remain in her hand for the taking, but she could not see past the immense surge of power to understand what was transpiring in front of her eyes—only the power was important in that moment. Natalie closed her hand into a fist, drawing in the power. The power was strong, sending a jolt through Natalie's arm and immobilizing her body. Her arm began to freeze inward, past her elbow and toward her chest. She could feel the frost seek out her heart, and it did, although the pace slowed. Natalie turned her frozen hand over, observing that the stone on her ring had changed color to an ice blue. She couldn't fight the power any more, and figured she didn't have to. Instead, Natalie embraced the power, taking it all in and directing her efforts at sending the frost back to the hand through her arm. The frost eventually faded, leaving the ring a light green color.

Natalie looked up to find Melissa repeatedly striking the companion with a brick. Then, the companion dissipated into a black and grey mist, reemerging behind them.

"You don't understand, Forester," said the companion. "I can't physically die as long as the dark witch lives."

The companion held out her hands in an offensive posture, and Melissa held hers out too. Lights and distorted specters of power began to manifest between the two combatants. Taking the force of as much power as possible, Melissa began to crumble backward.

"Go, Natalie! Go! I can't hold her." Melissa's body bent backward into an unnatural position. "Go!"

And Natalie did.

CHAPTER TWENTY-SIX

✿

BESTOWAL

Natalie made her way up a steep stairway, through a wooden trap door, into a small closet-like room that had several doors. She opened the center door, and peering into it, she realized it led to the back side of the arena—a familiar spot. Hurriedly, she rushed through the door, moved across another room, and found herself at the bottom of the arena, attempting to traverse the entirety of the full length of the middle section in record time. Natalie ran over the dirt so fast that she paid little attention to any unusual presence in the room— or any person for that matter. She ran past the dirt, hopped the gate, and crossed the track, but as she tried to turn the corner into the front room, she collided with a young, unknown woman and fell, scrambling, to the ground.

The woman, dressed in a black robe, gave off an aura of power—so much so that Natalie could feel her presence exude a force that touched her like shock waves. The disgruntled woman held her hand at her mouth, where Natalie's head had hit her, and gave Natalie a vaguely familiar look of scorn.

"Don't kill me," pleaded Natalie, crawling backward to put distance between them.

"My tooth has come loose, Natalie," said the somewhat recognizable voice.

"Ms. Haggle?" asked Natalie.

The woman sighed. "Who else would constantly be at the receiving end of your clumsiness?"

"But... You look so young. Not that you're too old... But—"

"I reserve my youthful form for more appropriate situations," replied Ms. Haggle. "Now, we have business to attend to. Follow me."

Natalie followed Ms. Haggle to the center of the arena, where she had prepared what appeared to be some form of a ceremony.

"The others have been assigned their tasks," said Ms. Haggle. "You and I are responsible for the dark witch herself. If you follow my instructions, we will be successful."

Ms. Haggle faced Natalie, placing both her hands on the Honey's shoulders. "I need your entire focus and obedience, regardless of what you feel. Do you understand?"

"Yes, Ma'am."

"Steal my power."

"What?"

"Steal my power. Now!" repeated Ms. Haggle.

Apprehensive, Natalie began to draw in what she could of the massive force of power that emanated from Ms. Haggle.

"Do not hesitate," said Ms. Haggle. "And do not bother yourself with what you see," she continued as she knelt down in an uncomfortable position. "I feel your uncertainty. Do not hold back, and do not mimic. You must take whatever comes your way, whatever is the easiest."

"I'm scared," said Natalie.

"Keep going," urged Ms. Haggle as she began to scream in pain.

Ms. Haggle fell to the floor, reaching out, and Natalie could feel the power circle around Ms. Haggle, and move toward her. The scene in the mural flashed before Natalie's eyes. Natalie leaned back just enough to allow the power to enter her body. Every muscle, vein, and bone in her body warmed slightly, stopping short of a burning sensation, as she could feel the power move about inside her body.

Suddenly, the connection between the two burst, signaling the rupture of the power drain. Immediately, Natalie rushed to Ms. Haggle's side.

"Are you okay?"

"Yes," replied Ms. Haggle. "Now, for your second task. Bring me the sword of power. You know where it is. Go back through the caverns and bring it here to me."

"Will you be okay?"

"Go!" shouted Ms. Haggle, and Natalie began to run. "Go the way you came; three niches past your statue, there will be a passage. You have my knowledge of the path from there on."

Somehow, Natalie could feel the way, but there was something else she could feel—the companion. Natalie made it down to the four corners, cautiously maneuvering her way around the stones. There, where they had battled the companion, lay a pool of blood. Melissa's? Natalie could tell that the body had been dragged away. But to where? As Natalie moved closer to the four corners, she could hear sobbing sounds emerging from the path back to the classroom—the way the girls had gone. The pool of blood did not run in that direction, but Natalie decided to explore the noise, hopeful that it was not one of the companion's tactics to trap her. Shortly off the main path, the sounds grew louder and Natalie could see that the exit was sealed off by dirt and stone. She looked around behind the rocks to find Emma hiding there.

"Emma!" gasped Natalie. "What are you doing here?"

"I was left behind," she managed between sobs and snivels. "Then, when the witch shot ice at Melissa, the cave collapsed."

"We need to get you out of here," said Natalie.

"But how?" asked Emma.

Natalie thought for a moment and made a decision. "You have to go back to the four corners and make your way through the cemetery."

"On a full moon night?" asked Emma. "No way!"

"Here," said Natalie as she took off her ring. "This will conceal you. You'll be protected as long as you don't use any spells. That's how I made my way through the cemetery on that full moon night."

Natalie put the now dark emerald stoned ring on Emma's right ring finger, and helped her up. "You can do this. Make your way out of the cemetery, and wait for help."

Natalie, her arm wrapped around Emma's shoulder, walked her down to the cemetery path, pausing to observe her mural once more. At the edge of the path, just beyond Arlene's body, Natalie gave Emma a gentle push and hoped for the best.

When Emma had gone out of sight, Natalie turned back to find her way to Ms. Haggle's home, but before she could make it to the third niche, she felt the presence of the companion nearby. Quickly, she darted to the opposite side, crouching under the arched walkway. Natalie now began to question her decision of giving away her ring.

Then Natalie saw her. The companion was almost floating down the dirt path of the cavern—toward Natalie. Natalie crouched low, hoping that the piles of rocks and bricks would hide her. Her heartbeat grew louder. She could hear her own breathing in the silence that enveloped her. Every rock, each piece of clothing, and even the dust seemed to make noise. Natalie crept forward to shorten her time of wait. The companion glanced her way, and Natalie lowered herself to the ground even more, trying to mimic the power of her ring. She waited, but the companion didn't move. The companion whispered some spells, but Natalie focused on the feeling she experienced with her ring on, confident she could conceal her presence. The companion moved in Natalie's direction, and stopped. Natalie froze.

"There are still children here," said the companion. "I will find you," she continued before resuming her slow drift down the path toward the cemetery, slowly moving away from Natalie. "Chil-dren," she slowly uttered.

Natalie waited for the companion's voice to fade. Then, she waited some more. Once she felt she was safe, she swiftly rushed to the secret niche, all the while wondering if it was possible for her heart to stop mid-beat.

Natalie searched the niche for a secret button or a torch, but there was nothing.

"Chil-dren," rang out the companion's voice, as she headed back toward Natalie.

Frantically, Natalie searched over and over again, but nothing. Was she looking in the right niche? She craned her neck to count again, and saw the companion coming back. Had Ms. Haggle been wrong? Even if she was, there was little room to hide in the niche. Finding herself panicking, Natalie inhaled deeply to calm herself, focusing on the knowledge she had acquired from Ms. Haggle. The answer, she found, was not a secret notch, but rather a mental route into the passage. Focusing her power, Natalie was able to transcend into the passage without so much as disturbing a grain of dirt.

Inside, Natalie could feel the direction she needed to proceed in; she traveled hastily, probably too fast, stumbling once or twice, even colliding into a sharp-angled wall once. But something was amiss: she was not alone in the passage. Natalie slowed and began to stalk the slow-moving creature that was also moving along the path.

Crawling on the floor was Melissa, making her own way to Ms. Haggle's house.

"Melissa!" gasped Natalie. "Are you okay?"

"No. But I'm alive," she replied. "We must get to Ms. Hag's."

"I know," said Natalie. "Ms. Hag is waiting for me to return. The girls made it back."

Natalie helped Melissa up, and together they followed the path that led directly to the inside of Ms. Haggle's home, through a trap door that was unnoticeable from the inside.

Immediately, Melissa limped to Ms. Haggle's table of liquids and mixed herself a drink. To Natalie's surprise, the shadow in the kitchen also made some noise.

"Bring me the items from the shadow," demanded Melissa.

Natalie went to the kitchen and returned with plants, liquids, and cravats for Melissa, who began to heal herself.

"You need to get back to Ms. Hag," said Melissa. "I'll be fine now."

"Are you sure?" asked Natalie.

"Go," replied Melissa, grunting in pain.

Natalie dashed to the fireplace and searched among the knives for the sword... but it was gone!

CHAPTER TWENTY-SEVEN

ॐ∾ॐ

How to Kill a Hag

"The sword. It's gone," said Natalie. "What do I do now?"

"What did Ms. Hag say?" asked Melissa.

"That she and I would take on the dark witch. The girls had been assigned their tasks."

"Then return to her," said Melissa. "I'll help the girls."

Together, the two girls left Ms. Haggle's house and made their way to the stables.

"Here is where we part," said Melissa.

Looking at Melissa's condition, Natalie understood what she meant. In complete silence, the two girls placed a hand on each other's shoulder, their bodies saying their final goodbye, and departed. Natalie passionately stormed into the stables and unlatched the gate to Galla's stall. As her expertise as a cowgirl came into play, Natalie mounted Galla mid-stride, galloping out like a pair that had nothing to lose. Natalie nodded as she passed Melissa; then she circled between the stables and the cemetery, not realizing that Emma was watching her travel to the arena through the back path.

Galla stomped down on the big doors at the side entrance of the arena, and barged in with full force, not halting until the two of them were at the center. Natalie's eyes rapidly scanned the perimeter as Galla trotted in circles, both failing to spot Ms. Haggle.

"Let's arm ourselves," said Natalie, motioning toward the armory.

Natalie dismounted in front of the armory and opened its doors to find the practice equipment intact; but that was rather unsatisfactory—it was the real weapons behind the metal doors that she wanted. They were locked and spelled shut beyond her capacity. Natalie searched the area, but the best she could find was a fencing sword with a melted tip—gear typically used for training. It was all she had, so she took it. Deciding it was time to wait, she led Galla behind the large doors under the rear balcony and settled down beside her horse.

Natalie did not need to wait long before a dark mist entered, circling the arena, eventually whirlpooling its way to the center. It took the form of a dark robe. The witch turned her way, but Natalie was unable to see a face. Inside the cloak was nothing but a dark amorphous shadow—resembling the form of something vaguely humanoid. Natalie cowered lower, but she knew that her presence was known to the witch.

"I have her!" shouted the companion from the tunnels as she grabbed Natalie from behind. Then she leaped and floated with Natalie to the center arena, dropping her—and the fencing sword—in front of the dark witch.

"Succubus or not, I have no time for children," said the dark witch. "Kill her."

Suddenly, Galla rushed in from the back room, fully charged. The companion rolled away, but the dark witch did not even blink as Galla pulled up in front of her, hooves in attack mode. The dark witch lifted her staff, freezing the horse in her position on her back feet. The dark witch then rose up and placed her hand on Galla's face, turning her to stone.

"This is my favorite spell," said the dark witch. She eyed Natalie, who lay on her side, propped up with her arms. "When you turn an animal to stone, the emotion captured is the purest and most beautiful. Even the greatest artist cannot create what I just made." The witch reached for a second victim, her hand extending toward Natalie's face. "It's a pity that witches never really appreciate this spell. You see, a witch of any level can do it, but what I do is irreversible. My level of power will turn you into a piece of art. You will become famous, forever."

Natalie closed her eyes as the dark witch's hand neared her cheek. She said a prayer under her breath, wondering if the ground shaking beneath her had something to do with her words.

The dirt across the arena bubbled like boiling water. Natalie felt her legs and hands sink into the dirt as if it were fluid. A large face began to form on the ground. It was of the youthful Ms. Haggle. Gradually, the shape solidified and transformed into a head and a body that rose up from the ground in a liquid figure of Ms. Haggle. Then, the shape and ground became steady, forcing all animate objects to float back up.

"No harm from power will come to her as long as I live," said Ms. Haggle.

"Your spell is wasted on my companion," mocked the dark witch, laughing.

"I see my child has stolen your companion's power," added Ms. Haggle.

The companion shrugged but remained steady.

The vehemence in the dark witch's reply, however, showed both her displeasure and her confidence in her strength. "It would take days for your child to steal all we have accumulated. All she gained was a mere taste."

"Why are you even with this woman, Millicent?" Ms. Haggle asked the companion. In a condescending tone, she continued, "Are you still upset about the death of your mother?"

The companion, Millicent, now trembled in rage.

"I was there," said Ms. Haggle. "I was there when Amelia from our order killed your mother. I watched your mother beg for her life, and you weren't even there."

Infuriated, Millicent lashed out at Natalie with a spell.

Natalie winced, awaiting death, but nothing happened.

"Fool!" said the dark witch. "Did you not hear her say that no harm from power will come to this girl? She has forbidden you from harming her with spells."

Natalie, swift in thought and quick on her feet, sped toward Ms. Haggle, making her way in a stumbling flurry.

The dark witch lifted her hand, stopping Natalie, freezing her in an awkward position. "Poor child," said the dark witch. "The spell has no effect on me."

Millicent walked over to Natalie and picked her up, taking the fencing sword and tossing it aside.

"So, where do we stand?" asked Ms. Haggle. "Because my body lies in another realm, and you know you can't kill me."

"And you can't kill me!" shouted the dark witch.

"The last dark witch I killed was far more powerful than you," replied Ms. Haggle.

"Yes," hissed the dark witch. "But I'm more prepared." The dark witch pulled opened her robe, revealing the sword of power. "You weren't looking for this, were you?"

"There are other ways to kill a dark witch," said Ms. Haggle.

"I know," said the dark witch. "But, there is only one way to kill a Hag."

"So, who are you really here for, Annika?" asked Ms. Haggle, refusing to entertain the dark witch's remark.

"I am sorry, but I have a grievance with your entire order. My revenge is not absolute until it is ruined to the ground, which will commence when my spell is complete—precisely two hours after midnight."

"I'm not sure how that can be possible," questioned Ms. Haggle.

"Do you still think I left the order willingly? Are you not aware that many within the order have betrayed it? There are some who have intentionally gone too far. Their indiscretions have helped me attain my level of power."

"Then take your revenge on them!" demanded Ms. Haggle vehemently.

"It's too late," said the dark witch. "Your order is culpable and has been targeted as a whole for the purpose of my revenge. I have the right to wipe it off the face of this world."

"And the children?" asked Ms. Haggle.

"Part of the order," said the dark witch. "As… if… you… cared."

"Killing the immortal is always a challenge I enjoy," replied Ms. Haggle.

"Not this time!" said the dark witch, motioning with her staff.

At that moment, Natalie broke free, rolled over to the fencing sword, and picked it up. The companion cast several ineffective spells before she realized that Natalie remained unaffected. With a full swing of the sword, Natalie struck the companion in the face.

"I cannot cast a spell on you, but I can still cast spells," said the companion, floating in the air, moving over to the stands.

Meanwhile, as Natalie repositioned herself to keep both witches in front of her, the dark witch conjured up a black cloud, which enveloped the outer rim of the stadium before it descended onto Ms. Haggle. Ms. Haggle stood motionless as the darkness entered her without any effect. Annoyed, the dark witch used her staff to shoot a black ray at Ms. Haggle—again, without effect. Ms. Haggle turned her back to the dark witch, with little concern. Taking this as her chance, the dark witch used the sword of power to strike at Ms. Haggle; but even that had no effect—merely passing through her body. Ms. Haggle turned around, looking grave.

"Like you said, there's only one way to kill a Hag," said Ms. Haggle.

"You mean by three or thirteen," said the dark witch.

Now, for the first time, Ms. Haggle looked dismayed.

"The demons have taught me, and it was easy to find thirteen scorned souls," said the dark witch, as she raised the sword and staff, crossing them over each other in a spell.

"I call on the thirteen binders of the underworld," she said.

There was nothing Ms. Haggle could do. No power would work against some forms of revenge, and this was one of them. Noting that she was indubitably confined to the arena, Ms. Haggle frantically cast one last spell before a ghostly figure appeared.

"I bind you," said the bluish ghost of a knight. Then another appeared. "I bind you," said a man dressed as a king. Then another, and another appeared, putting binding spells on Ms. Haggle, prompting Natalie and Millicent to stop and gape at the magnificent show of lights.

"You can't bind me!" shouted Ms. Haggle. "I bind you!"

"I bind you," declared an eleventh character, then a twelfth, and finally a thirteenth.

"I cannot be bound!" said Ms. Haggle. "I am unbindable!" she screamed.

Together the thirteen said, "You are bound by the power vested in us."

"I am power incarnate!" shouted Ms. Haggle. "I cannot be bound!"

Gathering around Ms. Haggle in a circle, the thirteen scorned souls lashed back.

"I bind you to primary spells," commanded one. "I bind you to primary spells," ordered another, and another, and another, until the thirteen overlapping voices were done. Together, they repeated, "You have been bound to primary spells." Then, one by one, they began, "I bind you to mortality," and when they were finished, they repeated together, "You have been bound to mortality." Finally, one after the other, they disappeared.

Ms. Haggle recoiled under her robe, shrieking, until she chose to rise—bound.

"And that is how you kill a Hag," declared the dark witch with jovial laughter. "You are nothing to me now."

"You might want to rethink that," said Ms. Haggle.

"You question me still!" shouted the dark witch as she swung her staff and sent more black rays at Ms. Haggle. Unfortunately for the dark witch, the rays had no effect yet again.

"You thought you had come prepared," said Ms. Haggle. "But I have also bound you. You were bound to my level of power and mortality while you were busy summoning the thirteen souls."

Enraged, the dark witch tried her power again. "Primary spells? Reduced to the level of a Forester! I will inflict painful death on all your children when I am done with you."

The dark witch drew the sword and repeatedly swung at Ms. Haggle with both the weapons in a two-handed attack, but Ms. Haggle easily dodged.

"You've been outsmarted," said Ms. Haggle. "You are restrained by my spell, and your binding on me will fail after dawn."

"I have two companions," said the dark witch. "One of ice, and one of fire. When my spell is complete on your castle, my companion of fire will help finish you long before first light."

"My girls have your fire under control. You have nothing left."

"Millicent!" shouted the dark witch. "Destroy the Hag. Hurry, so that my power will return."

At that moment, Ms. Haggle also yelled out to Natalie, "Rule of the two kings!"

Incredulous, Natalie placed all her trust on Ms. Haggle and faced off against revenge incarnate: a dark witch. Natalie knew that fear was her greatest challenge. Fear diminishes insight, weakens one's training. She must overcome her fear, and have faith that she can succeed even without power. She must do what many cannot: she must believe.

Natalie stood her ground and swung first as the dark witch approached her; but the dark witch blocked the blow with her staff, swinging at Natalie in retort with the sword of power. Natalie felt the wicked might of the dark witch, but she refused to fear it. The dark witch took charge of the fight—following attack with attack, challenging Natalie's natural fighting skills with both her weapons, one after another. Natalie, unable to counter a two-handed attack, backed into the low side wall.

Taking advantage of this, the dark witch stuck her staff into the wall on Natalie's right side, pinning her while she swung the sword from the other side. Natalie, without any thought, leaned backward over the waist high wall, flipping herself over, into the stands.

The dark witch hopped onto the wall. "I'm going to kill you slowly. Ever so slowly, child."

Natalie tried to run left, then right, but the dark witch was gaining more and more ground on her, backing her up the stands, toward the back wall. Natalie was cornered. The dark witch took a number of swings. Natalie was certain she would not be able to dodge and block this many attacks, but thus far, she was successful. Out of absolute desperation, Natalie lunged forward, poking the dark witch, but failing to penetrate her cloak, due to the safety weld of the fencing sword.

"You don't even have a proper weapon," mocked the dark witch. "And you think stealing my power will matter once you're dead? Don't worry, I'll make this painful."

"Ahhhhh," shouted the dark witch as she fell down, revealing the figure of Ms. Haggle, who had struck her from behind.

Without hesitation, Natalie scurried away, back to the arena center.

"What is wrong with you, Millicent!" screamed the dark witch. "She is limited to primary spells. You have the powers of the dark witch. Can't you take her out?"

"I need the sword," said Millicent. "She is still impenetrable."

The dark witch threw the sword to Millicent, who continued to pursue Ms. Haggle. The dark witch, however, remained where she was—in the stands.

Natalie knew that Ms. Haggle was at a disadvantage, and that it was up to her to make a move now. She needed to find a way to shake things up—a way to kill the dark witch.

"Are you scared of a poor, little child?" she taunted the dark witch. "Is a little Honey too much for you?"

The dark witch laughed. "You cannot vex me, child. I have endured far more than your pathetic taunts, far more than you could possibly fathom. If you want a fight, you'll have to step up."

"So be it," said Natalie. "I see that the anger in you won't subside." And with a deep breath, Natalie directed all her focus and determination toward a single objective—stealing power.

"Stop!" screamed the dark witch. "Stop stealing my power!"

"If you want me to stop, you'll have to stop me," answered Natalie.

The dark witch leaped to the ground, swinging, but without the sword of power, her primary spells were useless against Natalie's skills.

"Hurry," shouted the dark witch. "Kill the Hag."

Lights and elements of ultimate power blasted out at Ms. Haggle, who absorbed all the hits with the sole intention of avoiding the sword of power. Then again, the task itself was impossible, even for a Hag. Ms. Haggle was eventually struck in the arm. Immediately, she attempted to cover her blood-soaked upper arm, but her hand passed straight through the triceps and the bone, not stopping until it reached the muscle on the other side. Her arm was barely intact, held together only by flesh.

"Kill the witch!" shouted Ms. Haggle.

Natalie felt desperate, and gathered all the emotion she could. In her frenzy, Natalie welcomed an influx of power drain from the dark witch—even the power the witch had held back became available to her.

"You can't kill me," said the dark witch.

"Then why do you defend yourself?" retorted Natalie.

"You're nothing," said the dark witch.

Natalie ignored her, relentlessly pushing forward against the dark witch's frail attempts to counter with her staff. Natalie drew upon her experience in fencing to snap the staff back and forth, to opposite sides, in an attempt to produce an opening to thrust the sword forward and poke through the dark witch's cloak—a tactic Natalie realized was unsuccessful due to the limitations of her sword. Unfortunately, Ms. Haggle suffered another strike. She said nothing about it to Natalie, but she didn't have to— Natalie knew Ms. Haggle was close to her death, and that her protection would soon be gone.

While Natalie's attention was divided, the dark witch managed to whack her in the head, sending her crumbling down to the ground, next to the hind legs of her beloved stone horse—forever frozen in a rearing position. The dark witch hovered over Natalie, prepared to finish her off, exactly as she had envisioned in her nightmares.

"You had your moment, child. Now, you will see how true revenge feels."

Before the dark witch could strike, however, Galla's statue fell forward, nearly crushing her, but the dark witch's acute sensibilities aided her to roll away.

"Yes!" yelled Millicent, the sword buried in Ms. Haggle's stomach.

Natalie freaked. Think, she ordered herself. The moment was still hers and only hers. She looked into the face of her horse, who had once, twice, and now thrice, saved her life when all motivation had deserted her. As fast as she could, Natalie poked the fencing sword into the nose cavity of Galla's statute, snapping off the tip before accosting the dark witch.

"Time to die," said Natalie, stabbing the dark witch in the back.

"To my aid!" bellowed the dark witch, but Ms. Haggle held on to Millicent, restraining her.

"Get off me, Hag," said Millicent, but Ms. Haggle, even on the brink of death, was defiant to the core.

Natalie seized the chance, swiftly removing the sword and effortlessly striking the witch. Hit after hit she continued—in the face; on the shoulder; in the stomach; through the heart. Natalie grabbed the dark witch by the shoulder of her robe and thrust the sword completely through her chest.

Natalie beamed as she and the dark witch fell to the ground. "You've just been killed... by a Honey."

The dark witch's black silhouette transformed into flesh, and slowly, morphed into a human face. She looked at Natalie in disgust, grunting a few last worthless spells before a rattle crashed through the stadium.

From the spot where Ms. Haggle's body lay, beams of blinding light scattered throughout the arena; the earth shook relentlessly; holes broke the ground into fragments; and thunder roared to mark the death of a Hag. Subsequently, as legend would have it, Ms. Haggle's body sank into the ground in her own, self-contained funeral.

Tears ran down Natalie's face as she took in the sight before her eyes. But before she could react, the dark witch placed her hand on the soft, young cheek of a no longer chaste Natalie. Natalie gasped for air, but it was too late. Her face and eventually her entire body turned into stone from the touch of the dark witch.

Millicent stood—the lone survivor—over a dead dark witch, a retired Hag, and two stone statues of young females that were once innocent.

CHAPTER TWENTY-EIGHT

≈≈

LEADERSHIP

Melissa waited—her nerves uneasy, her brow clenched in angst, her mind vacillating. All her next moves were dependent upon an outcome of which she had no knowledge. For her, waiting, guessing were the hardest parts about being a leader. Making decisions was not the "coup de gras," so to speak, but for want of the details upon which the decisions were to be based. This has baffled leaders for as long as the existence of humans.

Melissa stood like shale—unbending to the wind, but ready to crack if hit. Her face sat unfazed atop a motionless frame as she stood tall with her robe wrapped around one side of her body while the wind flapped it back and forth on the other. She did not dare look directly at the green robe approaching in her direction, or the one that stood next to her, waiting for instruction. Melissa knew something had happened, and her moment of solitude was to come to a stop as the planning would begin.

"We found the spellbinder," announced Rebecca with just enough air in her lungs to spit out the words.

"Where?" demanded Melissa.

Rebecca gasped for air, then bent over, covering her side with one hand in an unhelpful attempt to ease the pain of breathing. Melissa waited, looking at Rebecca's reddened face from the combination of shallow breaths and the harsh cold wind that was typical about this area—a defiant sensation that Melissa had often felt was like spirits spitting in her face.

"I... I..." stuttered Rebecca, still trying to recover her breath. She pointed and said, "The east side."

"Exactly," said Melissa before turning to Isabella and pushing her. "Round up the others, and meet me behind the east hill."

Isabella darted away like prey in the open.

"Tell me about the encounter," said Melissa.

"Well, one of the Honeys found her."

Just then, two girls carried a wounded Honey toward Melissa.

"She's still alive," said Rebecca.

Melissa lifted the girl's head, brushing the brow with her fingers. "Yes, she's alive. Bring her with us to the east hill. Go!"

Melissa hurried away, oblivious to any concern about stealth or the girls falling behind. For her, timing and position were much more important than the cracking and rustling of leaves and sticks that would give away her presence to any person located within a hundred meters. Melissa could hear noise from every direction. By now, every girl was speeding to the east hill, eager to know the strategy. Only one thing was certain in Melissa's mind— the girls stood little chance without Ms. Haggle.

"Melissa, wait. We can't keep up," said one of the girls.

"Maintain your stealth," replied Melissa. "You know where we're going."

Melissa knew that she sounded contradictory with her "stealth" comment, but she needed time to think without any interruption. She had two advantages—just two—and they seemed miniscule in the context of confronting a witch with dark powers. She knew the lie of the land—that terrain is always the first priority in battle— and she had the numbers. Numbers are nice, but compared to superior ability, it pretty much falls short of an advantage.

"To the bunker," shouted Melissa to a few girls who were moving toward her. The bunker—her favorite spot for strategic gathering in outdoor games and gossip—made for the perfect place to plan an attack. And all the girls knew she'd be there for anything to do with the east side of the castle. There it was—the naturally carved hole in the back crest of the east hill where she had recently put nine overconfident Honeys in their place. Melissa knew she could fit a good twenty girls in there and be nearly invisible from every direction but the back side.

Melissa slowed when she neared the bunker in order to prevent anyone from zeroing in on her final position. "Shhhh," she whispered as she pushed her hands downward in a signal for the girls to stay low. "Where is she?" asked Melissa.

No one answered. Melissa peeked over the hill, but was unable to determine the answer. "Where would I hide?" she asked herself.

A couple more girls assembled behind the hill, but none made a noise, having been given the signal for silence by the girls already in the bunker. Melissa gathered her breath and embraced the knowledge that she would be expected to perform some miracle the moment the injured Honey and her escorts arrived. Melissa turned around. "You and you," she said, pointing. "Keep your eyes out."

The two girls, in good coordination, sneaked to the top of the hill with their heads just raised slightly above to provide a lookout. Melissa turned her back to the hill, and instantly—as more girls arrived—the group gathered into a circle, waiting for instruction. "Save your spells," instructed Mellissa. "We must make the most of what we have if we are to succeed."

"But what about Ms. Hag and Natalie?" asked one girl.

"Ms. Hag told you what to do. We must learn to depend upon ourselves now."

"But Ms. Hag—" tried another girl.

"Ms. Hag is not here," said Melissa vehemently. "We will give her a few more minutes, but as far as I'm concerned, we must make this happen ourselves. Does everyone understand?"

The girls nodded their heads in agreement, but Melissa could tell they were not ready.

"There she is!" said one of the lookouts.

Melissa looked in the specified direction and saw Millicent soaring above the castle. She knew what every girl there was thinking: Ms. Hag and Natalie hadn't made it. Were there two, three witches? Melissa knew the girls wanted to run, and she knew what was at stake. Melissa had never been one to run from a fight, even against insurmountable odds, although her role here was no longer of a fighter but that of a leader. Melissa needed the girls to be as strong as her, and though they weren't, it was her job to get a fight out of them. What she would give for ten more girls with her own stubborn will to win! But she didn't have that; she had children.

The injured Honey arrived, somewhat faint, but still able to convey valuable information. Melissa knelt down in front of her. "Where's the spellbinder?" she asked.

"Invisible, ten steps out. By the outer drain."

"That's why we couldn't find her," observed Melissa in disappointment. "She has cast a spell that won't allow us to see her until we're ten steps away."

"But she'll see us coming before we can see her," cried a girl.

"And the one above," said another. "We haven't a chance."

Melissa smacked the second girl before another negative thought could enter the girls' minds. "What do you think is going to happen come sunrise?" she asked. She was met with a resounding silence. "Do you think those witches are just going to leave the second our protection is gone? We're witnesses. We're avengers. They *will* find us. If not tonight, tomorrow, next week. Our fate is sealed with those witches trapped inside. We can go out fighting, or we can stay cowering in a corner. And I'll tell you something… if any one of you is going to take down our morale, I'll do you in myself, right here and now. Because our only chance to survive is by sticking together, being in synch, and giving these witches a taste of everything we have."

Melissa could see fear in the girls' eyes—the fear a woman experiences when she knows she must take a stand. It's a different kind of fear altogether—a drive; a step to see what she is capable of, as opposed to what may happen; a realization that she is in control of her destiny, and that she is responsible for both her successes and failures.

A sense of responsibility, if you will, set in. Now is when these girls would see who they really were, what they were made of. Melissa remembered this feeling from when she was seven years old, and she hadn't looked back since. These girls, if they managed to survive, had taken their first step into womanhood. She could only hope they were ready.

At this point, Melissa was confident she could spell out the harsh truth to them: help was not coming. "Ms. Hag is gone," she said. "We have to accept that, but we must also see that the dark witch is gone as well. Ms. Hag already explained to you how to break the spell. She gave us a chance by killing the dark witch, and we must make use of it. These are two witches, but we are junior witches, witches in waiting, and Honeys of many. If we can't find a way to stop these two, then our training was wasted on worthless souls. We have been prepared for this! We have the capacity for this! This is our home, and we have to fight for this!"

"I need fighters," continued Melissa. "If you're not ready... if you want to die a mile down the road... if you want to leave your protectors unprotected... raise your hand and you can leave. I promise not to be mad. You are free to go. Just get up and leave." The offer was clear; however, no girl raised her hand, all partaking in a newfound sense of duty. "I'm serious," added Melissa just to be sure. "You can leave, but if you stay, I expect you to fight. You will take orders, stand your ground, and fight to the end. That's what you will do if you stay. Are there any takers of my mercy?"

Melissa gave a strong ultimatum that could lose her the crowd. It was risky and she was nervous, but she felt she had to take the chance to evoke fortitude. She didn't have time for weak-minded fighters. She needed them to know that it was all-or-nothing now. She needed discipline, sacrifice, and service, and she would squeeze it out of them if it meant she had only two Honeys by her side. A girl started upward, making Melissa concerned; women can stand together in strength very well, but it just takes one to cause a doubt. Melissa knew she must not let anyone see her emotions, but she was relieved when she saw that the girl was just reestablishing her balance and kneeling back down.

"That's it," said Melissa. "We're in this together." Melissa inhaled deeply, but it didn't help. She was the leader, and she needed to plan the attack against, not one, but two dark witch companions. Technically, she was the only one capable of confronting a witch, and even she had failed earlier. "Is there anything I need to know about the terrain or about the witches that might help?"

The girls remained silent. Melissa was hoping to spark an idea, gain an advantage, or stall for a plan, but she gained nothing. "We have to break the spell at all costs," she said. "If we can disrupt the spellbinder, all the witches will come out and fight. We need not win to succeed, but we must merely break the spell."

Melissa cleared the dirt in front of her, and began to make a diagram on the ground with a stick. She was uneasy about sending the Honeys into battle. She did not dare tell them that they were mostly pawns, cannon fodder, and mere helpless distractions.

"Here's the castle," began Melissa with her instructions. "Here's the drain. Here we are, and here's the old oak tree. I need distractions. We are high in our numbers; so we can spread out—along here, here, and here. All I need you to do is get that flying witch off my back."

"You're not going to attack the spellbinder on your own, are you?" asked a Honey.

"Yes," replied Melissa. "All I need to do is break the spell, not destroy her."

"I'll help you," said Rebecca.

"Fair enough," replied Melissa. "But I need that witch off my tail. That's the priority. Fan out like this," she said as she mapped out the formation on the ground. "Nothing lethal, because it won't work. I need attrition and harassment. Hit and move. Hit and move. In this pattern." Melissa used the stick to draw an alternating pattern from side to side. "Got it? Hit from this side, then move and hide. Hit from this side, move and hide. Hit from this side, move and hide. She must not get the time to focus on one person, and she can't leave the spellbinder unprotected to follow you. This will give me, us, the window of opportunity we need. It's paramount that we have our protection. Ms. Hag did her job; you do yours, and trust us to do ours. If we are successful, the witches inside will do their part and finish it. Understand?" Melissa reiterated, "In being united, we succeed."

"But some of us can't do much. We don't have power," said one Honey.

"I don't need you to do much," replied Melissa. "I need distractions. Act like you have something. Act like you know what you're doing. Feign a spell, shake a stick, throw a rock."

The girls shook their heads and looked ready—well, almost.

"Everybody," continued Melissa. "Pick a position on my map, and I will tell you when you need to run for it." The girls all pointed to the position they were prepared to assume.

"No," said Melissa. "Isabella, Susan, Toddi, I need you here, here, and here, so we can spread out our power to make it look like we have more. Okay? Now, disperse. We move in two minutes."

Melissa pulled Rebecca and Isabella to the side while the other girls moved to the outer rim of the hole. "Isabella, I need you by the oak tree." Melissa opened her robe to show the two girls the extent of her injuries. "I didn't want to scare the girls, but I'm close to tapping out. Isabella, there's a good chance we won't make it to the spellbinder. You're most likely our real force. I need you to be ready to advance on the spellbinder when... if we die. You are the last hope."

The three girls held hands in the center of their little circle.

Melissa added, "If you fail, we all fail."

CHAPTER TWENTY-NINE

৯৵৶

ASSAULT

Melissa craned her head to look over the hill, painstakingly aware of her only goal: breaking the spell. Time felt like a luxury, but she paused anyway, not out of fear but from hope—the delusional hope that Ms. Haggle would arrive to protect them. Melissa knew that once her plan was in action, there would be no turning back, and also that this was a plan of desperation, with little real potential of success. She was ready to move. So ready, she could feel her heart pound. Her heart beat with such loud thumps that Melissa could swear she would be able to reach out in front of her chest and squeeze it. She could only imagine how the other girls felt, putting their absolute faith in her. Melissa wanted to come off as strong when she gave her next order, but her throat was dry; so she raised her hand as she prepared to speak.

"Ahem," she began. "Don't attack until *I'm* good and ready. Get to your positions quietly, but fast. And remember, hit and move, hit and move. If you're not at the same place, she'll have a harder time finding you."

Melissa lowered her hand a little, and then said, "Ready? Move." As the girls moved out, Melissa began to question herself about which act was harder—moving herself, or giving these girls the order that would likely lead them to their deaths. It was no contest: she would rather move with her full force and not care at all than send these unfortunate girls to their doom.

The moment of decisions and planning had passed. Now was not the time for strategic alterations, but rather for battle decisions—something that was often harder because everything seemed to move incredibly fast. Melissa reflected on all her battlefield failures, and how split-second decisions were impossible to avoid. This time, however, it was life or death—not just for her, but for everyone. Every woman and child here was dependent on her strategy and her ability to think on her feet.

"The girls are in position," Melissa informed Rebecca. "This fight is greater than any test or challenge. As of now, at this moment, we're witches. And we'll walk out there like witches."

Melissa released her foothold that was meant to give her a quick start, and stood up tall, prepared, and confident. She began to walk with Rebecca at her side.

All the girls watched her in shock and awe. They were absolutely mystified by the audacity, poise, and conviction that Melissa had. They saw that there was no doubt about their success in Melissa's mind, and therefore, they felt like a part of the winning team. Not only could this work, but Melissa showed them that it would, even if she had to raise hell to do it.

Melissa and Rebecca neared their destination, and were undoubtedly visible to both witches, but they stood unwavering. The flying witch, Millicent, threw a look of contempt at the green-robed girls, but let them walk within fifty meters of the spellbinder before taking them seriously. Melissa gave a shove to Rebecca's shoulder. "Spread out," she said.

Rebecca could not believe that they were just going to walk up to the spellbinder. Never in her life could she have imagined that they would advance this far. She was astounded at the boldness, but also felt a fire in her gut with every brave step she took. Not Melissa, though. Her veins were like ice—stubborn, cold, and unyielding.

Every set of eyes were on Melissa and Rebecca, and they knew it. Every survivor here would forever look back on this moment and see a role model, a leader, and the essence of a real witch. Melissa understood the impression that she and Rebecca had on the girls, and how the girls would see it—something extremely "cool." She couldn't help but play up the drama of the moment a little. Keeping her eyes focused on the goal, Melissa pointed her finger to Rebecca, and in a voice loud enough for everyone to hear, she said, "Spell up."

Melissa and Rebecca commenced their whispers, which initiated a series of events so quick that there was no time to think. Millicent stopped hovering and swooped down upon Melissa and Rebecca. At that very instant, a loud crack of thunder rang through the grounds. Before Millicent had entirely descended, Isabella was ready: she zapped the area between the women with a small, yet somewhat effective, diminishing spell. Rebecca jumped away, but not Melissa, who whispered, "Blurred," as she continued to walk, as composed as ever.

Thrown off by the spells, Millicent could not identify Melissa, and from the impact of the diminishing spell, she slammed into the ground. A pretty good start, thought Melissa, especially considering this wasn't a part of the plan; nor was the walking. Melissa realized that she was a fairly good group strategist in the moment and decided not the stop there. "She took the bait!" shouted Melissa. "Get her!"

All at once—again, not according to the original plan—every girl stood up and attacked, or at least pretended to attack, a grounded Millicent. Nevertheless, it worked. Millicent took back to the sky in defense against the uncertain threat.

Meanwhile, observing the commotion, Emma made her way down from the cemetery to stand near Isabella's side by the great oak tree. Uncertain about whether she was ready to do anything more than to hide, she cowered behind the tree, unable to move.

Within a good ten seconds, Melissa went from her first whisper to a full sprint toward her goal. The plan worked, and now it was all up to her. She did not need to wait for Rebecca; however, she slowed down to avoid walking into any trap. Melissa's vision was impaired by the witch's invisibility; therefore, she placed her trust in a hearing spell to pinpoint the location of the spellbinder. As Melissa moved closer, her fear strengthened. Her mind was tormented by the sinister laughs and threats that the spellbinder breathed out. Literally, Melissa could hear the air rasping out of her mouth. It was louder than the squeaky laugh. She never thought that sound could be so frightening, even more so than anything she had seen.

Melissa knew the witch was near, and that she would suddenly appear. The thought was terrifying, and the anticipation was killing her. She wanted to rush in to end the fear, but decided to continue with her successful string of choices. Rebecca had caught up, and Melissa instructed her to swing around. Together, they took in the entire perimeter of the targeted area.

Melissa, armed with assistance, was now willing to invest less thought in the distraction above, which remained effectively inundated. The girls had alternated efficiently, and Millicent was quite preoccupied; nevertheless, she was a force that demanded strict attention.

"Ahhhh," cried Rebecca as she flew backward.

Melissa compelled herself inward, utilizing the trajectory of Rebecca's flight to sense the whereabouts of the spellbinder. There she was, looking intently at Melissa and Rebecca at the same time—with two distorted faces emerging from one. There would be no multiple advantage here. Or could there be? Melissa didn't move closer, but defensively circled away from Rebecca's position as the faces grew more and more faint to keep in opposite directions. Rebecca stood up, and with one Forester on each side, they began to spell off with the witch.

The hovering witch noticed the action, but she knew that the threat to the spellbinder was miniscule. Her job was to figure out the extent of the outer threat, which she quickly realized was equally miniscule. "They're children," she screeched. "Children! Heeeeeeee."

Millicent covered a circular path around the area. "Children!" she shouted again. "Children have fear. Fear," she repeated. "*Fear me!*" her voice crackled in a spell, and the girls did.

Isabella shouted, "Maintain your discipline!" as a couple of Honeys began running back to the east hill bunker. But not Emma—whose only movement was to dig herself deeper into the old oak tree. She had peeked out once, only to look at what she feared in the day, let alone during the night—and that was even before the fear spell. Isabella, repositioned somewhat away from Emma, shouted, "Fight, Emma. Fight!"

Millicent zoned in on the apparent leader of the outside group: Isabella. Leaving the spellbinder unprotected, she landed next to the oak tree, between Isabella and Emma.

Out of absolute fear, Emma cast a spell of courage.

"What do we have here?" croaked Millicent, turning around in surprise.

Emma, no longer concealed by the oak tree or the ring, looked past Millicent, at Isabella, as if to cry, "Help me."

Isabella knew she had two duties, and neither of them was to protect Emma.

"How could I have missed such innocent blood?" said the witch as she crept closer to Emma. "It's been a long time since I've tasted Honey."

Emma shifted to the far side of the tree with her back pressed so tightly against it that she could be a part of the bark herself. At the moment, she definitely wished she were. Please just go away, she prayed, but her pleas went unanswered as the witch's steps sounded closer and closer. Emma's heart raced faster with the crunch of every dry leaf she heard. "Crunch…crunch…crunch." She swore the witch was standing on the other side of the tree, but she was too crippled with fright to do anything about it.

"Run!" shouted Isabella. "Run! Get out of there!"

Emma couldn't though. She simply couldn't. "Why won't Isabella just help me?" thought Emma. She couldn't understand that Isabella was responsible for a second attack on the spellbinder, at all costs, which included Emma's life.

"What are you, seven, eight?" asked the witch. "Do you know what a young Honey's blood does for my spell casting? It's not often that I have such an opportunity to feast."

"Crunch," went the ground as Emma's ears amplified the sound of each step.

"I feel your heart," said the witch. "The last time I sneaked upon one so young, her heart exploded before I could reach her. Will yours explode?" Millicent's voice echoed, creepier still—something Emma had thought impossible. "Or will you see the horrors I have in store for you?"

"I'm at the tree," said the witch. "Will you run, fight, or just collapse?"

Emma whimpered as tears ran down both her cheeks.

"Run, Emma. Run! She's right there! Run!" shouted Isabella.

"I want you to look at me," said the witch. "Turn around. I want to see if you can. I want to see the look on your face—the look in your eyes when you see true fear." Millicent stepped a little bit more around the tree.

"Melissa, hurry!" shouted Isabella. "You have to do it now!" Isabella looked around at the devastating outcome of the fear spell. All the girls lay low, and the attacks had ceased altogether. Isabella considered rushing the spellbinder in a triple attack—figuring it was no good in waiting—and prepared herself accordingly.

"Tell me," said the witch. "Will you die when you see my face? He-he. No, that's not the question. How will you die? Will it be from your heart? Will your breath stop? Or will it be when I'm sucking the life out of you?"

Millicent's hand reached around the tree, nearly touching Emma. "Boo!" she shouted as she jumped around. Emma froze with her mouth open, unable to breath. The witch placed her hands on Emma's cheeks, pulling her closer.

"Now, that was slightly amusing," said the witch. "But fun time's over; it's payoff time." Millicent opened her mouth abnormally wide. Then, there was a sound—as though her jaw had unlocked. She opened her mouth even wider, bringing it closer to Emma's head. Her mouth was so unnaturally open that Emma suspected the witch was going to devour her whole head. Emma was petrified— she only prayed for it to be painless.

"Get away from her, witch!" shouted Isabella as she shoved the remnants of a large branch into the witch's gaping mouth.

The witch screamed the best she could as she flailed about to remove the branch. Isabella, in a violent rage, cast on Millicent every spell she knew, following it up with a physical flurry of claws, feet, bites, knees, elbows, and even a head butt. If Isabella had it, she used it.

"We have to move faster," said Rebecca. "The witch is on the ground."

"I'm trying," replied Melissa.

"Melissa, our spells aren't working."

"Then let's throw down," said Melissa as she marched forward.

A rock suddenly shot up from the ground, toward Melissa's head. Melissa blocked it and countered with a protective and then a proactive spell. Then, she charged at the spellbinder, Rebecca in her wake. Melissa landed a hit, knocking both faces back into one, but only because the spellbinder was busy pushing Rebecca to the ground. The spellbinder turned her attention completely to Melissa and smacked her hands together, sending at her a flash of air in the form of a concussion blast. But Melissa was ready, and she magically slipped through the rippling energy that simulated the power of a grenade. Then, Melissa struck again. The spellbinder took another hit, and then flung her hands outward into the air to create a bubble that circled her; consequently, her invisibility spell ended. Melissa and Rebecca continuously struck at the bubble, but were unable to affect the witch. The witch knelt, cross-legged, inside the bubble, concentrating all her casting ability into two spells—one over the castle, and the other on her bubble.

"We have to spell her out of this," said Melissa.

Melissa and Rebecca started casting a series of spells that appeared to lighten the bubble. They continued, their words working faster than the mind could comprehend. The bubble began to flutter and fade. Suddenly, the witch—her ghostly essence remaining inside the bubble—briefly lashed out at Rebecca in a stream of light, returning inside before her kneeling image vanished completely. Rebecca fell to the ground, motionless.

Melissa continued her spells alone, ready for a similar attack. And it came: the witch, suddenly flying out of the bubble, made a physical attack. Melissa easily repelled it. And another attack. And another. The witch was stymied, and the bubble was breaking. The attacks stopped, and Melissa drew closer to cause some more harm, but the witch began chanting two spells with the same mouth, and Melissa was thwarted back. Melissa, never one to be outdone and an expert imitator, thought that she could probably do this too, and began to speak two spells at once. She drew closer again, and the witch, desperate, made another futile attack, her stretched arm merely leaving the bubble. Melissa, confident that the witch's physical ability had weakened, prepared to vigorously press forward with her assault. However, she saw the witch's mouth divide into two mouths, casting four spells simultaneously.

Melissa's protection quickly fell apart. Another strike by the witch, followed by a concussion attack and two facilitating spells proved too much for Melissa. She hit the ground, hard. Another concussion attack struck at her, and then another. Melissa felt her insides crumble and blood gush out of her mouth as she mustered the last bit of her energy to crawl a safe distance away. She was done. On the one hand, she had failed, but she knew she was close. Otherwise, the witch would not continue the attack on her had she not been a threat. She had held her own and had certainly gained the witch's respect; but respect was nothing more than a worthless consolation prize when death was on the line. Melissa's previous defeat, combined with this beating, was too much for her body and spirit. Victory, if possible at all, was up to Isabella now.

⌘

Isabella sat on her knees, spent. Exhausted from using everything she had within her, she fell down to her side—useless—as the witch blithely stood by her. Millicent laughed viciously. "You can't hurt me, silly girl. But I... I can easily hurt you."

Millicent leaned over Isabella, and with a squeak no louder than a mouse's call, she said, "Break," and Isabella's forearm broke in two. As Isabella screamed, the witch said, "Oh, did that hurt? Maybe this will help. Break." Isabella's other forearm also broke. Emma watched helplessly in horror as the witch carelessly repeated it two more times. "Break. Break." Isabella's upper arms were now broken, and all she could manage before passing out from the pain was to make a despondent eye contact with Emma.

At Millicent's gesture, her stick floated into her hand; the witch glanced at Emma and playfully said, "Don't you go anywhere. *We* have plans."

Then, Millicent's face and body transformed: her teeth grew long and sharp; her eyes shrank; her facial bones protruded outward; and her spine bent oddly into an exaggerated curve as she hopped onto her staff, her complexion now a dark green.

The girls, no longer under the effect of the fear spell, immediately reinitiated their alternating attack when Millicent took to the air. She, however, hovered over one spot, unaffected. Then, Millicent screeched and laughed over and over again, oblivious to her surroundings.

"She's gone berserk!" shouted Toddi.

"Ha, ha, ha," screeched Millicent—again, and again. Until, she called out, "Break," and a Honey's leg broke. "Break, break, break. Ha, ha, ha." Three more bones broke. "Break… Break… Break, break, break." The witch continued to chant in a rhythm that seemed more important than the act she was performing—the breaking of bones and spirits.

Accepting their defeat, the girls scurried, hopped, and crawled away from the area—at least, the ones that could.

CHAPTER THIRTY

❧❧

HOPE

Natalie's face, frozen into stone, revealed signs of life as the marble fragmented into sections and movable crevices that cracked and ground against one another. Color returned to separate patches of her skin. Natalie, unaware of what to expect, fought away the spell that bound her in a semi-permanent shell of artful suffering. Despite how much she hated to admit it, she understood the truth regarding the dark witch's comment about the spell's inert beauty. In some time, Natalie was able to break free of the rocky prison that her adversary had cast on her with her last breath. She was once more alive, collapsing into the empty cloak and staff of the dark witch, which by no means took her life as intended.

Natalie glanced at her dear friend, Galla—still locked in stone. She then brushed away the last of her rocky skin, realizing that her fate had turned favorable only because the dark witch had been restricted to primary spell abilities at the time.

Quickly, Natalie took in her surroundings. Ensuring that she was safe to move freely, Natalie grabbed the dark witch's staff and made her way to Ms. Haggle's final resting spot. At one end of the arena, Natalie noticed Ms. Haggle's empty black robe with the brooch that had changed color from onyx to pure white—establishing her death as permanent. But in this death, she saw hope. Entangled in the robe was the hilt of the sword of power, barely reaching out from the spot where the earth had engulfed her dead mentor.

"Lightweight," she said, brushing away massive chunks of dirt from the area. Instantly, Natalie was able to make a deep hole that revealed her current predicament—the sword of power locked in the stone coffin of Ms. Haggle. Natalie knew that her chances of success would increase significantly with the sword, but soon realized the strenuous effort that would need to be exerted in retrieving the weapon from the rock. She was faced with a huge dilemma: assist the girls fast, or spend valuable seconds hoping to recover the sword, or even use it. Holding the dark witch's staff in one hand and the hilt of the sunken sword in the other, Natalie's decisiveness faltered: was the sword worth her time?

Meanwhile, Melissa lay flat on the ground, motionless—only a trickle of blood continued to flow from her mouth. This act of playing dead served two purposes: it was her only protection from repeated concussion blasts, and it gave her time to recover a little, as she lacked energy to move. Even her head lay flat to one side. Defeat and depression were slowly taking control of her mind. Reality and pain were the same in Melissa's mind, as she realized that living through one's defeat and eminent demise is unmatched in agony. Correction: knowing that she was responsible for the death of others aggravated her sense of misery. Melissa had not shed a tear since she was seven, sworn never to do so again; but now she was on the verge of breaking the promise she made after her mother's death. If only victory and glory were entwined, then Melissa would be ready. To be honest, she had always been ready. She just didn't want to go in the same way her mother did—in shame.

For the first time in a decade, Melissa showed some signs of being human. "Mother," she cried. "I miss you." Tears flooded over her nose, going over her other eye, mingling with other tears and then falling to the ground. "I'm sorry. I'm sorry I let you die. I'm sorry I wasn't strong enough. All I ever wanted was to make you proud."

Melissa heard a couple Honeys whimper in pain, and took in a few sharp breaths, sorrowfully crying, "Mother, comfort me!"

Just then, as Melissa wondered if her time had come, she double-checked what she saw before her eyes: her mother approaching her from afar. "Take me with you!" she cried. "Release me from this pain! My loss!" The woman Melissa saw as her mother, dressed in a black witch's robe, ran to her. "Come mother, I'm ready," cried Melissa, giving in to the pain. As the woman in the black robe moved close enough for recognition, Melissa's mind was shrouded with doubt, even though the woman's face was covered by the robe. The woman, as it turned out, was not running toward Melissa. She ran past Melissa—Melissa's hope to be whisked away to her death, crushed. "Stop your wicked games, witch! You torment me, and I will not die so easily!"

The black-robed woman continued toward Rebecca, bracing herself for a concussion blast. After the blast, she cast a spell, "Featherweight," and picked up Rebecca with one arm, followed by a grunt. "I really need to work on that spell," she added. Then she approached Melissa.

"Come quick," she said. Melissa got up as the woman helped her.

"How?" asked Melissa.

"Let's go. I have a plan."

Putting her arm around Natalie's shoulders for support, Melissa felt something hard inside the cloak. "What's this?" she asked.

"Hope, sister. Hope."

"The hovering witch?" asked Melissa.

"Hold on!" interrupted Natalie as another concussion blast hit. "Over the castle."

"We can attack," said Melissa, desperate for success.

"She's watching us right now. I have a plan. Trust me."

"Gather," Melissa cast a spell. Then, she said, "Motivation."

The girls who were still mobile began to move toward the bunker.

"Carry your weight," said Natalie.

"Ummph," tried Melissa. Coughing up some blood, she began to move again. "The robe?" she asked.

"It's Ms. Hag's. See her brooch?"

Just then, they arrived at the bunker behind the hill. Only a few other girls had gathered there. "Listen," Natalie addressed Susan, who was nursing a broken arm. "We don't have much time before the spell comes complete, at 2 a.m. Gather as many girls as you can, and bring them here."

Natalie laid Rebecca down and checked for a pulse. "She's no good," said Natalie. "I need a witch. Where's Isabella?"

"I don't think she made it," replied Melissa.

"I need a witch who can move and fight."

Melissa heard Natalie and understood what she meant. She sat herself up, turned her head to the side, and spit out some blood in a grand gesture. "You got one," she said.

"Trade robes with me, and listen carefully," said Natalie as she removed Ms. Haggle's black robe. "Now, you know the pictures of the former witches in the hall…"

As the two women strategized, Honeys piled in, determined to take a second chance. Susan took charge and began to determine who was missing and figure out ways to rescue more girls.

"I can do my part," said Melissa. "But can—" Melissa began to cough profusely. "Do you think you can do your part?" she finished.

"I have to try," replied Natalie, wiping the blood from Melissa's mouth. "Are you sure?" she asked back.

"I'm the woman for this job," said Melissa, standing and wobbling around. "Now that we know their weaknesses."

Natalie closed the clasp of Ms. Haggle's brooch over the robe to complete Melissa's outfit. As she did it, Natalie noticed the brooch change in color from a clear white to onyx. "Somebody's with you," said Natalie. "Someone strong."

"I'm just badass," joked Melissa, trying to laugh; but it turned into a cough, and then a gasp for air.

"Well, let's just hope it works." Then, Natalie checked with Susan. "Report."

"Everyone's accounted for, except for two."

"Where are they?"

Susan lowered her eyes in grief. "Isabella and Emma are by the oak tree." She continued, "Isabella is down hard, and Emma won't move."

"We'll have to continue without them," said Natalie. "Melissa, you ready?"

"Gather round," said Melissa. "This is my final order. I want you to make me proud." Melissa began to cough excessively. "Okay, now that it's come to this. I need spells. Every last thing you have. Protection, gift, assault, demeanor—everything you have. I want spells cast over and over onto Natalie. She's going to make a run. Our final run."

"What about the hovering witch?" asked a Honey, fearful of being slapped.

"That's my responsibility," said Melissa. "I'm taking her on, alone. Nobody must help me. Toddi, you keep track of the time. The spell completes at 2 a.m., sharp."

"But that's in like ten minutes!"

"Well, if it happens, we're done. Everyone else, your absolute priority is to support Natalie in fighting the spellbinder. No matter what you hear or think, do not stop until you are certain the task is accomplished. Well! Spell her up!"

"I have something special for you," said Susan. "*Premonition*," she uttered in a whisper. "You'll see things just before they happen. You're going to like this one."

Natalie stood, almost engulfed in a meditative trance. Not only could she hear the spells, but she could feel them as the girls cast them—"haste," "sight," "dexterity," "sure shot," "confidence," "wisdom" to name a few. She donned Melissa's green robe, opening it up to see the initials MT engraved on the inside—initials that yielded great meaning to her.

"It fits you well," said Melissa. "Good travels."

"Good travels," said Natalie. She gave one last look to all the girls supporting her, and then turned to Melissa, saying, "Mitzi. It's been a pleasure… for me."

"You're welcome," replied Melissa.

Natalie began to speed away before she was stopped by Melissa's voice.

"Nat," said Melissa. "Me too."

Natalie smiled. "Use the forest; you have protection there," said Natalie, as she trotted away.

"Now what?" asked a Honey.

"Pray, spell, enjoy the show," said Melissa. "It's all out of your hands."

Susan stood by Melissa's side. "Anything I can do?"

"You've done all you can. It's in her hands now." Melissa placed her hand on Susan's shoulder. "You have a good group here, and you've led them well. Take good care of them. Many don't have mothers, and they look up to us. You're the next witch up."

"But what about you?" asked Susan.

"It's your time, sister."

"But—"

"It's your time. I have to go." Melissa began to walk again toward the spellbinder, but not in the same manner as before—now she was less determined and more serene.

Natalie arrived at the oak tree and knelt by Emma. "How you doing, Em?"

Emma, in deep shock, lay motionless until she finally raised her hand to point to Isabella.

"I see," said Natalie. "She's going to be fine. This is all going to be over soon, and you'll be asleep in your bed, trying to forget. But, until then, will you do me a favor?"

Emma didn't reply.

"I want you to remember that I love you, and I won't let anybody harm you. Okay?"

Emma nodded and muttered, "Kay."

As Natalie began to move away, Emma moaned, "Nat."

Natalie turned back and fell into a vice-like embrace with Emma. "I killed her," said Emma as she began to cry. "I killed her."

"No you didn't," said Natalie. "No you didn't."

"I let her die. I watched. I watched her. I didn't do anything. She's dead because of me. I wouldn't move. I wouldn't move. She's dead. I did it. I did it. I did it. I did it," continued Emma as she rocked back and forth.

"Calm down," said Natalie. She looked at the night sky and realized she only had a few minutes. Melissa was in position, and waiting. "I have to go. I'll be back for you."

"That's what she said!" cried Emma.

"But I don't lie," replied Natalie as she gradually pried Emma off herself and backed away from her young friend.

Natalie began to walk toward the spellbinder. Almost in perfect synch, the witch turned to Natalie's direction and Millicent came into sight from her position over the castle. Then, without delay, Millicent pulled lightning from the sky; but Natalie, anticipating this move, jumped out of the way.

"Easy prey," said Millicent as she swooped down from the sky, but again, Natalie rolled out of the way.

"I have to learn one of these premonition spells," said Natalie. "I do like it."

Then, Millicent landed, standing between Natalie and the spellbinder. "You're a Honey," she said. "Just a poor, worthless Honey." Then, fast as lightning, she swished forward and grabbed the green robe, tugging on it. "You don't deserve this. You haven't earned it."

"Millicent!"

Millicent scowled. "Who dares speak my name?" she asked, letting Natalie go and taking to the air again.

"I do," said Melissa. "I speak your name because I am your master."

"I will kill any person who makes such claims after the dark witch is dead."

"Then kill me now. Or, am I right?"

"No. No. You're not right."

"Then how do I know your name? And why won't you kill me?"

"No. I must know. I must know who you are first."

"Because you have a master, you must know. And that master is I."

"*Show yourself. Name yourself,*" demanded Millicent, casting spells.

"Your spells do not work on she who has killed your kin."

"No!" said the witch. "No!"

"Yes, it is I, Amelia," said Melissa as she took off her black hood. Using a spell, she had transformed her face to match the picture of Amelia—the woman she had known from the picture in the hall of witches. "I killed your mother. I killed her as I am to kill you."

Melissa began to move away from the spellbinder with undetectable haste, toward the forest, where she had laid layers of protective spells over the years. Natalie composed herself and patted her wrist to show Melissa that there was little time remaining.

"What's the matter?" asked Melissa. "Are you afraid to die?"

"Never!" shouted the witch.

"Then why won't you face me?"

Millicent looked at Natalie, and turned back to Melissa. "I will tend to you shortly."

"Coward!" shouted Melissa. "Just like your mother. The cowards are so easy to kill. She died at my hands, Millicent. At my will. I killed her with my bare hands." Melissa turned and ran, yelling, "I killed Millicent's mother! She was a coward! Millicent is a coward!"

Millicent roared like thunder. "Never!" she shouted as she followed Melissa, who was now running for her life, her legs rustling through the knee-high grass that marked the path to the forest. Never had Mitzi Forest seemed so distant!

Natalie made a break for the spellbinder, who held out her hand and slowed Natalie's approach. Concussion blast; Natalie braced herself. Fireball; Natalie weaved. Lightning strike; Natalie rolled. "*Fear*," said the witch, but Natalie stayed strong. "A Honey you are, and a Honey you will die. You can't break the bubble, and my soul won't leave."

"I killed your dark witch. What makes you think I can't burst your bubble?"

"Ahhhhhhhh!" cried the witch. "I... won't... leave."

"Then I will kill you right where you stand," said Natalie as she began to move inward.

The witch stretched out her arm far from the bubble and grabbed Natalie's throat, throwing her away, to the ground. The witch retracted her arm inward and waited.

Natalie stood up and approached the bubble again. "If I can't break the bubble, then why do you attack?"

"For pleasure."

"Liar!" screamed Natalie.

"Liar, you call me. He-he. Liar, liar, pants on fire," said the witch, causing a ring of fire to burst up around her. Another explosion, and Natalie was thrown back again. "Rise," said the witch. "Rise." And the fire grew higher.

"How much more time?" asked Susan. Toddi held up two fingers.

The younger girls, now sitting in a circle at the top of the hill, held hands and continued to cast their spells with vigor. Suddenly, they heard something disturbing: Melissa's voice rang out from the forest, screaming for life.

"Continue with your spells!" said Susan.

"I will rip you apart piece by piece, you hag!" promised Millicent. "I have a lot of pain for you. Pain that will make you wish you were dead. Pain to the hag. *Pain.*"

"Ahhhhhhhhhh."

"We have to help her," said a Honey.

"No!" shouted Susan. "More spells. Get that fire down!"

The fire began to dwindle and Natalie rushed in again, cutting through the heat as she slightly glowed with the fire protection provided by the Honeys.

"One minute!" shouted Toddi. "You have one minute!"

"Help!" shouted Melissa.

"No," said Susan. Despite the horror she saw in the young girls' eyes, she insisted, "Keep the anti-fire spells going."

Natalie rushed forward and reached into her robe.

"Gotcha," said the spellbinder as her arm stretched several meters outside the bubble and tightened around Natalie's neck. The witch slowly brought Natalie back toward her as she squeezed the life out of her. "I can reach through the bubble, but no Honey can. Not even with a staff, regardless of who it's from. If you weren't so hopeless, you'd know this."

Natalie pried her fingers between the spellbinder's hand and her neck, gasping for air so loud that even Emma could hear her. Emma shrank, realizing her fate. Fear set in, but it was not her strongest emotion. Emma finally turned her head to see Natalie dying right before her eyes. She looked at Isabella—wishing she would wake up—but it was of no use. Emma had to watch as two girls died before her! Never mind what the hovering witch would do to her later. Death would be good for her in the absence of her friends. Emma turned back and looked away.

"Now!" shouted Toddi. "Now!"

Natalie was pulled closer to the witch's face, now frantically fumbling through her robe while gasping for air.   Emma looked at Natalie again, hoping someone would help, but she knew there was no one—no one close enough but her; her and Isabella, if she was even alive. Alone, who was she against a real witch? Just a little girl.

Then, when Natalie was near striking distance, the dark witch's staff fell from her robe. Instinctually, she reached for the staff with both hands, but bungled it, and watched it slip through her fingers. The staff dropped helplessly in front of the spellbinder, who quickly whisked it away, then lifted Natalie higher until only her toes were touching the ground. Natalie, unable to resist anymore, submitted to her reflexes and gripped the spellbinder's wrist with the palms of her hands to pull herself up for gaps of air while she stretched her feet for the ground. Her eyes began to close—she was dying from suffocation. Eventually, her hands fell to her sides, limp, and her eyes ultimately closed.

"Time!" shouted Toddi.

Natalie already knew her time was up, her last sight was of the castle beginning to fade and disappear from existence altogether, but all she could focus on at the time was staying conscious.

"Sunlight!"

The spellbinder was suddenly blinded by a bright ray of pure sunlight, and she instantly dropped Natalie to her knees.

"Air," said Susan, who had just been waiting for her chance to cast the spell.

Natalie's chest expanded as oxygen blasted its way into her lungs and rapidly surged into her veins. Unhesitating, she lunged up, grabbed the sword of power, hidden under her robe, and swung it into the bubble, slicing through the witch.

CHAPTER THIRTY-ONE

৵৶

PROMISES

Susan, Toddi, and all the girls watched in delight, worry, and hesitant relief. What had just happened? What would happen now? They held hands in dire hope.

"KANK. EEHHHHHHH," sounded the castle, not quite in its most structurally sound state. "BAM!" Scores of witches burst out, shrieking, through the top of the castle and into the air. They were so quick that it appeared merely as a blur of light to the girls. Once free, the witches from the castle flew toward the forest, toward Millicent.

Natalie looked down at the spellbinder—both halves of her. Then she wondered who... Looking to the spot the sunlight came from, she saw Emma standing next to the tree, in self-disbelief, still pointing.

Past where Emma stood, Natalie could see rapid, recurrent lights shooting out from Mitzi Forest. Taking a much needed break from the constant worrisome thoughts, she reflected how upset one must be to set fire to her own forest. With that thought, she allowed the sword to drop to the ground and made her way to Emma in the best way she could.

৩৪৩৫

Two days later, amidst the fire-ravaged forest, Natalie stood next to the spot where Melissa had breathed her last—preoccupied with the events and circumstances of the past few days. Ava approached Natalie from behind. "Are you ready?" she asked.

"No," replied Natalie.

Ava put a hand on the back of Natalie's newly replaced honey-colored robe. "She was alive when we found her. She knew you succeeded, that she succeeded. She was ready."

"Why doesn't it help?" asked Natalie.

"You've experienced a lot of loss. It's normal."

"Loss?" asked Natalie as she turned to Ava.

"No," said Ava. "Your reaction to loss is what's normal. Loss leaves behind questions, doubt, pain. Time will heal. New relationships will help."

"It hurts to know that I will never have another relationship like that one. What we went through... How she forced me to grow... And then to learn to trust, to build teamwork, and to achieve success. She had a way of inspiring, bringing out one's best, and getting them to follow her. She will always be special for me. That... and our time together—I will never forget. I would have followed her anywhere."

"Maybe you were meant to lead instead," said Ava.

"Maybe, but I've learned something more—about them, myself. Every one of these women filled with hate, or anger... they were all hurt. They were all hurt to the same extent they hurt others, if not more."

Natalie, glaring far into the distance, allowed tears to roll down her cheeks before bringing her eyes to look into Ava's. "I don't want my hurt to turn me into that."

"It won't," said Ava.

"How do you know?"

"Because you won't let it. Those women weren't worried about other people's feelings, but you... you have shown that you care. They started too young with their pain—before they could develop compassion. You... You have it already. Your mother made sure of it. She protected you until you were ready. You proved this, two nights ago, and yet again, right now. You're just like your mother, and I'm proud of that."

Natalie embraced Ava and continued to weep.

"Are you going to be okay?" asked Ava.

"Well, it just seems that every time I finally get to really know someone, they die."

"Ahem," coughed Ava. "For the record, we aren't really that close, are we?"

"Right," laughed Natalie.

Ava brushed away Natalie's tears; it was strange how it felt like the umpteenth time of them saying goodbye to loved ones together. "Let's go pay respect to some women who have earned it."

"Can I have a moment to myself?" asked Natalie.

"Of course."

Natalie bent over the spot where Melissa had lain— the imprint of her body still marking the ground. Natalie dropped to one knee and held out her hand. When she opened it, she had Melissa's leadership pin on her palm. "We made a great team, didn't we? You were a great leader, teacher, and friend. I will always remember you and draw strength in the memories. I'll miss you."

The cemetery overflowed with hundreds and hundreds of witches from different orders, arrived to pay their sincere respect. Robes of red, purple, grey, blue, black, brown, green, and honey decorated the area in a never-before-seen spectacle. Two caskets were placed on the cemetery altar, ready to be laid to rest, in the Hall of Heroines.

All the attendees were hooded, except for the two women who stood just outside the cemetery—Ava and the headmistress—waiting for Natalie. "Do you think she'll make it?" asked the headmistress.

Ava did not bother to show any surprise at the faulty question. "Of course she will. She has her mother in her, more than she'll ever know."

Natalie joined the two women. Facing them, she said, "I wish Melissa was still alive."

"Hold on to that thought during the ceremony," replied Ava. "It will do her justice."

Natalie smiled, and the three women began to walk, with Natalie on the far right, the headmistress to her left, and then Ava—a formation that was a huge sign of respect toward Natalie. Natalie glanced down the hill to look at the grave of Melissa's mother, but the lone grave at the bottom outskirts was missing. "Whaaa…" began Natalie.

"She belongs in the witches graveyard, and has been moved accordingly," said the headmistress. "A dying wish I personally granted."

Natalie stood proud. There was no greater gift that Melissa could have received in her sacrifice. As the three entered the cemetery, they pulled up their hoods before passing a number of honey and green robes from their order. Rebecca and Isabella greeted Natalie with hugs. Natalie felt a surge of warmth through her body. She stood taller, more confident. Only one sight saddened her:

the number of broken bones in white casts peppered across the line.

Natalie was escorted to the line, but before she could assume her position at the head of the procession to honor the two heroines, she noted something eerie—one of the witches eyeing her unnaturally, as if there was some kind of history between them. Nonetheless, this evening was not about her. She now stood at the altar—the first to view the coffins of Ms. Haggle and Melissa. Ms. Haggle's casket remained closed, but Melissa lay in an open casket, dressed in a black robe. Natalie forgot about the odd look from the strange witch, and smiled as the headmistress patted her on the back. Words entered Natalie's mind: "I thought you'd like her in black." Natalie looked at the headmistress, who also smiled.

No one left after the ceremony. All the witches from the surrounding orders remained in attendance for a second occasion.

"May I have your attention," spoke a woman in a red robe with a black sash over her shoulder. "Never have I seen so many red robes, so many orders, at peace, gathered in one place, but today we honored a woman whom we all knew, and who knew us—a great protector of our way of life. It gives me great pleasure to honor one more person. Natalie, will you come forward please?"

Natalie was surprised and nervous. She knew nothing about this woman with the black sash, but she could tell that the woman was someone really important. Her presence not only commanded respect, but Natalie could see that she was being given utmost regard from every person present there.

"Natalie," said the woman as the sisterhood's headmistress joined her. "It gives me great pleasure to present you with this green robe."

Natalie would no longer be a Honey! Today, she was officially a Forester. Ava helped Natalie remove her outdated Honey robe. Well, the sisters had been issued new robes for the ceremony, but "for Pete's sake," thought Natalie, "it was old."

The woman with the black sash was handed a green robe that seemed a little worn and tattered, not quite what Natalie was expecting. Weren't there any new green robes? Ava then proceeded to assist her niece with the robe. When it was on, Natalie viewed the inner lining. Inside, she noticed her own initials right above two others: MT and LT.

"It's Melissa's!" exclaimed Natalie in pure delight.

The headmistress replied, "I hope you don't mind? I did get her permission."

"No. Yes. I mean, of course," replied Natalie in a joyous voice.

The woman with the black sash produced a new, shiny leadership pin. "If you accept it, I would also like to present you with the leadership pin for your order."

"No," said Natalie unequivocally.

The crowd went silent.

"If you don't mind, Ma'am, I already have one." Natalie held out her hand to reveal Melissa's leadership pin.

"Of course," replied the woman. As she took Melissa's old pin and pinned it on the green robe, she said, "I wouldn't have it any other way."

SCARLET REIGN

Malice of the Dark Witch

Call for Independence

War of the Orders

Fate of the Realms

ACKNOWLEDGMENTS

Shoshana Regos, from inception to publication, you were there—listening, encouraging, contributing. Your role was far more important than you realize, as this book would not have existed without you.

Katrina Bradley, I am indebted to you for your honesty, your open mind, and your expertise.

ABOUT AUTHOR

R.D. Crist is a psychotherapist who generates creativity via long walks and majestic views of nature. True inspiration, however, derives from personal hardships that have sparked a desire to help others manage life's various struggles.

Although R.D. Crist has only released one book, three have been written and several more begun, which span a variety of genres. The focus of these stories are intended to center on Crist's favorite dynamics of a story—personal conflict, relationship development, inner growth, and social revelation. Each story is created with a greater purpose to stimulate a person to reflect on common challenges, be they personal, interactive, or in principle.

Childhood influences include Ray Bradbury stories and character conflict movies like *Twelve Angry Men*.

Socializing, listening to people's stories, spending time with family, and relentlessly exercising (as if those last ten pounds cared) are some of Crist's favorite ways to pass the day.

COMING SOON

SCARLET REIGN: CALL FOR INDEPENDENCE

War is brewing amongst the orders, and the sisterhood has lost its infamous protector to the dark witch. Tough decisions are on the horizon for Natalie, the renowned teen leader who saved the Sisterhood, and is expected by some to do so again. The council, however, bears no respect for Natalie's opinion in choosing a side, or declaring independence: a state that requires more than she is willing to sacrifice.

Meanwhile, old flames and foes vie for Natalie's attention as she expresses desires to leave the order altogether. Natalie will need all that she has learned, her natural talents, and more, including new gifts of light bequeathed to her by her mentor. But all will be for naught if she cannot learn to materialize her powers in time. Will she move on from her sisters in what will be seen as an act of betrayal, or will she stay and fight?

SCARLET REIGN: WAR OF THE ORDERS

War is a fact amongst the Coalition of Orders and, despite the betrayal by a superior mother, Natalie's pure wit and determination has gained autonomy for her remaining sisters. However, that may be just the start of her problems as some have begun to suspect that the war is a ruse with ulterior motives.

Natalie, tired of standing aside during needless hostilities that sees friends and sisters fight against each other, decides it is time to challenge the legality of war altogether by secretly entering when the opportunity arises. Her actions bring all who trust her to the brink of joining the battle, as she risks everything for a chance to heal her relationship with one man and avoid the threat of another. Does she have the acumen to manage love, politics, and war? Or will she demand too much from herself and ultimately lose everything?

CONTACT US

We would like to know your opinion. R.D. Crist is currently working on three books from other genres, but if you truly appreciated this fantasy novel, and the audience is large enough, R.D. Crist would be more than willing to set aside those projects to accommodate these fans and continue the Scarlet Reign, four book series.

www.scarletreignbooks.com

29144575R00183

Made in the USA
Columbia, SC
21 October 2018